# BOOMKITCHWATT
## don hendrie jr

# BOOMKITCHWATT

A NOVEL

BY DON HENDRIE, JR.

JOHN MUIR  PUBLICATIONS
*SANTA FE*          *NEW MEXICO*

*Fair acknowledgment is given to the following:*

"White Rabbit" by Grace Slick. © Copyright 1967 by Radio Corporation of America. "Happiness is a Porpoise Mouth" by Joe McDonald. © Copyright 1967 by Vanguard Recording Society, Inc. "Martha" by Paul Kantner. © Copyright by Radio Corporation of America. "She's a Rainbow" by Mick Jagger and Keith Richard. © Copyright by Gideon Music, Inc. (BMI)

*And more:*

Cover by Peter Aschwanden, based on a design by Hendrie, using an original photograph by Judith Steinhart. Author photo by David A. Batchelder.

Portions of this book first appeared, in quite different form, in SILO 11 and in CONFLUENCE, to whose editors a friendly gesture is made.

First Edition, November, 1972.

Published by:
JOHN MUIR PUBLICATIONS
Box 613
Santa Fe, New Mexico 87501

Distributed by:
BOOK PEOPLE
2940 Seventh St.
Berkeley, California 94710

For Susan Blue and Phineas A.K.J.

*My own suspicion is that the universe is not only queerer than we suppose, but queerer than we can suppose.*

J.B.S. Haldane

# PART ONE

Fancy *Wolliam Victor Flute*

My father, Andrew Eliot Flute, who speculated in soybean futures, fancied the entire five syllables. Curling his thin loser's tongue around the first misdone O, he played my name into the air until, by the time I began to talk with myself, I was a quick and flat *W.V. Flute.* And I've continued to address myself this way ever since---in times of peace, trauma, humor and death. Yet my wife Kate, whose sense of what's silly is sublime, has always called me *Flute.*

"Flute," Kate cried outside my window, "we're a long way from California." You're right, you're right, I mouthe, pretending there was glass in my window, instead of clear New Hampshire air.

We are far from the wreckage, far and away.

"Flute," she shouted from the well just a Saturday ago, "won't you come outside? Why do you stay in there?"

"I'm unable," I answered. "I'm mortgaged here, don't you see? I'm *stuck!*" And I continued to favor the walls of my room with a third coat of flat-white latex.

Now, late in September, my walls are dry and bumped, plain but painterly a friend might say. I like this steady whiteness all around me, interrupted only by the changing fall colors which muffle through my two open windows. The only other interruption is the print Jones gave me years ago; it has been in all my rooms. A knight in orange tights and motley jerkin drifts in a tiny skiff with only his battered orange lance to stave off three fat and luminous sea monsters. Erect and braced, Paul Klee's Sinbad the Sailor is getting the best of his attackers; he's on top of the situation.

I'm fond of control myself. That is, I'm neat. I'm just as apt to *try* to organize the past as I am to foolishly project ordered visions of our future in this new life. But for now it is clear enough to me that, if my objects occupy their assigned place, why, then any surprises will be that much easier to absorb. I hate surprises. They waste my brain, paralyze my muscles; I choke up, Kate says with typical astuteness. In my room here I keep my disorganized past stored in three rectangular banana boxes. Unopened, they form a three-foot stack against one nubbled white wall. I like the symmetry of their three blue-scripted labels. To violate the neatness of the stack, to rip into its mash of contents is, of course, what demands to be done. But meanwhile there is the high and most *orderly* delight of arranging my real and necessary objects.

For a desk I have a solid draftsman's tilting table, which Kate recently waxed to the color of honey. It is precisely in front of the well window and adjusted so that I am able to peer out on the rocky lawn and stone well---my window vision stops abruptly at the wall of trees marking the end of my property. On the plain of my desk I have put: a high intensity lamp, a letter-file empty of letters, and a metallic mug containing an eight inch scissors. This typewriter, a gray portable I bought while a student in California, sits squarely on a rubber pad which keeps the machine from falling into my lap. The desk chair, the only one in the room, has an intricate wicker bottom and was made in Prague. That's it. Sparse, I think, even impermanent, but everything has its place. Except, perhaps, me.

The gross business matters of living having passed from my control out of my caring, I am comfortable when I see Kate at her own desk dealing a deck of bills, scribbling at checks whose color and numbers are strange to me. At the end of August, when we sought the mortgage on this house at the town bank, Kate was a maximum of force and efficiency. She knew the going interest rate, the points the bank would gouge, and the state of the property deed for all past years. It was a curious and pleasing situation for me; before, I was a great one for handling such rituals, legal and illegal. You can be sure W.V. Flute has inaugurated a deed search or two, delicately and discreetly handled large sums of money, and with fine skill manipulated bank officials, judges, and bureaucrats. . . from Pasadena to Eureka.

But now I'm retired. And my lady is quite adept.

She guided me into the bank by an elbow, sat me one chair away from the official, then took her own place next to the man's swabbed and porous face. He registered formal surprise when Kate mentioned the down payment we were prepared to put up for the unfinished house in the village of W_____ (population, once we moved in, 36). Seeing the cashier's check from Jones's estate for eleven thousand dollars, the bank representative dryly agreed to participate in a discussion of a ten year mortgage on the remaining balance of the house price, nine thousand five hundred dollars. Then it is my impression that Kate magically extracted a "home improvement" loan of two thousand dollars, with which we might finish the house (abandoned to the bank by its impoverished builder)---shingles for the barren tarpaper, an extension of the heating system to all the rooms---the balance to be used for furniture.

The Flutes arrived in New Hampshire with a Jeep automobile, their costumes, a portable mesh crib, the banana boxes, typewriter, Sinbad, and the impeccable check.

"What is your husband's occupation, Mrs. Flute?" Despite my silent passivity the man pushed his swabbed face past Kate and offered me a curious, banker's glance. Forgetting the absence of my moustache I pursed my naked lips and watched his face tuck back to the safety of my politic wife. Kate did not tell him I was a refugee, something of a wreck. Instead, she lowered her voice and said, "My husband has a guaranteed income of eight hundred and twenty-five dollars a month for the rest of his life." While the words of this public sentence batted about in my head, Kate handed over the papers necessary to prove the assertion, unfortunately true. I crossed my knees, made a pass at my sunglasses, and reflected in my heavy-handed and repetitive fashion that Jones, when the whim struck him, could be as thorough and officious

4

as I once was. Despite the efforts of his executrix mother, the trust that produces this grand income is irrevocable.

"Are you employed, Mrs. Flute?" Of course she's not! I placed a fist beneath my chin and stared at nothing. From Kate's lap, my new-born daughter Ann began to cry. The bank arranged the mortgage four or five days later. No, I have never been arrested, tried or convicted, Kate lied for me.

At twenty-seven; refugee, father, property owner, I have my habits. Lightly and rapidly I shall put them down. Statistics don't bore me. I am five feet, eight inches tall. I weigh a hundred and fifty pounds. On a quiet day, here in New Hampshire, I smoke eighteen to twenty-five Camel cigarettes, to the nub. There are nicotine stains on all ten of my fingers, stains which Kate periodically scrubs off with lemon juice and boraxo. My teeth are tidy enough, but the daily flood of coffee and smoke has colored them saffron. My hair is the color of strong tea and is receding, I calculate, at one eighth inch per calendar year. During the expanse of a day, my eyes run a spectrum from navy to water blue. For size seven and one half feet I own: elk moccasins, tennis shoes, and a neat pair of rubber and leather duck boots. Naked, Kate sees me as a "healthy twig" or, in more fiery times, a "peakéd mantis." Directly beneath my throat grows an isoceles triangle of blackish hair, the inverted apex of which points snidely to the lowest depths of my sunken chest. Clothed, costumed to my satisfaction, I resemble a seedy troubadour, a drooping lackbutt.

Could such a narrow and stained figure be burdened with a dramatic, a recordable, a *necessary* history? Suspended here in front of my window, like a hairy seed in some fresh still liquid, I know so, Yes!

But. But this cool New Hampshire stability. This organized, safe room. This peacefulness Kate urges that we feel amongst the granite humps and burning swamp maples. . . .I am falsely soothed! My boxes remain damnably closed, irrelevant and neat---fearsome

5

against the wall. Perhaps I should heft and fling them to the center of the room, walk circles around them until finally--nerved-up for chaos---I pounce, rip into them from every which way. . .until, magically, I come to terms with their scattered contents. But how to do it? Is it as simple as Kate suggests?

This morning she came and stood outside the well window, her lovely head just above the sill, ready for our morning ritual. I sat at the desk and watched the breeze blow swatches of brown hair across her eyes. I felt we had been rehearsing the conversation for days.

"Why don't you unpack those boxes?" she demanded, pointing her chin at the mute cardboard. "You just sit. Are you out of *order*?"

"How's Ann this morning?" I began. "Did she eat her cereal? Did you comb out her hair wishing yours were as fresh?" She smiled patiently. "Did you canister that foul morning diaper? Kate," I said, "how is your daughter?" I leaned back in my chair and waited the necessary beats.

"Ours," she said. When I didn't respond she rapped a knuckle on the window sill. "That stuff won't work, you know. I'm taking care of my part, doing *my* job." Her hand moved from the sill for a swipe at her blowing hair. "But you're. . .look at me!. . .you're not on top of your situation. Are you."

She got me, surprised me: This wasn't part of my plan.

"You think I should get to it, do you?" I asked, looking at her.

She snorted. She'd reached the point of exclamation, passed out of the days of gentle prodding, and come to bold chiding. "I think you should quit dickin' around, Flute."

All right, Kate. To it, and good-bye.

I need no opened boxes to produce this collection of names, all it amounts to for now: Jones, Claude D'Mambro, Julius Stein, Molly Noel, Bobbi Love, Jacob Maven Bogue, Phineas Clingsmythe, Robert Quell. And: Sandor Moody, Oyd Fikes, Margaret Pickel. How neat they look, these names; this orderly list. Here in New Hampshire, on Sinbad's diminished skiff, I can at least see to that. Because *here* I am the center of the universe. This New Me. Young/Old Artificer; liquid man of Notions. Surely I must be capable of the thick spurts of fancy Jones recognized as the Truth of things. I know my head can create. . .can speak a variety of voices. . .can murder or not-murder. . .can act or not-act. By the list, I see there are enough voices to encircle that woman's absurd murder of my foolish and wondrous friend Jones, now dead.

JONES, to tell it, was born in April of 194—, near Halifax, Nova Scotia. Nothing special attended his birth; no cataclysm split the land. It was a sunny, still day. Seventeen years later, in Palo Alto, California, he received a copper plaque naming him the *Optimist Club Boy of the Year*; and in the late sixties he earned a Bachelor of Arts Degree from Stanford University. Shortly after his graduation he flew to Asunción, Paraguay, where for one year he helped his friend Loman Pence manage the cattle ranch which occupies nearly all of that area of Paraguay called the *Chaco*.

Pence, who was later to commit suicide by leaping off the Golden Gate Bridge, wrote to his father in America: ". . .you were right enough to call him [Jones] invaluable. Is he going to replace me? For a change, why don't you tell me what's on your mind? The Guarní [Indians] call him 'boss of the sun'. . . . But do you know the flaw, Daddy? There's a quirk in his backbone. He won't admit it, but twice now his back's locked on him, and the second time he was driving a Unimog and nearly killed himself. How can I talk to him? I never know where his mind is. . . ."

In Southern California, shortly after his return from Paraguay, Jones met and married Linda Saint Thomas, of whom he later said (to a group of puzzled friends): "She's alive, you know. Like all of us." The day after his marriage he inherited a sum of money reckoned at very near one million dollars. This from his maternal grandfather, a Canadian lumber king. After his divorce (guilty of "outrageous and absurd mental cruelty," said Linda S. Jones), he went to Nova Scotia and passed a year in a gray clapboard house on the Bay of Fundy. Celibate, he dug clams, learned to fly an airplane, did small carpentry, wrote infrequent letters, and read with abandon in the more than two hundred books sent to him from San Francisco by W.V. Flute—his agent, adviser and friend.

Jones returned to San Francisco, to California in an April fog. And for a time stayed in Palo Alto with his mother and father. He said: "Amos asked me, probably for the first time, if I knew what I was doing. I allowed that I did. My mother said that money was a tremendous responsibility. I agreed. Amos brought out a bottle of that fine bourbon, and we chatted."

To Flute's Green Street apartment, just up the hill from the San Francisco Marina, Jones eventually brought the several cartons of books he had used in Nova Scotia. He took to staying in the city, on Green Street, for days at a time, until finally he admitted his habit, and arrived on May Day with a leather tc'let kit, a few clothes, and a new down sleeping bag.

"This is only temporary," he said. It was.

One midnight, he explained his next move: "I had dinner with that crazy Stein tonight, in the Chinese-American beanery on Polk Street. I think Stein. . .Julius Stein, you know. . .I think he was miming different characters who live in Chinese restaurants, when suddenly I had a brain bong." He laughed. "It wasn't Stein, it was a girl who quacked at us over the booth wall. She quacked. Stein froze. From where I was sitting it looked as if she just sprang alive from Stein's hair, quacking her blessing on the both of us. Stein ducked and. . .bong! The whole place seemed to vanish, even Stein, and there I was with this quacker, this lovely Kate Ximines."

At the end of May, Flute purchased and registered in Jones's name a surplus United States Army weapons carrier in the best of condition. On the instructions of Miss Kate Ximines, this small truck was that same day painted a vivid yellow and black shapes over its entire surface.

Some days later, Flute drove his ancient and maroon Morris convertible to Eureka, California, two hundred and eighty miles north of San Francisco, where he engaged a room at the Honeydew Tavern & Hotel. While in Eureka he undertook visits to several realtors, a lawyer, and an individual by the name of Oyd Fikes, the owner of a sizable piece of land on the Pacific coast south of Eureka.

In early June, while Flute was returning to San Francisco, Kate Ximines broke the lease on the Polk Street apartment she shared with Jones, and the two of them went to his family home in Palo Alto, where they stayed one night. The next day, mounting a weapons carrier loaded with books and camping equipment, Jones and Kate drove north to Red Bluff for a brief, angry visit with her father. On the fourth of June, in the abandoned mining regions

9

near Weaverville, they met by accident an itinerant, Claude Augustus D'Mambro.

I, Claude, am speaking.

I was up. Hunched low on a soft grassy canyon lip with a good view down into the grasses and scrub chaparral at the bottom, I watched the two of them thrashing and making the two-back, frog-legged beast. In the knee grasses closeby a cold black stream they made the beast for my eyes only, on top of what looked like an old duffel coat, lined with blue.

I was up on the lip under a hazed June sun---in north California maybe a little too cold for the beast. Calm, relaxed, crouched on my knees, I felt the damp nuzzle up from the soil. Calm enough for seeing her a minute before, seeing her jackknife out of a pair of pale jeans and fling them out of sight in the grasses. She was spread-eagled, empty and talking into the sun until the looming man hunched himself onto her, his butt all white and rubbery in the sunlight.

My eyes froze unblinking on what I saw. Inside my head Piro giggled---and I saw a flashing picture of him, my buddy, flying our Cessna over the Michigan beach. But still, I watched the people in the canyon below me. And still, I watched them on the beach in Michigan as we swooped down on a thick slide of clear air, Piro whistling over the controls. They were there in the low slash between two dunes. I saw the girl's face twisting out under his shoulder. The engine belched and the man backjumped back off the girl, snapped his head at the dopes in the sky. Sure, Piro giggled when we saw him raise his fist, middle finger up; the sound spilled from his bent mouth, mixed with the engine whine, mixing now with the sound of my own heart, here in California on my grassy lip, without Piro for a while.

But he was not far, not far at all. Every noon I left him down on the Trinity River, on a skinny gravel bar shaking an aluminum pan, grinning each time he came up with only dull pebbles or gritty sand. I left him and made for this warm spot on the edge of the canyon, old buddy Claude who preferred sitting in the sun with a warm spam sandwich to panning for gold more than likely not even there.

11

So I saw them.

He was pissing, a gleaming yellow arc in the afternoon sun. She stood by with her hands tucked away in her jeans. I think they were laughing. He finished and zipped himself in while she watched. They walked apart some. He threw pebbles at her when she eased into the thicker scrub near the stream. He loomed out of the grasses, cocking his thick arm for each throw, controlling her movements like a herder. Tall in the grasses, light hair laid back tight against his skull---he was an impatient man with his stones. She yelled at him, just her head showing above the green. He stopped throwing and waded in after her. She moved to him, afloat, dogpaddling through the grass. They were saying things I could not hear, just the two heads, one above the other. Hands fluttered up and they came together, heads merging to a lump that thrust from the swaying green surface.

He stepped back and began to trample the grasses until he had made a rough circle, a lair of flattened green. She took off the duffel coat, spread it out on the ground, stood at ease in front of him, tiny, hands tucked away in the pale jeans. She put her face up at the sun, at me, and with a swift set of motions had her shirt off a top white as cloud against the green. The nipple things, like far-off pennies, were red earth color. She was down, out of the jeans, talking silently into the sun when he moved onto her. In the midst of all the thrashing her legs rose and fell, feet treading wild circles in the air.

I was calm.

I could see my path down to the canyon floor as if it was marked with lines of white lime. I scrambled over the soft lip and crawled, slid, dropped down to the canyon's bottom. Creased into my eyes was the final sight of her hands beating and scratching over his tight-muscled back. At the stream I lay flat, listened, looked across for some sign, but they were hidden---safe lair. I heard over the wind and moving water sounds a hard pounding like a palm beating on packed earth. Then she was talking fast and breathy,

12

"Jones, you—Jones!"

Quiet.

The soft rushing of the water took control of my ears. An ant groped over my palm, and I tasted dirt in my mouth. My chin had burrowed a trench in the soil. I lay still and locked Piro out of my head, refused to hear my old dancing friend. Through my palm I did think I caught the beating of her heart; through all that soil and water and root it reached me—a tiny muscle engine without a governor, a frightened animal in the cage of her chest. I smelled a new wind of damp flesh, sweated hair, a clump of grass freshly wrenched in two. In the midst of the throbbing fell a groan—his large-bodied groan. Still as calm as a stick I worked myself backward using my knees, my elbows, until I was a hidden part of the stream's caving bank. "Boy, I love that." Her voice rose from their lair, crossed over the stream to my ears, cups for the liquid sound of that smooth, eased voice.

I saw her.

Across the stream, my eyes on a level with the sooty gray of her tennis shoes. I took a breath of air and dirt. She was there—all her colors bashing my eyes. Calm, I watched her bend, saw her smallness, pointed tits swaying off gently from her chest. She bent and cupped cold stream water into her crotch. My hands tingled and numbed like the early morning when I first shoved a pan into the river. She scooped again, rubbing hard, searching. Her hair fell forward over her head and flowed down to the ripple of the water. She went up straight and looked directly at my hiding place. I closed my eyes, didn't breathe, and still saw her. "Come wash," she said, and I saw myself leaping over the water and landing easily beside her.

"I will," came his grass voice.

I gave my eyes a harsh squeeze and opened them. It was shaggy and dripping clear drops of water where the dark V came to its

13

point. Her belly was a piece of clean white sheet above the wet clutching curled thing. The pressure seemed to flow up through the soil and the grass; it entered my own belly where it took hold of me, pushed me up while holding me down. I tried to cling to the ground with fingers, mouth, knees, elbows. . .but I was up, standing; it was shaggy and dripping clear drops.

"Come wash. Hurry," she said.

And there I was, standing, taking up air and space, moving lightly. But something caught and Piro's giggle followed me as I tripped and fell flat down to the cold water---seeing how she was seeing me fall.

I lay face down, a hulk of wet, unmoving Claude. My ears took the pressure of the shallow water. I felt it throbbing just the other side of my ear drums, crazy to get into my head and chill my still brain. I was calm.

I might remember that I pissed my pants, but I don't, and I didn't. Jones snatched me from the water. I lay on my face, oozing on their side of the stream long enough for them to climb into their clothes, long enough for him to prod my backbone once or twice with a hard boot. What kept my face down, my eyes shut, my breath held until I thought I would bust, was plain shitless fear.

I heard the air explode through my lips. "He's conscious," she said.

I wanted to clutch deeper into my own mud, disappear, but two boot-steps, another poke for my backbone, and I was jerked right up off the ground and set down hard on my feet. My knees wouldn't hold, but he had a good grip on the scruff of my neck, the seat of my pants. I dangled there some seconds, enough time

14

to open my eyes and see his open palm come whistling at my face. Just as his hand thwacked into my cheek, I sensed he was smiling. And an instant later, through the water that had spurted into my eyes, I saw it was true. By then his hands were off me. I had my footing and was looking into his wide face. He looked like a handsome gorilla with his broad flattened nose, and right above the ungrinning blue eyes a kind of rolled-out ridge of bone, light skin stretched taut over it. He stepped back, a little crouched; his long arms swung easy but he kept his hands near a waist as narrow as the girl's---though he stood a good six inches taller than me.

"Well," he said, lips thin, pale pink.

A matter of talking, I thought with a shiver. I kept my eyes bolted to his, dead sure the girl was not five feet away, but just as sure it would be a dirty insult to look at her then. "I'm Claude D'Mambro," I croaked, trying my damndest to look him straight in the eye. He chuckled coldly. For a second the wide-set eyes gleamed with something, but quickly returned to chilliness. I shuffled a bit and felt the water in my boots pressure up between my toes.

"Well. . ." he said again, and waved a heavy-muscled arm at a section of the canyon bottom, at the blasted stream. "Are we trespassing?" I watched; he was serious, a straight question. In my silence the girl stirred, maybe had a terrible chuckle of her own. "Is this your property, do you work here. . .or are you out bird-watching."

The girl laughed easily. He didn't even smile.

"I don't know whose land this is," I said. "I was eating my lunch up yonder, up there." I pointed and we both looked to where I had been. Looking down, I saw the light skin along his jawline tighten. It was so quiet I was sure he could hear the blood pounding into my face and up to my ears.

"I hope you enjoyed it." she said from behind me. My neck

15

muscles went rigid, and sliding my eyes right I just made out the tan jeans. In the space of a long blink I saw the wadded ball of waxpaper, trash of my spam sandwich, falling away into space right before I saw them, saw her legs treading circles in the air. I still didn't have the guts to look at her.

In the quiet, he swallowed. "And what do you *do* around here, bush-whacker?" He spoke the final word heavily, made my belly knot. But his face was relaxed.

"I pan for gold." I talked out clearly, right at his strange face. He laughed. The eyes still chilled into me.

"Just you?"

"No, me'n Piro."

"Piro," she said.

"Yes ma'am. He's probably over there now. We've got a shack on the Trinity about three-quarters of a mile from here. . .kind of a shack." I felt her eyes on my cold back, his on my front, watching me, expecting something I couldn't guess at. He sat down on the grass, right on the spot where the beast had loved. Had to keep talking. "You know the floods last spring?" He nodded once, up and down. "Piro says they knocked hell out of the riverbeds. Nuggets ripped up the size of your fingernail." The edges of his mouth rose a hair. "But we sure haven't seen any." He was still nodding, pulling words out of me. "Some people have."

From the matted grass he stared up at me, eyes shaded by those thick yellow brows. "I know," he said, angling his head to look a-round me. "Kate, Mr. D'Mambro speaks in sentences." He raised his left hand in a sort of shrug or salute. "I'd like you to meet Kate Ximines. My name, maybe you know, is Jones."

She said hello.

16

And I looked at her. I just cocked my head over my right shoulder and we had a stare. Simple. She smiled and the brown eyes went wide open until I thought I would fall back to the ground. She got up, very small, and came towards me just as I had enough sense to turn my head back, and shake Jones's offered hand. She stood beside him. "You're cold," she said and smiled again. I looked away, not knowing worth a damn what I should do, or what they wanted me to do.

Jones, still down in the grass, was chewing on a stick, eyes fast on me, as if they had always been that way. He said, "Kate, please get a blanket from the vehicle," without breaking his stare. My mouth must have fallen down. She laughed, then started off through the grasses. Her hair hung thick and brown down to the center of her back. "Thank you," I called out. She kept going, didn't turn, but raised a hand and kind of flipped it back at me.

Jones threw the stick away, took a cigarette from his shirt pocket. Finally he was watching the ground, not me, so I hunkered down in front of him. He put the Camel cigarette between his thin lips, pressing them together enough to pinch the end of the cigarette. He lit it, sucked hard, took it away from his lips with thumb and forefinger, then blew a fan of smoke into the air like a man emptying his lungs of all trouble. "You'd understand if I didn't mind my own business," he said.

I hesitated. One of his eyebrows twitched. "I guess I didn't. I mean. . ."

"It's all right, man." Another suck on the cigarette, a whoosh of smoke. "Want one?" I shook my head, confused—his offering me anything at all. "Piro," he said so low I could hardly hear him, "means fire in Greek."

"It does?" I tried to smile. And couldn't keep down a quick, rainy gray picture of Piro cackling over all those pans of speckled river grit. "He's my buddy. We. . .travel together. Lots of jobs. You know." I suddenly thought Jones did know, knew everything in

17

my head *before* I got it out.

"Drifting."

"Yes sir," I said.

His eyebrow flicked again. "Who decides things?"

"He does, I'm kind of stupid. . .sometimes."

Jones smiled broadly, which confused my vision and hobbled my tongue. "Well. Where are you from?"

"Ohio, I guess," I answered.

"Farmer?"

"My daddy was. A truck farmer."

He carefully buried his cigarette stub. "Besides prospecting, what else can you do?"

The sun wasn't warming me a bit. "Not too damn much." I was trying to keep my teeth from knocking together. "Carpenter stuff, and I know somethin' about engines."

"I like tools," he said after another pause. I didn't say anything— the trembling was spreading all over my body. I had to get up from my hunker. I stamped my soggy feet and tried to pry my pants where they clung to my gooseflesh. "Do you think you're free?" he asked.

"What. . .?"

"Nevermind," he said quickly. "If I saw some folks copulating in a canyon I might join them in some way myself." He smiled, but not quite at *me*.

"I'm sorry, Mister Jones, I was off my head."

He kept smiling, stayed quiet for a while, and then said, "Yes, Kate can do that. You're forgiven, Claude D'Mambro."

"I am?"

"Jesus!"

"I'll go."

"No, stay. The blanket's coming. Relax, it's a beautiful day."

I did my best, believing the hardest part to be done with. No. He lay back in the grass and started the damn *watching* again. I wanted the girl back. "Piro is a shit, isn't he?"

His question shocked me---booming out of the blue like a gun shot. "Piro? I-I reckon he's mean, if that's what you're. . ."

"I like hunches," he said to the sky. "I'm seldom wrong."

Before he decided to undo the silence again, Kate arrived with a folded patchwork quilt clutched to her chest. She held it out, I took it, wrapped up, closed in the chill. Watching her, I stopped thinking *he is a shit* and simply enjoyed the way her chin pebbled when she smiled, the slight turning up at the end of her nose. And I was still watching her when he spoke again. "Would you like to go to the coast with us?"

It seems I almost fell straight down to my own muddied ground. In my confusion, I looked up, above Kate---who didn't seem one bit surprised---to the canyon rim where I'd eaten my lunch. Impossible, but Piro was up there, standing out tall and stark as a lone tree in a plowed field. In his tar-paper colored jeans he stood with a hand cupped over his eyes, peering down at us. Surely his cackle would carry over the distance, and Kate or this strange Jones would turn, and catch sight of my leering friend. But no sound. Perhaps he didn't know me in my patchwork. Quick as a bug I caught my balance, lowered my starting eyes and said, stupidly, "Where?"

"You heard," Kate said gently. "Jones, you're so abrupt. You want him to leave his partner in the lurch for no reason?"

"Why not? Isn't he free to do what he wishes? Or is he Sancho Panza?"

"Cut it out," she said. "I assume this is serious."

"It is. I am." He got up, came at me and stood very close. Looking up, I could see his teeth, white and skinny, with gaps between. When he spoke again his voice was higher. The words came out in funny short spurts. "I have a sense about you, D'Mambro. . .a hunch. I'd like to have you around."

"Come on, don't scare him," she put in. "It's not a very subtle way of picking him up." She was chuckling enough to make it all seem normal.

He waited for her to shut up. "Right. I'm buying some land south of Eureka. We're going to *live* there. I think you know the world is less than fair; it's corrupt, perhaps a kind of illusion."

"Jones, take it easy," she said, and laid a hand on my trembling blanket.

". . .it's breaking up and America is leading the way. Does instinct condemn us to violence? I don't think so, but *something* is rotten. For now, for me, it's cities. The city is the garrote of the spirit." Kate moved away from me to put a hand over his mouth. "It's the great úncivilizer." She stopped him up.

"Claude, I'm sorry, trips and fields make him pompous."

"I'm only trying to tell him something," he said. "How else to

20

say things?"

"Maybe you could be a little more *basic* about it. Are you trying to convert the poor man on the spot?"

He looked at her for a while, then laughed. "Pardon me," he said in my direction. "I just have an idea about how to live, away from a lot of ugly things. And any worthwhile person who wants to come along is welcome."

"While everything else blows to kingdom come." She seemed to poke at him with her words, but there was no visible reaction from him, none at all---though he lit another cigarette.

A pause for me to check that Piro was still there. How could they miss him? Kate moved closer to me. Now I was half-boxed-in, and I suddenly wanted to run from whatever pulled me to them, whatever made me want to believe anything they said.

Jones's smoke filled the space between us. He trapped my eyes. "I need a handyman, a driver, a mechanic, whatever you are, or want to be. You'll get room and board and. . .what? A hundred dollars a week."

"And some mighty odd company," Kate said.

Jones smiled, sucking the cigarette, ducking his head. His scalp glowed red through the sparse golden hair that clung to the top of his head. He seemed *less* than a giant for the first time since I watched him pissing in front of her.

"Will you come with us?" Kate asked. Again, she touched my quilted, unshivering shoulder. "Steady work, good food, and no need to mess around anymore in freeze-ass streams. We'd like you to come, at least try it out. None of us knows how it's going to work out."

I know how to cook," I said, or maybe I croaked.

"Beautiful," she said.

"I'll do it." I spoke out clearly, and loud enough, I hoped, to carry over the wind to Piro's crusty gray ears.

In New Hampshire, late October, I am beginning to see the skeleton shapes of trees. Caught up, as I am, in my fancied crust on distant ears—the necessary effort to *see* what I never actually saw—too often I fail to see what is happening immediately in front of me: on the other side of these windows of mine where, perhaps, changes more subtle than falling, harlequin leaves go on and on.

This morning Kate appeared in the backyard, the piece of it taken in by my well window, carrying a giant bamboo rake which she proceeded (I saw) to wield with efficient vehemence. Soon she had manhandled several rusty piles of dead leaves mixed up with gray twigs and even larger blowdown from the bordering trees. She fetched an old poncho, laid it out next to her first pile and then carefully raked the remains onto the rubber surface; seizing the poncho's four grommeted corners, she hefted the drooping packet out of my sight. And again and again, until there were no more piles, and the trees had sent down a slew of newly dead leaves.

Later, she appeared at my open window, sweaty and as defiant as any wife who knows she has been watched, but not helped in a job of work. "Hey, voyeur. . .you want lunch?" She frowned through the silvery shadow of the screen.

"I've got some coffee here. Is Ann sleeping?" At my busybody question she screwed her face into irritated furrows that sent me ducking into my coffee mug.

"Yeah, she is."

"What's the matter?" I asked, immediately regretting the words that had become too familiar, an idiot litany.

"Nothing. How are *you* doing?"

"Well, I don't know," I said, wary. "You've seen all this stuff, haven't you?"

"Umm."

"It's a beginning, a start." I tried to sound casual, in command. "It's not easy."

"Blowhard." I thought she was kidding, but she took a sharp breath and sent a loud pronouncement through the screen: "*Education puts pits in your eyes!*"

Even in the act of saying, "What do you mean?" I knew that somehow she had me dead to rights, though I also knew that whatever *she* thought would have to not-matter for now, that my method now had its own momentum, and could not be influenced by her scrutiny or even the violence of her reactions. She met Claude D'Mambro much before I did, but suchlike ironies could not stop me now. I was gone, on *my way*. So, stubbornly, I tried a feint. "What do you mean? Are you talking about so-called intellectuals, people like that Bogue? I've yet to put a single word down about him or any of that *psychology* ilk."

"Quack-quack." She pressed her nose against the screen. Humoring me? "Don't worry, love, I'm on your side."

"I hope so."

"It's just that a lot of people are underestimated. By you, I mean, and you should look into that more, a fellow like you who's stuck in a room with a bunch of boxes and a brain full of stick figures."

"I don't need any leaf-raking kibitzer," I grumped weakly.

She snorted. "I'm just saying be careful how you mix up the truth with that fancy you're so proud of. I mean, your friends are

24

watching. . ."

I shouted, "What do you know! Go away!"

Which she did, but not before hissing through the screen, punctuating the exchange, "Cartoonist."


Now, in the afternoon, with the succor of hot and sweetened tea, I am fair recovered from that well-reconnoitered assault. Perhaps militant wives *allow* themselves to be humored and endlessly flattered, but I doubt they can ever be put off or silenced, not this one. I once saw Jones throw his wife Linda across a room and into a wall—on the principle (I think) of his own privacy, which she believed she had an absolute right to invade. But he was wrong; I'll never be able to lock my room, conceal the facts, or protect my fancies from Kate. Who, after all, was with me as we fled across the country in our Jeep last August.

She and Ann waited tolerantly, if not patiently, for me to burrow into the Fulton County, Ohio, archives for traces of the long-disappeared Claude D'Mambro. I discovered that he had, as he always said, been born in the town of Delta on June 6, 193—; apparently the only child of Julius, a produce wholesaler, and Melodie Rose. These are careful facts I mix in here; the reality of flesh and blood, not the splinters from a stick-figure (Kate, be patient!). The same records indicated that Julius D'Mambro had his name engraved with sixteen others on a war memorial erected in front of the courthouse in 1946.

And the enrollment sheets at Bowling Green High School, Delta, show that D'Mambro completed only his sophomore year, 195—. And he *was* honorably discharged from the U.S. Army at Fort Benning, Georgia, in April of 195—.

But Melodie Rose D'Mambro died, Cook County Hospital, Chicago, in December of 1961. "Indigent."

And I drop this, from the "Harbor Springs [Michigan] Light" of April, 196__, into my oblique "cartoonist's" scheme:

### BUZZER NABBED

*PETOSKY. The Civil Aeronautics Board (FAA) representative for the lower peninsula district, P.G. "Pud" Lowery, today suspended the private license of Mr. Piro Samuel Webster, the owner of a 1948 Cessna 120, a single engine aircraft.*

*Mr. Webster, it was charged, continually annoyed the residents of Harbor Springs, Bayview, and Conway with persistent low-level buzzing. One man present at the hearing, Mr. Dick Yvor of Indian River, stated that Mr. Webster's plane had threatened the life and limb of both himself and his fiancee, on April 14, while they were sunning at Spring Beach on Lake Michigan.*

*Mr. Webster, presently unemployed had no comment after the verdict was spoken. A companion, Mr. Claude Demambri said, "It's not like they said. Piro never means to harm." Demambri, an unemployed cook, did not elaborate.*

I found Piro in a squat behind a thick spiny chaparral pea; discovered his hideout after scrambling back up the canyon wall and followed the path he must have taken back down to the Trinity when he'd had his fill of watching us. I came in sight of the river only to have my eyes light on the empty gravel bar and the mirror glitter of an aluminum pan. It flashed in my fresh eye as I heard his leafy fart. He giggled and thrust his head through the thorny oak leaves, ogling me like I was a three-balled horse. I faced him just outside the thicket, stood in my drying clothes---cool, calm, stuck.

"Where you been, humhead?" he asked, his voice snickering through his nose. He stood out of the scrub, jerking up his tar-paper jeans. "Looks like you fell in a barrel of horse piss."

I snapped, "You bet, Piro."

His oily head sprang up from his fly buttoning. He threw me a hard look. "What! Hey, tell me something, humhead. I saw you down there with them. Cozy, huh?"

"I saw you," I said, watching for the signs, ready for anything.

"Who are they?"

"It's none of your business." He bared his teeth. "But I'm leaving, I'm going with them."

He snickered. "Is that all?" In a flash the grin showed up---a bad sign---and I could see the one snaggling yellow tooth poke out from a corner of his bent mouth. Click, he changed, sneering "Nice, nice, nice." His head was bobbing and he started his sly foot-shuffle. "You just take your goddamned leave, just like that." He giggled enough to disarm a rat.

I stood my ground. I seemed to be watching him from high in the air. Piro, I thought with a happy flash, go to hell, old buddy, I said, "I'll get my stuff from the shack."

"Wait! Where do you think you're going?"

"Eureka. Jones said that," I answered, cautious, and already regretting having said the name.

"Jones huh? And that girl, what does she say, Claude?" He grinned. I didn't answer. "I smell cunt in this." I hit him. Full on where the one yellow tooth peeked out. It bit into the tight skin of my knuckles. I heard him whinny, watched him stagger back and grope for balance on the riverbank's loose soil. His head was bobbing, giggling. A thin froth of blood covered the tooth and bubbled down his chin. "Chickenshit," he sputtered. Even in the light of day his eyes shone greasy red. I had seen it before, this crazy rage, but he'd never turned these funny witch's eyes on me.

I was ready though, with maybe a small clod of laughter sitting lightly in my belly; I had somewhere to go—for sure. So I hopped around on the riverbank like a rooster, with my fists up and wagging at him. "I'm going," I baited, and watched him sleeve the ooze from his lips, breathing hard, eyes shifting gear from mad to sly, sly to mad, a crazy clicking going on in his head. He's going to beg, I thought with a happy twitch.

"Listen to me! You can't quit, we're gonna make it here.

"Why'd you hit me? Bust my frigging tooth.

"What the hell can you do on your own? Look at this blood!

"We talk, don't we, Claude? We always talk.

"Can't leave a buddy, always told you. Don't do it.

"No damn gratitude. What I've done for you the last two years.

"You gonna tell 'em what's wrong with you?"

28

"Now goddammit! Why'd you hit me!"

And burbling spittle from his bent and bloody mouth, he shouted, "Goddammit, you unfucked baby, you won't leave me!"

I was running. Across the shallow part of the river and onto the gravel bar, my heavy foot going thwang on the pan, sending it whimpering and skidding across the gravel and into the water. It sank in front of me and he shouted behind, "I'll get you, mother-fucker! You watch!"

And in the water again---running, lifting my knees, losing way, forcing the current, highstepping to the opposite bank, and all the while behind me I knew that Piro ranted and frothed. I reached firm ground and was up the hill, into the trees, my feet thudding and smashing grasses, branches---I made the shack. It was quiet. Except for my thrumming heart and aching lungs, it was quiet as trees in summer.

I carried my clear head into the rotten inside of the shack. I pulled my denim ditty-bag from underneath the bunks, pawed off my soggy boots, and traded wet jeans for Piro's old fatigues. Some dry dusty socks the color of leaf mold, and back into the stiff boots. Collected for the ditty bag: shirt, jackknife, skivvies, brush, razor; and on me I put my grease-slicked canvas jacket. I jerked the draw-strings of the ditty-bag, fingered a shameful poke of coins in the jacket pocket, and turned hard into the door jamb, a good blow, solid enough to shake the uneasy boards. I loped into the trees, bent on the highway at the other end of Jones's canyon. Where they had to be waiting. I was free.

My father, Andrew E. Flute, who did his sidework in soybean futures, fancied his gambler's self urbane. By controlling and manipulating his thin but buttery tongue he rose to a middling height within the western branch of the business machine cartel. Gambling during lunch (tastefully served by his broker each noon), he became a familiar name in the desperations of the commodities exchange. At sixty, the cartel retired him to his paid-for home in the independent city of Pasadena, where Andrew, the dapper stucco-owner, was abruptly noticed by his family---that is, two sons and a wife. She, my mother, grown fat with living the private, unnoticed life of the fifties, decided that the regular presence of her husband in his home was adequate and numbing cause to take to the bottle. This she did with a will so unfettered that she died before the sixties had barely got started.

After her funeral, in the neighboring city of San Marino, Andrew met and married the lovely but aging Dulce Tobuat---and her three children. Perhaps fearing a vodka-swollen spook, he moved his newer clan to a glassy highrise on Sepulvada Boulevard in South Pasadena.

So that one day---it was nineteen hundred and sixty-three---I drove south from my placid university, pulled off the freeway in Pasadena to find my home occupied not by A.E. Flute, but by James A. Lovato instead.

From this urban displacement I escaped into the library of my great university, inhabited its bygone stacks for perhaps a year before I emerged into the sunlight with the sure knowledge that the *matter* of philosophy, fiction, history, mythology and mysticism could not provide an easement, a haven from whatever it was that had already made me arrogant, gregarious, urbane and facile: the worldly mutterings in my ambidextrous head.

Perhaps I graduated.

I did move to No. 6869 Green Street, San Francisco, California.

From this New Hampshire advantage, at the end of two or three years in that city, I believe I still projected urbanity, gregariousness and, certainly, facility. Indeed, I was a Young Man About Town, a Dandy, a Sartorial Fillip, even a Cafe Name in the city's chattering newsprint.

Only a very slight shift of mood here, and I become (then) a man without: commitment, scruple or substance. Nevermind. After three city years ( I assert), I was the *only* one to hear the hollow sound of my own business, social and rhetorical genius.

There are two possible cures for this inner mush: psychology or calamity.

Enter Calamity, dressed in stately weeds.

Into my tinny, echoing utopia fell a draft notification, a summons of no mean substance.

After three years, Wolliam Victor Flute became speechless.

I have just eaten the lunch Kate prepared for me. In a pint of cottage cheese, the large curd variety, I found several fractured slices of cucumber chips, splotches of corn relish, pepper, four sections of hothouse tomato, an infusion of mayonnaise, several gherkins, and a surface of paprika.

"*Real* history is a subtle mix of anecdote, speech and image," Kate murmured as she left.

31

The psychologist, Doctor Jacob Maven Bogue, shrink to the down-trodden, the hung-up, and a few matrons of wealth, occupied a comfortable office on Bay Street in San Francisco.

In keeping with modern psychology, his reception room was a gallery of abstractions. Shy teak tables supported magical boxes of electrical strobe or hazy photos of the female reproductive system. In one corner of the room was a lengthy phallus shape made of stainless steel, rounded at both ends and suspended from the ceiling by invisible wires. A casual patient might peer through the quartz eye of this cylinder and discover, in complete three-dimensional detail, dozens of Hieronymus Bosch figures copulating colorfully amidst a flaming hell.

The dominant artifact in Bogue's reception room was a massy, upthrusting cluster of grays and blacks—a sculpture whose surfaces seemed to be made entirely of grotesque and filthy nylon stockings, gone rigid beneath a coat of some obscene shellac. Closer inspection might reveal the artist's intentions. "Apocalypse."

Near this piece sat Miss Molly Noel, secretary to Dr. J.M. Bogue. A charming, moustached young man of recently arrested interests, W.V. Flute, entered this room one day in June. It was not for the first time, and it was not long after a business trip to Eureka, California, at the behest of his employer Jones. Flute greeted Molly Noel as he had many times before, with restrained pleasure; his current mistress was as lovely as he had seen, and Flute, of course was not as dissociated from fleshy matters as he (and perhaps Bogue) wished himself to be.

Flute was soon with Bogue.

"You know me as a psychologist with twelve years of training," says Jake Bogue. "My income? The stability is the checks of quirky fat matrons—sexual bleaters. The satisfaction? Convincing people like you of spiderweb conspiracies, impending disasters. That good grass has virtues above and beyond big money or literary orgasm."

Grey-eyed Bogue turns on twice a day.

So does Molly Noel.

Bogue's comments are not always so opaque. "Who really sent you to me, Flute?" he demands. "What Russian Hill anarchist first spoke my name?"

W.V. Flute does not answer. The questions are often repeated, irrelevant, Bogue's method of beginning.

He continues, "You're making progress though. This afternoon may end our weekly sessions." He walks to his window and (Flute imagines) peers at Alcatraz.

Flute crosses his knees, mulls it over.

"Any kind of therapeutic progress requires proof," Bogue says from the window, "and I'm sure I can convince you. Did you know that underneath San Francisco Bay is a large, ignoble crack?" Bogue has repeatedly indicated that he digs the San Andreas Fault. "Is that too elliptical?" He sighs. "The problem is you come here wanting things: answers, predictions, instructions, letters of certification. Why can't a man who craves deferment simply sit and converse with his shrink?" Bogue turns from the window to face his mute patient. "And when I really come down to it, which I often do, I think Molly out there may be *all* you want."

In the face of this civilized accusation, Flute sits knowing that Molly is in the reception room at her desk, where she consumes sunflower seeds, sips tea. More interested in this image than in Bogue's elderly suspicions, he yawns. Bogue returns to his appreciation of the late afternoon June light. Alcatraz glows like a Greek Island village in August.

He says, "My own life is hindered by the American Urban Plot. Even this city. . .no matter how beautiful it might appear to you, its foundation is slipping laterally on greased rock."

Flute nods at Bogue's long, narrow back, uncrosses his knees, fingers his thick, apricot-colored moustache. Twelve years of train-

33

ing cannot be scoffed at. So he listens. "Your current and traumatic dissociation from the *particular* reality you find undesirable
needn't extend to me. You do a lot of staring, you know. Right
now your eyes are jabbing me below the shoulder blades. Perhaps
staring is a form of therapy.

"You do listen though; you're no fool. And Molly agrees, as she
should. So. . .you're making progress." He leaves the window and
returns to his molded leather chair. "Shall we blow some grass? I
believe we've some of yours left. The afternoon is dying. We sit
here like pimples on this cancerous city, surrounded by its lovely,
but crack!-able surfaces. Maybe we can get *higher* on the city's
superb muscle tone. Encouraging?" He laughs to himself and presses a pearl button on the arm of his chair. "Electricity is abstract,
a highly groovy mystery. I've sent for Molly electrically. She'll
come chemically. She does, doesn't she?"

Afternoon shadows make Bogue's tanned pointy face a play-
ground of dark threats. The overhead light, a ricepaper globe,
illuminates. The light drives away Bogue's imagined grimness and,
as his secretary enters the room, Flute comes near to deciding that
he may have cuckolded the wrong psychologist. W.V. Flute plays
a fresh game of checks and balances. On a level with his eyes,
Molly Noel's apple knees pass in front of his chair; he checks a
faint lust. She takes a chair next to Bogue and opposite Flute; the
lust falls in smoothly with his love and balances his impulse to
flee the entire situation.

Molly smiles, knees together, prepared (as Flute has noted before)
to be what they want her to be. The possibility of conflict makes
her lovelier than lovely. Flute knows her eagerness to *watch,* and
falls to staring at his reflections in the tips of his Spanish leather
brogans.

Bogue gazes at Flute, perhaps composing his thoughts into a calm
and amber jealousy. "We were discussing the earthquake," he says,
not looking at Molly, though he must know her hair is glinting in
what's left of the Alcatraz sun. "Light the pipe." He indicates the
small copper hookah she holds beneath one silk-covered breast.

Two months before, Flute entered his apartment's baroque portal

34

on Green Street. Lifting an oxydized brass lid no different from eighteen others in the line, he discovered: an orange flyer from a flip men's store, a greedy alumni envelope (Stanford '6\_); and the not unexpected rectangle -

CALIFORNIA LOCAL BOARD NO. 7

SELECTIVE SERVICE SYSTEM

1975 WALKER ST.

PASADENA, CALIFORNIA

- a manila postcard which said to him, "this is to certify that Wolliam Victor Flute is classified in Class 1-A until \_\_\_\_."

In Flute's head gross movie trumpets bellowed, his intestines crumpled like wax paper. His body spun about three times there in the dusky portal, three revolutions about one firmly planted brogan inside which his five toes curled desperately in upon themselves. The other foot dragged uselessly, until on the third spin-around it lazily kicked the new wadded postcard into a dark corner. Flute went inside.

Relaxed in Jake Bogue's office, they pass the hookah politely and gracefully from one to another. Molly takes the mouthpiece tenderly between her teeth, breathes short once, twice, passes on to Bogue who pokes it into one corner of his mouth and sucks deeply once, then leans forward to allow Flute a turn. And Flute, more prudent, holds the mouthpiece just to his lips---takes brief stuttering tokes. The hookah's sherry-flavored water bubbles merrily for him while the office fills with the ripe smell of Acapulco Gold gently laced with Laotian hashish.

At his armed forces Physical Examination in Pasadena, Flute, chest concave and geometrically hairy, stood in plain underdrawers in front of a thoroughly bald armed forces psychiatrist.

35

"What sympathy I feel for you, young man! From what I read here you are not only totally familiar with the faddish drugs, but you also say that homosexual experiences are not beyond you. Then I see that you are or have been a member of three organizations on the Attorney General's List. And now you stand there and owlishly tell me that the Army experience would be most detrimental to your mental health. Do I know everything?

"You just watch what I'm about to do. You people are all alike. Mindless. . .unsubtle. Balls to the *lot*! Take that!"

The doctor handed Flute his set of papers. Rubber stamped on the first page -

FOUND FULLY ACCEPTABLE FOR INDUCTION

- and below this was inked the psychiatrist's enraged signature.

Remotely, the Presidio military cannon pops off the hour of five o'clock. Meanwhile, Flute, Molly and Bogue are as high as the mixture will allow. Molly's knees relax inches apart, the flowered green silk of her skirt barely shrouds her thighs. Her pale, queen's face floats free and supple for both men—she regards them with steady black pupils as the slack Bogue places the hookah with its bowl of white ashes precisely on the cranberry rug next to his chair. The ricepaper light washes them all, and offers Flute a special late afternoon distortion.

Flute thinks: I cannot guarantee that the necessary proportion will remain in this room. We all seem to be slipping quietly past each other, never separating, building the pressure like Bogue's San Andreas Fault. Molly is a fulcrum. Across from him her tongue arcs slowly across her upper lip, punctuating his swelling conjecture. He recalls taking her to lunch the day, in late April, of his first session with Bogue.

He watched her warm tongue trundle a fried potato back into the possibly sweet darkness of her mouth. The sight of Molly's lips, prettily glazed with chip oil, was so distracting that the backbone and flanges of his most recent dilemma flew continually from his bothered mind. The thought of working his way into the fugue state that Bogue had just outlined (he also called it a "purple funk," or the supposedly simple dis-connection of most terminals to the *real* world) as Flute's only means of escape from an absurd Presidential decree -

(GREETING! YOU ARE HEREBY ORDERED FOR INDUCTION INTO THE ARMED FORCES OF THE UNITED STATES, PRO-CEED THEN DIRECTLY TO OAKLAND ARMY TERMINAL, OAK-LAND, CALIFORNIA, ON JULY 2__, 197__, AT 8:00 A.M., FOR INDUCTION PHYSICAL AND EVENTUAL TRANSPORTA-TION TO BASIC TRAINING CENTER, FORT ORD, CALIFORNIA)

- was quite too much for him to handle in the face of Molly's delicate consumption of fish and chips. Her lips caressed a straw, siphoned a dark cola into the mysteries of her slender throat.

Flute has a tremor just as Molly pries into the lengthening silence in Bogue's office.

"I'm so glad this is happening," she says. Bogue inclines his head in her direction, his white-ash hair neatly curled back over his ears. "I always feel like a Billy Burroughs soft machine. Isn't that strange?" She laughs. "I'm a soft machine made of mushrooms and silky caterpillers. Or a pot of cream cheese, a caramel bush." Flute considers. Bogue sucks in his breath. Molly laughs again and says, her voice like a vaulted lute, "I'm thinking Flute is a sprocket with a twisted tooth. You see, that would never happen in a soft machine. Any twisted tooth would slip back into shape."

Bogue interrupts quietly, "The earthquake dooms all of this, you know."

Molly, staring secrets at Flute, seems not to hear. "But my nipples are like Eagle pencil erasers. Flute is so *odd* over there," she says,

37

and Flute has a second pleasurable tremor, a vision of Molly rising nude  from the flames of San Francisco's '06 quake.

Bogue is determined. "A psychological deferment, a 1-Y it's called," he continues, his voice rising, "sounds absurd in a time of cop-out, Flute, even if it's only a sham? Why this single-minded pursuit when all around you men are being assassinated, asphyxiated, and are soon to be sucked into chasms. Yet you're pathologically concerned with a measly deferment. . .and turning my secretary into a mindless, oscillating piece of bubble gum."

"I like fish and chips," comes Molly's second non-sequitur.

Flute's apricot moustache dances a slight lateral motion. Molly and Bogue, he knows, watch the crowtracks beside his eyes squinch as if he has had some paltry inner twinge. Bogue, with stiletto two-and-two perception, injects: "Have you balled this lady?"

Flute's apartment on Green Street is less than sparsely furnished. Two small rooms, plus a kitchen and a bath, contain: a table for eating, a chair for eating in, an army cot with air mattress and quilted puff the color of chocolate, a desk made of an empty beer keg supporting an ellipse of thick plywood, a soft chair for reading newspapers, a floor lamp, a poster of W.C. Fields palming his four-flusher's hand, and arranged against a wall of one of the rooms, twenty-two rectangular banana boxes containing well over eight hundred various books.

"Are you still balling this lady?"  ·

Yes. The first time, on the army cot no less, beneath the chocolate quilt, she provided a joyful easing for the liquid gloom of his novice fugue. With chip oil fresh on their tongues, the soft machine clutched at him and she said, "Hold on," four, five times while the cot teetered dangerously on its three X-supports. And when he came angels beat tattoos on his eardrums. Slow, selfish seconds passed, until he realized that underneath him she was out cold. Fainted. He found that it happened each time they coupled;

the night before one of the political murders, she was gone a full five minutes.

Why doesn't he stop? repeating, ". . .have sexual congress with this female."

"The external fact of anything at all is pretty doubtful," Molly says, an answer to Bogue, or perhaps a warning to Flute.

But Flute, unfashionably uptight with the draft, and in the slight pall of Bogue's seeming jealousy, realizes that any form of rational proportion still cannot be handled in the office, and so he continues to deny himself speech. Though suddenly the question—the hope—Will this fantasized earthquake occur the day of my Induction? bobs vigorously in his brain.

It is the cocktail hour in San Francisco. Across the street from Bogue's office in *The Silent Woman*, eighteen established professional men of Flute's acquaintance order Johnny Walker Red on the rocks—in the space of fifteen minutes, Flute envisions. Or: in front of a dipping platinum sun the Golden Gate looks like the devil's lacework.

"It's ironic," Bogue says, "that my first positive, if paltry, act against this sick society and its obscenities, my careful instruction in *funk*—in funking-out as it were—should turn out to be not much more than a sleazy scenario for an archetypal and commonplace triangle." He stares at Flute with wide gray eyes. "You know, Flute, you're an extremely unaware person for someone with your background."

He touches Molly's nearest thigh with one extended forefinger. "I've *enjoyed* this."

She does not react, hardly seems to be listening as Bogue goes on. "I have, Flute, and I shall continue. . .if you hear me."

At Flute's requested hearing, Local Board No. 7 glared fiercely at his moustache. The High Official spoke: "Young man, this psychologist, this Bogue, is required by the letters of the law to provide us here with a written and confidential statement of your alleged unfitness to serve your country in an armed capacity in these times of peril and shall we say, prevalent draft-dodging yellow bellies. And even should this Bogue do this for you, Mr. Flute, you will have to report for induction in July as previously communicated to you. We feel very sure that the people up in Oakland will treat you with the greatest suspicion.

"If you have no comments, son, we'd surely appreciate your sending in the next appealee as you leave."

Bogue continues, reflectively. "Yesterday was Sunday. Molly, tell us where you were yesterday."

"On Sunday he was as quick as silver," she sings.

"Oh dear, this is beginning to give me pain, in electrical arcs," Bogue insists with a queer, possessive glance at Flute. "The philosophy of silence, in your case, is painfully comic. . .or comically painful."

"I died and died," Molly murmurs, looking directly at Bogue, either teasing or stabbing him with gritty abstractions.

Bogue closes his eyes, says, "I'm sure of this earthquake. I'll have to pack up my revolver, sell the apartment, liquidate my securities."

"Such prudence, Jake."

Flute senses holes in the office vapor, a change in the room, a return to some kind of logical proportion, a realism with its sharper edge somehow pointed at him---all a very unpleasant invasion.

He recalls an earlier meeting in this same office. Bogue spoke: "What I can do for you is help you to convince them you're the victim of a type of oscillating fugue, a state something like the in-and-out dissociations of the L.S.D. experience, an inability to *fasten.* No, don't worry, we won't actually have to go that far. We'll use a little grass maybe, a kind of referent. And my girl out there, Molly, is always helpful."

Or the third session, when he began to wave his arms and shout: "You're not paying attention! There must be a *reason* for your behavior, or it's no good. It's empty, it's shallow. You've got to be *driven* into the funk by the WORLD, by its insanity." He stopped abruptly, excused himself, and continued more calmly. "The problem is somehow disguising the fact that you're a wispy dandy, a sensualist existing in this world of bombs and gore. . .on his facile wit, an unscrupulous wit that proceeds, I believe, from an emotionless vacuum."

And the first prediction: "This city is going to be destroyed again, and in less than a year. Molly and I and my lawyer friend Phineas Clingsmythe are simply going to leave it, perhaps when I get done with you. The expedition of the wise professionals, ha ha!"

Flute had appreciated the prediction, thought of it as part of the insane therapy; he was grateful for all forms of aid in the midst of his distress. But Molly, of course, was more and more with *him* as the sessions progressed, and this was a situation, a calamity, that Bogue seemingly had not anticipated.

Poor Bogue, thinks Flute, twelve years of training can be scoffed at.

"Jake has the kindest perceptions," Molly said, in Flute's cot one morning in May. "In my bed he's devoted but vague. He's not a saintly man. In fact, slipping as he is, he's probably more dangerous than that fault." She laughed. "I love fanatics."

In the office, Molly's voice overlaps those in Flute's head. She speaks vehemently but, Flute thinks, lightly. "Perhaps this earthquake of yours is just an excuse for splitting from responsibility."

"No, no," Bogue says, "I've no responsibility for this pusing urban

41

rot. And I have no desire to blow it all up. It's just that it *is* going to happen anyway so there's nothing for it but to go away and watch from a distance." He smiles, leans forward and hisses, "Listen to this city burst like a great pimple!"

The last curve of sun is swallowed by the Pacific.

With growing pomp, Bogue continues. "Flute here is a summing up for me, a final hopeless gesture. When he's done, and free, I can leave. I can forget wars. . .pollution, hypocrisy, murder."

"Then what, Jake?"

"I think it's impossible," Molly says with the same queer lightness around the edges of her voice.

In the electrical whitewash Flute notes the twin seams that frame Bogue's proud nose and downturned mouth. And, wondering again just where in the scheme of things comes the earthquake, Flute is moved to say, "Bullshit."

Not so much in accusation, as from a longing for relief. In celebration of this brief independence, he stands, crosses, and kisses Molly's startled hand. Then he turns and smiles to make the wispy ends of his moustache point to the ceiling, and walks out on Bogue with a light step.

Snow---strange to us---fell today, the middle of November, Kate tells me. For the sake of our daughter Ann, and perhaps in celebration of my imagined ability to deal with past psychological trauma, no matter how lightly, Kate persuaded me out of my room and into the outside, our entire "atomic" family (her terms) of three taking careful steps over the thin crinkling of phenomenal white that smothered the hibernating grass. Kate carried Ann through our homestead's first snow, Kate in a light yellow parka and Ann soundly muffled in a snowsuit of faded blue. Her red corduroy cap was a beacon for me as I paced off to one side through the blowing early mushflakes. My feet were crisp and thin in the duckboots, and I felt a brittle relief in this my first outing since mortgaging myself to New Hampshire's suspicious banking system; it was a harsh relief, like a lung-suck of icy air; for the beginning of things, for the tentative, varied, oblique steps into the balky, sometimes exploding past.

Feeling inflated and falsely powerful, I mushed on with my wife and the small creature, until we came to the trees and found a bit of unblowing shelter where we could turn and look down on our house, a tight arrangement of boxes united against the outside. My own windows, now two panes thick for this storm and those to come, glowed amber rectangles at us.

Of her arms Kate made a tidy seat for Ann so that she could peer at the dotting whiteness. I leaned my sallow indoor face into hers and made a series of fatherly but soprano noises until she grinned bare pink gums and blew a breathy steaming laugh at her father's chilly face. And Kate said, "Your old man's finally come out, Annie," with a squeeze for the child and a hopeful wink for me.

But not for long was I out. We walked some more, completed a

43

well-marked rectangle around the house, and with Ann's cheeks bitten red by the cold, went inside.

Where, in time, Kate came into my room and began to gently but persistently rail at what she thinks is the crazy way I'm running certain chronologies, narratives, people and descriptions. "Just look," she declared, pointing at my sheets, "you've gotten ahead of yourself and into a mess."

I laughed and said, "No. It's clear enough. Besides, fast foot shuffles can solve quite a bit." Or the verbal equivalent of a shrug. But she wouldn't be put off by my lightness. A breath of chill outside still lurked in her face and near her hands.

"What are you going to do, flash us a title card? I can see it. Wolly Flute, the skinny impresario, skitters across the stage wearing a sandwich board---'meanwhile, back at the ranch'---and we'll all hunch up, prepared for high western drama. . .a screw for every climax."

Bending away from her small thrusts, I said, "Maybe you shouldn't keep reading this. What's *really* diddling you?"

She snorted, "Who's diddling whom?" she demanded in a low-down mutter.

I thought I knew what was bothering her; at least I flashed a quick, still-photo of Molly Noel lying nude, slack-jawed and unconscious on the rickety army cot. I said, "But fiction is only a verbal bang. It's an invented hard-on. Doesn't it leave women dry as old whitewash?"

"Fiction!" She grabbed the back of my expensive Prague chair and dumped me very painfully onto the cold floor. "Not me," she spewed from above. "You're offensive with your apple knees and silken tits."

"Okay, okay," I said, trying to get out of my prone chair. "But it's just history---it's made-up."

44

"Yeah, the history of my husband's willy-nilly penis."

"This is insane. You *know* all this. You were there."

"Phooey! You've got this whole thing arranged so I'm just a chick being screwed in somebody's paisley meadow. Spread-eagled and empty---what a load of crap!"

"Invention," I yelled, in true pain, my brain flooded with waves of self-righteous blood. "It's the only way to get where I'm going."

"You couldn't invent your way out of a soap opera, you and your five minute orgasms."

"For Christ's sake, Kate." She bent down and unloaded me from the chair as if she were wielding a wheelbarrow. I went sprawling even closer to the arctic floorboards. When I tried to get up she pinned me---very dense for her size. And continued to shout her pricked sensibilities into my ringing ear.

"Here I am. . .lovely small tiny me. . .with my glinting hair and tilted nose." She whipped her clout of hair around with enough force to sting my eyeballs. "Damn your words! Feel these. . .can you feel my copperpenny nipples through my sweater. . .my pencil erasers. You jerk!"

With a cowardly bellow I eluded her on the floor and fled to a corner of my much too bare room. She crawled after and tackled me into a squat, my back wedged into the corner---a hunkered stalemate.

"Why don't you come out of your self-indulgent fog, out of this *spiffy* room. . .see what's in front of you, what's real. Can't you disconnect your romantic-fuck brain and make love to your wife. . ." She was crying. "Me! Do you know how long it's been, do you?"

"Kate, I hear you." With that fragile punctuation I rose slightly from my crouch, and pitched forward so that in a trice we were laying together on the abused floor. Her face was beneath and inches away from mine, a profound exchange of attitudes. I knew I had to go very damn carefully. "Where's your sublime sense of what's silly? Huh?" And, thankfully, she responded with a soft, teary laugh. Safe, for the moment.

She said, "I know when to attack, and you're getting off easy," and, at the same time, managed to insert a hand, still warm from the struggle, into the area covered by the seat of my thick trousers. "Lackbutt. That's *one* true thing you've written this fall."

"Thanks."

She kneaded and fidgeted over my rear end, and eventually we arrived at that most familiar, still most-sound arrangement of two bodies—the Missionary Position. The softest of kissing lips. "Are you here?" she asked after a time. "If you are, I welcome you back, and I love you. . .for fear you've forgot." Both of her hands were now doing god's work over my tail.

"My poor knees, my turgid groin," I complained.

"A rare proof," she responded, a mite too quickly. Chuckles in my ear.

"Your point's made. Maybe you don't attack me in my room often enough."

"Why should I have to attack you at all?"

"You. . ."

"Even if you are a *refugee* trying to survive in the Maine woods."

"This is New Hampshire."

"Sure. It's all this passion distorting my sense of place." And then, by design I think, she arrived at the dark backside of my frothing balls. Fingertips unsullied by nail edges. I forgot to maintain my sore, kneecap and elbow equilibrium, and allowed my stricken body to fall onto her ribcage. "Oh boy," she whispered, "I haven't felt this kind of weight since Ann was born."

Quickly catching myself, I kissed her mouth, sparingly at first, and received a nip of her tongue in reply. I went right ahead with my own tongue, into the most accepting of mouths and tasted, now: something metal like new snow or fresh anger; a hint of Ann's clean hair; a rush of urgent Kate as she swept into my own mouth and gave my front teeth a glad tap.

She said, in a minute or so, "You really are here, Flute."

"Please. Let's go up."

"Upstairs? To make love?"

"Yes."

"And you won't come back here and write it all down exactly as it didn't happen?"

"If you tease me I'll go limp as this tit," I said, and very nimbly, despite my deadened knees, jumped to my feet, pulling her up with me and even into my cradled arms, enough balance remaining to stagger to the door, into the hall, up the stairs, and to the quilts and downs and sags of our tarnished brass bed....

Should I try to remember the progress of yeaterday's, last night's copulation? I sit here, bussing with that effort. I think, on the one hand, that no sexual favors should be *performed* in anyone's

47

delicate marriage. I don't want to wield my body like a proper tool, while my sad brain is haunted and wrenched. Kate, Kate, you say sex is *everything*: we live by the cock or the cunt. But where is this ideal state? Where must I soar to find it? Last night, for sure, I was not there. Forgive me, forgive me my mere *performance*. But. . .see it!

It begins with the act of flying an airplane, which I do only in frantic dreams; at times my body is the entire fuselage, other times I am the helpless passenger. Now, the stick is something near my navel---I grip it there. We go. A brief, upchest motion and together we enter a steep climb. Watch Out! Telephone wires crosshatch our infinite space. . .with the ballward motion of the stick, we are committed to an agonizing power dive, stitching our way through the living wires. I level out. With a punch of power to the groin, we are away from the wires, free for now. Going smoothly on into the waiting fog which is suddenly like sheets of white canvas rippling around us. I waggle my wings, but my soupy shroud doesn't clear, not a bit. Kate is speaking into the muffling fog, talking into bread. "Why don't you go? Go!"

But I don't know where I am. Both of us crane our tuned necks in search of the ground, which isn't there. Wait, see the dark ribbon aquiver down there; it's a snaking grease smear below our wings/limbs, a highway, is it? A chalk strip twists down its dead-center, and I congratulate our mutual vision. "See that road curving." But already it's gone by, there is nothing but to re-enter the kiss. Kate's tongue, a swollen triphammer, taps my teeth clean out of my soaring head, but I do not let go the stick. I am flying by the seat of my pants. My heart is in my asshole. Careful, lady, if you go in there I'm a goner. We will crash.

Flying on, I'm in danger of losing my companion in this purest fog imaginable, as white as our sheets. I must adjust my knees to this altitude; Kate is an engine winding up in a circle over the small of my back, pumping my juggernaut body until the parts must give way from strain.

Now a new smell of salt, the fog is suddenly shot through with salt. The sea? A wet throbbing in all of our viscous fluids: I'm down, going down to this ruby conundrum; let me open this new mouth, peer into the coral. The drops of saliva turn me into the very mucous. There are smooth membranes in this sea salty fog. I see strings of opaque spit traveling one membrane wall to another. Sweet womb, I want no contraception in this lovely anonymous sheath. Reversing, climbing back up to the pilot's seat and, remembering to navigate, I reach for the stick and encounter one soft hassock of a breast. Where is the *mother* stick! We are rudderless; flapping; I fumble with the trim-tab, for we are out of kilter. A damned female with a snail's bush is interfering with my flight. Please give me back to the fog; I think I know what's at the end of it. My god, she's flipped us, and I'm head down in a field of gay fog, beset by gravity, and something soft and warm puffs over us. She keeps sitting up, going erect, kneeling on the stick, and meanwhile her neck tendons turn to ice. Come back, I call, a gentleman-pilot is here to console you. Up with my knees, slide my hands to her rear until they both meet over that other, unmentionable center. Smoothing it down, gliding in, our bellies extended and at work like regulated pistons. Ahh! I'm returned to my righteous pastures, these white foggy pastures in the air. But the salt is back, like a tumor in my nose, and I hold to her lower cheeks for dear life. Her laughter greets another flip of bodies, but I hold to the liquifying fog; great droplets of water appear behind my eyelids. Blindly, I crouch in front of her, pushing, pumping until she gives way; she's jumped the plane. Gone. Must I radio what I see, what I hear? Because I do hear Jones, the fog voice saying, "I'll hump your dreams, Flute." Didn't she kill him? I cannot listen to *this*! Not while my part is sunk straightaway into the woman who chose *me* over the ghost dying in my head.

Kate reappears beside me, pulls the throttle and puts us into a seventy-mile-an-hour glide through the gleamy white. The muscles in her shoulders are tight, like Jones's biceps. . .Shut up! Zooming

49

now, past the point of no return, though his voice is still shooting off into my brain, ". . .hump your dreams," and I'm jerked up short in flight; the plane is empty again. The dim gray outline of some mammouth rock dances before me in the fog. Stopped, suspended alone on Jones's tether. "Why don't you go!" Yes, *she* goes on and on in the dark. I wrap both arms about her slender neck, holding myself rigid above her while she slaps onto my suspended stick, reaches for my dumb balls; I come unstuck, rejoin her---though my head is still in interrupted flight. "Like that, yes." I'm there, moving fast, presenting the favor, but barely moving, and her neck tendons might snap any second. Let me go!

I think, I am immobilized. But the hand is back, fingers doing a hornpipe around my asshole. In. And I'm on my way, right at that mothering rock, a gleaming sea monster which I immediately recognize as the Point Sur Coast Guard Station. No mistake. Kate is moaning in my ear---she's taken care of---but her sounds fade, she fades, as I leap to my hundred-mile-an-hour glide at the rock, fifty small white explosions of fog ripping along my arms/wings. My heart is going on all cylinders until the liquid rising makes me deaf. But its not the Coast Guard Station at all; I've made a terrible mistake. Jones stands on the rock's battered summit, the sun breaking on his amber head. He looks up, grinning a splendid welcome---I flair out to land just as I see the blood spilling out from his mouth and nose like sacred, suppressed liquid. And suddenly, horribly, I'm going off into his lady to beat the fucking band....

So. Having seen this film, this dream, this haunted dreamfilm, I'll say the obvious: I'm bothered, itchy, unsure of myself. I'm not feeling so lightfingered anymore. Must I say good-bye to you, Kate? Should I now lock these guilty papers away from you, permanently entomb my soaring, babbling privacy? But you're on to me, you are; you'd *know*, whether you had access or not.

At supper tonight, over Ann's bologna, Kate pulled me slowly over the coals. But so calmly and peacefully did she do her work that now I almost welcome an approaching return to the warm safety of facts, the verbatim details of that old life.

"Can't you just forge ahead?" she asked. "You really don't have to do things so nervously." She came across the kitchen and touched my face. "I feel good, Flute. You're with me."

"I've still got a ways to go," I said, trying for a self-possessed tone.

Her arms circled me, hugged. "Of course, and that's okay. But get the past straight before you start making connections in the present. You know, go forward. . .the plain style, the simple form." She was positively gay with *her* vision.

"Well. . ."

She stepped away from me. "Come on, you know what I'm talking about. Like what happened when Claude ran out of the woods to the highway, free as he was?" Somehow her mood was bending at the wrong angle. Ann whimpered from her high chair. "Aren't you going to *make-up* his narration of that?"

"He's. . ."

"Don't look so smug, I hate it when you do that."

"Damn you, I'm about three thousand miles from being smug!"

"Boy, a speech. How brave. I'm sorry, I know you're going to go back in there and continue your logical and sequential narrative." Her sarcasm fell like shards at my feet. She moved swiftly to the stove, then she was beside Ann; bending, coaxing, feeding. "Flute, I *know* you're confused, bothered by all those things that were beyond the whole goddamn world's control, but you think you're so special!"

"No I don't," I said automatically.

51

"Oop, sorry, sore spot again." She straightened up and regarded me for moments and moments. "Okay then, how about some plain old rootin' tootin' action to keep the remorse off your back."

Seizing her clear offer of an easy out, I smiled, then laughed, and Ann joined me, her mouth like a small black pit. While Kate fussed over the stove with her back to her children.

Now, back in my room I grope for the momentum necessary to follow her advice, which, as usual, I was too proud to acknowledge to her face.

Definition: *For some of the people in my collection of names Jones was a kind of free-form prism, a translucent center, a man who would focus the chaotic and blind energies of his random satellites.*

(Kate, good-bye, for sure. I will see you.)

Recall, then, that W.V. Flute, the ubiquitous millionaire's vassal, the subdued victim of fanatical psychology, the unwitting tool of the mute forces of conscription, embarked on an automobile journey in late May to the northern California city of Eureka. After a few days at the non-existent Honeydew Tavern & Hotel, his employer told him by phone, and circumstances allowed him, to return to San Francisco; where Flute had other, psychological obligations. Thus, on an early June morning, Flute entered his Morris convertible and bent his way south. Meanwhile, as noted, Jones and Kate drove the fantastic weapons carrier north for their arbitrary rendevous with Claude Augustus D'Mambro. This accomplished, they soon arrived (all three of them) at the infamous Honeydew in Eureka.

It was here that D'Mambro was visited by a nightmare in which many white sheep of a certain flock became mixed up with his recent, garish memories of Piro Webster. On this same night, that is the late evening of the day of bucolic fornication and accidental voyeurism, yet another mythic political figure was assassinated. It

52

is apparently true that the following events occurred more or less simultaneously: D'Mambro dreams of sheep and disruption; Flute and Molly are copulating on his teetering cot; a single small-calibre bullet zaps this political-god; Dr. Jacob Maven Bogue dines on spaghetti and steam beer; Jones and Kate speak of abstract matters in the Honeydew Bar; and before they can all, together, reach a state approaching sleep, the politician is pronounced absolutely dead.

Just after sunrise the following day, Kate, D'Mambro and Jones drove thirty miles south of the village of Honeydew, on the western edge of the Humboldt Redwoods State park, in the King Mountain Range. A bank of the Mattole River provided a location for their presumably somber breakfast. Jones then drove the gaily colored weapons carrier southwest until the third-class dirt road gave onto the property and house of sometime songwriter Oyd Fikes.

Fikes, at that time, was widely known in the area as the composer of "Whereat My Ramblin' Rose?" which was nominated for a Country & Western "Grammy" in 1961 or 1962.

In the celebration of this run of factual material let me be clinical about the three people who have just stepped out of their vehicle, and are about to confront tunesmith Fikes. Jones is six feet three inches tall, thick with muscle, blonde hair laid back on his skull like fine wire. His clothes are a pair of light green Levi pants, leather walking boots, and a blue tee shirt. He is colorblind, twenty-five, and classified *IV-F* by the Selective Service System.

Kate's head reaches to within five inches of the knob of Jones's shoulder. The sun glints in the brown of her long, smooth hair. She is a small, twenty-six year old woman, short in the leg, wearing white jean pants and a worn duffel coat with pockets that forever hide her hands.

Next to her, but hanging back in the shadow of the weapons carrier, is D'Mambro, with a knot of dusty hair above a face that seems to be in perpetual motion, a face that looks freshly burned no matter how much it has been in the sun. Medium in size, there is a suggestion of pudginess along his jaw and belt line. He slouches in bluejeans and a stained cloth jacket. D'Mambro is thirty-four years old.

The three of them stood on the edge of the neat Fikes lawn—looking, smelling the fresh morning air, shuffling in the dew—until Fikes came out of the house, and surveyed them from the porch. In the safety of the shadows he squinted over his holdings: his lima bean shaped swimming pool, the swaybacked barn, the yard. . . .and the three visitors standing in front of an incomprehensible black and yellow truck. Fikes moved out of the shadows and trundled down the porch steps. Near the pool he rested again, blinking at the strangers. Who, likewise, regarded him. They saw a man dressed entirely in khaki, the costume of a rancher who has finally moved beyond physical labor.

Despite the distance between Fikes and his visitors, it is clear that he is even larger than Jones; and well gone to fat. What is left of his physical dignity remains above his shoulders. A noble head of slicked-back gray hair, slight jowls, a handsome snout, and, most noteworthy, bushy ears the size of fists.

One hour and thirty minutes after this mutual sighting, standing beside the spanking new swimming pool, Jones concluded, with a handshake, an agreement with Fikes that the latter would sell him his five hundred acres of coastal property, his two-bedroom house, his barn and pool, for the cash sum of $150,000.

Reinstalled in the Honeydew Tavern & Hotel after this quick exploit, this grand liberation of a chunk of soil, redwood, beach, sand, concrete and vinyl, the three drank some whiskey in the bar and spoke very little while the TV rendered a public funeral three thousand miles away, muted drums and all.

Late that evening, Jones placed a call to Flute in San Francisco. I submit this verbatim transcription of the conversation:

Jones:    Flute? Who?

Molly:    This is Mistress Nell. Are you royalty?

Jones:    Molly? I want Flute.

Molly:    Everybody does. 'R you in heaven?

Jones:    Is he there?

Molly:    That is not the question. He's barely. . .

Flute:    Hello. Get out of the way. (*laughter, both ends*)

Jones:    Are you folks drunk there?

Flute:    Not drunk. Now. . .am I not efficient? You didn't have any trouble, I'm sure. Do you ever? (*laughter, Flute's end*)

Jones:    Will you listen?

Flute:    Always. I've discovered that neatness counts. Funerals are very *neat*.

Jones:    Okay.

Flute:    Okay? What's this okay? Dammit, Molly! You're right, sir, this is Jack Daniels burble, and the conversation is deductible. It's really swell to be on your team. . .in time of ca-catastrophe.

Jones:    Do you still go to that brain shrinker?

Flute:    Sure. It's a business venture, you know. He has a very untidy intellect, and his sex life is a shambles. Goddammit! Molly. Excuse me. I'm sorry, this is a waste of your money. What's up?

Jones:      Fikes agreed to the deal.

Flute:      Yeah? What kind of deal? I'm *sick* of everything. I
            got a yen to accept the Army's offer; the military
            takes care of you. . .underwear, scrambled eggs.
            It's a very safe, bloody system.

Jones:      I said Fikes accepted.

Flute:      He's a fascist, you know. I set him up for you;
            charmed him silly. He's a down-home boy all right.
            Homespun. . .he'd fuck your granny for some extra
            steel in his eye.

Jones:      Shut up, Flute. Here's what I want you to do.

Flute:      You *are* a hard son-of-a-bitch. What is it? Why
            don't you get me and this deranged lady out of the
            city? (*laughter, Flute's end*)

Jones:      Just get the money business arranged, and I'll see
            you down there on Friday.

Flute:      Right, friend. Bye.

"Call the place *Eureka*, then," Kate suggested after hearing Jones's
account of his attempted conversation with Flute. Not to imply
cause and effect, but rather to suggest some unknown irony that
might have occurred to her while she watched the bar TV and
sipped her weak bourbon. I know she's capable of these ironies
from time to time. But onward!

The next morning, Jones called Fikes and after an exchange of

56

pleasantries, convinced that jug-eared coot to take Claude D'Mambro into his home until the Fikeses could straighten their affairs,
gather their possessions, and take leave of their property. Fikes
was assured that D'Mambro would be a help and a boon. D'Mambro drove the weapons carrier south late that same morning. In the
afternoon, Jones and Kate went to the Eureka airport, where
Jones rented a single engine Cessna 180, and flew himself and Kate
to Palo Alto.

A week passed. Flute (still sadly *I-A*) placed Molly Noel in the
Morris, and the two of them made the trip north to the city of
Eureka, and sometime in the middle of this June, legalities neatly
arranged by the efficient Flute, the Fikes land was deeded to
Jones at the Humboldt County Courthouse, in the presence of a
clerk, Flute (with Jones's Power of Attorney), Molly, and both
Oyd and MaryJane Fikes. Flute and Molly immediately returned
to San Francisco.

Two days later, a Monday, returning from Palo Alto in the rented
airplane, Jones flew over his latest purchase---identifying its eastern boundary with ease; the blue lima bean shape of the pool
stuck like a perverse eye just in front of the Fikes roof. In the
midst of this mash of date and names and skeletal but factual
events, I take some pleasure in noting that as Jones sailed over his
land, beside him Kate was helping out of the plane's left hand
door, Miss Bobbi Love, a twenty year old friend from San Francisco. Bobbi Love jumped from the plane, a yellow parachute
strapped to her back and an insulated box of rock records belted
to her waist.

By the skyhole pool I stood barefoot in a shimmer of blue heat. I was pushing the odd lightness of an aluminum pool skimmer against the back force of the water, picking up a wilting yellow banana slug along with snakes of dog hair and weed. And I was listening—listening over the underground humming of the pool's filter device for a door to slam, for Mary Jane Fikes to come out with a stub of sweating beer bottle for me. It was hot and squint bright, and my toes had got rubbed raw on the new concrete of the pool edge. The front screen door of the house cracked shut, and I peered up at the shadows of the porch. In the hot blue brightness I couldn't see anything.

"You, Claude!"

"Ma'am."

"Come get this beer."

I looked up above the sun-grayed boards of the Fikes's house, above the easy rise of shortweed behind the house, and made out the dark brushy tops of the giant redwoods at the edge of the state park, maybe two rolling miles away.

"I haven't got all day!"

"Coming," I said to a Mary Jane Fikes I couldn't even see for the porch shadows. I dropped the skimmer beside the pool. It made its light clatter, and right then I heard a metal coughing, a sputtering noise high above me and toward the redwoods. Where before the sky was an unbusted blue, now there was a small green airplane that looked to be coming out of a long glide near the tops of the trees. But the noise had not come from that far off.

"Claude, you quit that mooning. We've a lot to do before Oyd comes back." Mary Jane was not happy about leaving her home.

"All right, I'm coming." A swooshing sound right above me. Something bashed into the pool. The water burst out of the pool

58

all around. Mrs. Fikes whinnied from the porch. Dumb-still and dripping I sensed that something was settling down on me, that it wasn't so bright anymore. I looked up, water running over my face and blurring my eyes, and saw that the above was all yellow, bright yellow, and whatever it was was settling faster and faster. Then I saw the thick white cords trailing down to the pool, where they gathered at some white thing. A person dressed in white thrashed and sputtered and threw even more water on me.

The yellow stuff kept on settling in a soft circle until it blocked out the house and most of the front yard, leaving me trapped in this tent along with the wriggling figure down in the water. "Hey you!" he said. The yellow parachute stopped falling, held by the hot wet air rising from the water. "Help me, I'm all tangled, I'm all tangled UP!" A girl's voice.

Outside, MaryJane Fikes set up an awful wail, jolted me out of my dumb standing. "Claude, what is it? What's in there?" she scream-ed. "Are you all right? Where are you, for pity's sake?"

I leaped into the water that was now gold with the sun shining through the silk chute. I hit bottom hard and through the under-water blur I saw her boots flailing to keep her up. With my raw toes I pushed against the bottom and slowly sailed up to her. When I broke out I saw that most of the trouble was because she couldn't undo the soaked chinstrap of her crash helmet.

"Be limp," I said. "I'll tow you. I said I'll tow you." She finally heard and stopped struggling. I grabbed hold of the harness release that was a dark metal circle on her white chest. My knuckles pushed into softness as I got a good grip on the thing and began to pull.

"You, Claude, what's that you're doing?" I looked up from my tugging and saw MaryJane's face, like a spying mouse peering through a flap in the chute. "What's that you've got?" she shriek-ed through the narrow slot.

We were sinking and water was flooding into my mouth from the girl not being limp anymore. "I'm helping this lady," I gurgled.

"Lady? Jesus!" She disappeared from the bright slot-hole.

With some struggling, and more water heaved into my mouth, and the girl thrashing like a caught fish, I managed to fetch out my knife and cut away the shroud cords. We were sinking more than not. But I cut through enough of them so we could make the edge of the pool without much resistance from the billowing parachute. The material began to sink down to the water, falling softly over our heads. With an elbow on the concrete curb, I worked loose her helmet strap. And she ripped it off. Fistfuls of wet honey hair tumbled down from her head, clung to her face and fell to her shoulders and below, down her back where I couldn't see. It clung in swatches and curls to the lightly tanned and smooth skin of her face---a tiny face with a narrow nose and a mouth as small as a nut. Her hard round chin thrust up and out at me a ways below eyes the same green-blue color as the pool water. We stared and shared some seconds of noisy panting. She made an 0 of her small mouth; her eyes shined and dappled like still water in the bright sun. "Wow," she said, and followed it with a breathy laugh that she couldn't keep the nervousness out of. We floated easily in the water with our elbows on the curb, in a deflated yellow tent, staring at each other. I felt heavy and light at the same time. "That was some landing I made. I mean, I looked down and saw you and the next thing I knew I was bamming right into the water."

"It was a shock," I said.

"It was beautiful," she said.

"Kind of dangerous."

"I've never done it before, and now I have. Haven't I?" She was teasing.

"I guess so," I said, still in the shock of her face.

"Hey, help me with this, I forgot." She began fumbling around her waist below the surface of the water.

"Hold on, I'll do it." I poked under the water, in the direction of the box on her waist. I could see the pink skin showing through where her white jump suit was stretched tightest. By the time I stopped seeing that, she herself had got the thing loose and up out of the water on the curb. A plastic, glossy orange box which stuck up into the folds of the chute like a thick tentpole.

"I bet they're all wet and warped," she said.

"If it's records I guess they are."

"Yes," and she laughed the shaky laugh again.

I said, "There's Mrs. Fikes out there. Maybe she's fainted."

"Then we can stay in this cocoon for a while, old Claude." I should have expected it, but her speaking my name startled the hell out of me.

"What a peculiar face."

"Who *are* you?"

She rose up out of the water, grabbed my leaking head with her fists, and tried her best to duck me under. We struggled and churned the warm water to a froth; I found one of my arms wrapped around her narrow waist, the other supported us both on the concrete. The chute rustled around us, and against my own soaking chest pressed the skin that peeked through her jumpsuit. "Bobbi Love, dummy," she laughed, inches away from my face.

In the midst of her first kiss Oyd Fikes came crashing up in his Ford truck. We heard him yank the handbrake, the slam of a door, his heavy boots on the grass.

"Claude's in there, Oyd." MaryJane had come to life.

I could imagine Fikes pulled up short, calculating over what he saw.

"What's happened to that pool, MaryJane? How 'bout you telling me that first."

"It's that Claude," she wailed. "And a girl, she came right out of the sky."

"Don't be 'sa stupid." Fikes stamped up on the concrete and ripped up the part of the chute that covered our heads. We both smiled, me with my face still warm from Bobbi's kiss. "Aw right," he growled---fat man with a shovel face and lantern ears that glowed red in the afternoon sun.

"Mr. Fikes, this is Miss Love," I said.

". . ."

"She's with Jones," I offered.

Fikes crouched with hands braced on his knees. "Don't say?"

"Yes sir, Mr. Jones dropped her off."

"Just dropped me," Bobbi said, pinching the soft flesh of my side and laughing.

MaryJane came round and stood in her dumpy body behind her husband's bulk. "I knew it," Fikes exclaimed. "Something damned funny about you people. Not a one that ain't odd, MaryJane."

62

"The neighbors 'll be a long time forgiving us," she echoed. "Margaret Pickel's going to have a hissy. When I told. . ."

"Shut your face. Claude, get that thing off the pool, hear."

We got out, and while they stood like brood cows watching us, we gathered up the parachute and managed to stuff it back into its pack. Thin as a twig in the soaked jumpsuit, Bobbi bent down and pulled off her boots. She stood barefoot with her hands on her hips and said to me—paying no attention to the Fikeses—that we ought to go to the beach and dry off.

"There's work to do here," Fikes put in. "Don't think you can just gussy off. Who's gonna load the rest of our belongings? Tell me that."

Bobbi laughed. Fikes flushed as red as his ears. "Look, old man, Claude's ours, not yours."

We went to the ocean; took towels, bottles of beer ("That's it, get loaded on my time!" "Dry up, Mr. Fikes. You're not paying him, and this place isn't even yours anymore.")' the weapons carrier, and went bouncing over the humped dirt road that runs in a squiggle along the north edge of the property, to the deep cove on the west edge. We climbed down the steep-cut cliffs to reach the ginger sand, and once down we were sheltered and private from all but the wind and the sky and rolling smash of the Pacific.

"Put the beer in the wet sand," she shouted. The wind made tatters of her words.

When I came back she had spread the towels together on the ruffled sand. She sat crosslegged on one blue towel and her hair, still wet, fanned out over her back, lighter than Kate's but just as

63

long. When my shadow fell across her she leaned back on stiff arms and half-turned to me; the thin stuff of the jumpsuit stretched tight over her nipples. "I'm inside." she said. "I don't like it. I don't want to be inside anything." She unpropped one arm and tugged at the collar of the suit. "Take off your shirt, old Claude." Odd grains of wind-sand skittered across my bare back. "You're as white as a fish's belly. You are." She sang a song with no tune -

> *Soft belly...*
> *White belly....*
> *Push-belly Claude*

I dug my fists in the hot sand, and the hard wind blew around my wordless head. Then I lay back, with no idea of what to do or why or anything, and closed my eyes. The sun flushed a bright yellow through my lids. I heard her get up and go off. After some time, a spray of sand fell into the palm of my outstretched hand. I opened my eyes to the blue of sky and a dark edge of the seacliffs behind us. A low laugh. I turned my head, blinking, and saw a big knot of blue work shirt sleeves at the top of her dark, skinny legs—she'd knotted my shirt around her middle; she wasn't inside anymore. Above the shirt was nothing but smooth brown skin, small breast hills with nipples like shadows in the glare.

She laughed again and kicked sand over my belly. "I'm the sun," she said, and came down on her knees to blow the sand from my chest and stomach. "Do I burn?" She kissed my rigid neck with dry lips, then slid them over my stubbled jaw and found my own. The mass of her hair blotted out the sun, and I put a shaking hand to rest on her arched back—brought it up along the bumpy ridges of her spine and found a home at the back of her downy neck. She hummed over my face with her lips, came to my ear where she stopped long enough to blow an easy roaring into my softly exploding head.

The knotted sleeves of my shirt pressed my lower belly. The whole length of her body was there beside me, going against me. The knot disappeared, no cloth, and she was saying, "Oh good, good," into my ear, and for the first time I acted on my own. I kissed her, and our hands made wild treks all the while, I hardly knew where. I heard the wind and water sounds as loudly as the grains of sand we jolted together underneath us, and I was knowing nothing and seeing nothing until out of my head's bright glare came a blue waterspout that rose up from nothing and smashed me dead.

"Come to the water now." I wasn't answering for the moment. "Come on, Claude. . .or your prickle will burn like a ruby."

"Uhh."

"Here, this'll get you." She took hold of my numb bent part as if it was a lever to be gently tugged.

"Hey!" But I thought I would fall in two with tired joy. Finally the whole business had happened, and it was simple. We got up and went bucknaked to the ocean where, like Kate, she cupped cold water into her crotch.

"That was nice," she said later, stretched out on her stomach on top of the towel, while I sat beside her and ran my hands over her back and butt, which was not much bigger than my two hands--- and the same tanned brown as the rest of her. "Didn't you think so?"

"Sure."

"They didn't tell me what a cool customer you are."

"Customer? I-I. . . ."

"Easy," she said. "It's a figure of speech." She calmed me, wiped out the flashes of Piro's deck of dirty whore-pictures. "Are you a fretter? I say that's the only sin in the world."

"I dunno. . . .I'm glad, if that's what you mean."

"Good."

In front of us the waves shot forward, lifted and dropped heavy and foaming into the trough they'd battered and scooped just off the beach. "I don't understand," I finally said. She rose up on her hands and cocked her head at me. "Why are you. . ."

"Now you're fretting." She scrambled around on the towel until she was sitting cross-legged beside me. "It's simple. I like you." She touched my chest. "And for a while I'm going to be with you."

"Just like that?"

"Don't be dense. We can do whatever we want." Her finger pushed hard into my belly.

"I'm a handyman," I said thickly. She flung her head back and laughed at the sky. "I am."

"Okay, if you wanna see it that way everybody is. Jones is a handy person. He can do *anything*!"

"Where would we. . .stay?" I asked, startled by my nerve.

"On the ground, in the barn, the trees. Everywhere, fatso. Does it make any difference?"

"It gets pretty cold up here."

"Let's get it straight. I'm here for the summer; most of us are, I guess. I'll be back in the spring, maybe even Christmas. Did he say you'd be here the whole time?"

"Jones?" She nodded, staring over my shoulder at the cliffs. "He didn't say."

"Do you know what a dome is? That's where we can stay. We'll put one up there, and make love on the beach every morning. Okay?" She smiled and casually touched the light, fluffy hair of her crotch. "Don't look away. I'm looking at you."

And after a moment, by damn, it didn't bother me a bit—as if we had been sitting naked together for months, years. She reached out and held my part in her hand, like a bird, staring all the while at the scrabbled towel between us. "Let's drink a beer," she said. I rose up and marched off, exposed, to fetch the beer.

I handed one down to her and sat with my back to the water. She was on her side now, with her head propped on a hand near my waist. After a couple of swigs from the stubby bottle, she said, "Those other human beings should be here pretty soon." She sounded sleepy, not looking for any kind of reply from me. I looked up at the cliffs, thought calmly of Piro, of Oyd Fikes grunting and sweating without my help, of this funny girl beside me in her skimpy body. I saw a movement, a flash of red against the dark rocks above me, but at ease as I was I didn't pay any attention.

But Bobbi Love wasn't so lax. "Somebody's up there," she said under her breath. I tensed, looked around for my pants, but she didn't move a muscle. "Don't do anything. If that's the way they get their kicks, I don't mind." Did she see me blush? I revolved slowly on my butt so that my back was to the cliffs. "Do you know the neighbors?" she asked, taking a sip of her beer.

"I know Mrs. Pickel a little."

"Sure!"

"Yeah, she lives about three miles toward Honeydew."

"People are weird. Whoever it was is gone."

"Trespasser," I muttered.

She laid her hand on my leg. "Don't sweat it. When the people come we'll get to work, put the place together."

"Who is this Flute guy?"

She giggled. "He's a *handyman* who works for Jones. Wait 'til you see him; he's a very fancy dude." She wrinkled her nose and upper lip. "I don't know, he vibrates wrong. My friend Robert, his brother says Flute deals drugs, but. . .you don't care about that."

"Kate likes him."

Bobbi shrugged, began to run her fingers over the insides of my legs. "You'll like Stein, I expect. He's a painter or an environmentalist or something, and he's beautiful. Ever since I knew him he's been trying to own a live giraffe."

We both laughed. She got onto her knees, leaned over and kissed me. When it was over she pulled back, very serious in her eyes and mouth. For sure, she'd gotten my mind off whoever it might have been on the cliff. "One thing," she was saying, "you'd best know about Robert." I couldn't help it—I jerked back out of her arms. "Listen, Claude, he really is my best friend, and he's sort of flipped-out, loony, Robert Quell. It's like brothers and sisters." I relaxed. She ran her palm over my chest. "He's in the nuthouse." I nodded, automatically trusting her just like everything and everybody else. Then, for the second time in my life, and forgetting the watching cliffs, I made the beautiful beast with Bobbi Love.

Winter is amok outside. Inside, Kate, when I see her, is strangely quiet. She spends hours with Ann, sometimes carrying her through the crusty snow strapped into the back pack. But for two days now, a great storm has been upon us; still, Kate moves through the house without a sound, and when she has occasion to come into my room she smiles as if I were just another child in her house. She brings meals and liquids, pats me from time to time, makes soft remarks that seem to indicate she has been lax in keeping up with these pages---or doesn't care. What omen is this? Does she no longer care to prod me with her special chiding? I suppose the vacuum is pleasant, but I am edgy.

Well, Christmas is coming, perhaps a seasonal excuse to break fast habits and find my wife among the tinsel and mistletoe. But for now, while this storm batters my blind windows, at least I can limn an historic topography.

*Eureka*, one hundred and fifty thousand dollars worth, was the shape of an elongated V---a wobbly V with its legs slightly bowed. The house, barn and pool clustered at the narrow end, the apex. From there the land rolled and spread west to the Pacific cliffs. A shallow stream coursed out of the pure stand of redwoods two miles behind the east of the house. It flowed near the house, side-stepped the barn, took a slow curve north, and then ran straight to the ocean a half mile away. The land west of the house sloped in short ridges and wide pastures to the sea, broken here and there with scrapple stands of shorter redwoods mixed with bastard fir and spruce. In several areas grew thick clumps of madroña scrub hung with fat yellow berries.

Mornings, through that summer, fog slid in off the ocean. Balls and fingers of it crept through the trees and over the house. But it was gone by anyone's breakfast.

By the end of June, on top of all this, and in residence, were several of those whose names I have been bandying about. Gone were Oyd and MaryJane Fikes; those gentles went sour-faced and grumbling to a rich suite in the immaculate city of Eureka, fully intending to live out their life in the golden light of Jones's social security.

And yet another ploy, this from the "Weaverville [California] Weekly Gazette":

### GOLD!

*FAWN LODGE, June 18.*
*Not in vain are all you fellows sifting our streams and rivers. Today the Gvt. assay office reported that Piro S. Webster had discovered a small but by no means unsubstantial quantity of gold in the bed of the Trinity River.*

*Chuck Woelful, of the assay office, said Webster's find was of a good and pure nature, about $700 in this crazy new market.*

*Webster opined that there should be no rush to this area as he had cleaned out what little gold there was.*

*When asked his plans, the Michigan native said, "I got my goods. I'm going to Eureka."*

*Keep up the work, men!*

At least my present isolation leaves me free to play these newspaper gambits. Apparently there is no danger of Kate bursting in to hiss "melodrama" in my lonely ear---the shaky confidence of a man subject to his wife's moods.

The storm continues yet, seemingly burying my house in snow,

70

as I reach for another foredoomed definition: *He was an organizer,*
*a man of many skills, both practical and esoteric. From his squat*
*architect father he learned carpentry, electrical matters, a little*
*plumbing, the proper use of good tools; not to slight the more*
*sacred cant: personal responsibility for all actions or inactions; the*
*value of money; the sanctity of the family; and a morality based*
*on love, the Golden Rule. Whatever it is, do it perfectly, or not at*
*all. Amos Jones raised four boys to be competent, fastidious, nit-*
*picking gentlemen.*

Or perhaps TRUE DEFINITIONS flow more naturally from accurately arranged FACTS: Jones decided on the geodesic domes
before he bought the land. In June, he and D'Mambro built three
35' square platforms of unfinished pine, each raised a foot off the
ground on a foundation of 6' sections of spruce logs buried five
feet in the spongy soil. They located one platform in front of the
pool, another farther west perhaps two hundred yards, and the
third close by the seacliffs. The framing struts for the dome triangles were to be made of redwood cut on the property. The
Gant Lumber Company, out of Eureka, agreed to provide the
machinery necessary to make board out of tree. But, early in
July---the first Monday---there was an interruption of sorts.

I woke up Monday morning at six, before Bobbi did. Most mornings she pinched my chest and blew hot rushes of air into my ears until I came to and flailed happily to make her stop. Not this morning. We slept on the floor of what once had been the Fikes's bedroom, slept curled and wrapped in two sleeping bags zipped together. Nights, Bobbi's habit was to spread the two bags over the floor---a soft field for us, she said. Not soft; it was hard as the bunks Piro and I had on the Trinity. What woke me this particular morning was the floor poking up at my backbone. I opened my eyes, as usual, on a window full of fog. I could see it sliding secretly by the house on its way to the state redwood stand. Drops of water clumped together on the bare glass of the window; some drops had slid loose, making wet brown trails down to the sill. I got up and went to the window. Behind me she made small movements and sighed out something. I pressed my nose against the damp glass and tried to make out the feathery tops of the distant trees. But it was too gray, too blank. I couldn't see much beyond the crumbling stream bank fifty feet behind the house.

"Claude." I turned. On her back, she stared up at the ceiling with squinched eyes and just a fleck of a smile on her mouth. "What're you doing? Is it a new dawn?"

"Nothing," I said. "It's Monday morning."

She sort of gasped, then rolled over and stared at me. "Oh, Claude, you're so definite. Come back here."

I suddenly felt choked by the fog outside, the girl inside. "There's a lot of work today."

"Great, swell, chop-chop, bang-bang. Come down here, I'm cold. Get in this bag."

I did. And while the room creaked in its bones and the fog squatted outside, we made the wordless morning love she favored. I was quick, and when it was done I got up into the gray damp air and found I had a funny knot in one corner of my belly, and her calling me a "rabbit," even if she was laughing, didn't make it any better. She wasn't always easy, or simple, this Bobbi Love.

In the kitchen she tried to make eggs and coffee, something she was poor at. Stein and Flute were lumps on the floor near the fireplace. I watched her, not saying anything, until a gob of hot fat lit on her hand. She cursed. "Turn the gas down," I said.

She turned away from the stove; the front of her jumpsuit was speckled with grease. "You do it," she whispered. "Get your own eggs, grouch!" She picked her way over Flute and Stein and went out the front door to the porch. Through the window I watched her walk past the swimming pool and disappear in the fog.

Stein sniffed the air, hawked, got up and followed his great black-haired belly to the bathroom. Jones came into the room and kicked Flute, who shimmied out of his sleeping bag and grabbed his buckskin trousers while Jones sought out a cup of coffee at the stove. Dressed, Flute came and sat on a box next to the stove---he was red-eyed and messy, not much of a dude in the morning. Jones padded around the room in his straightup, erect way. Without a shirt, his stomach muscles stretched taut above his belt.

"Flute," I said, trying to find something I could do right, "I will make you some eggs." His rusty little moustache twitched. I began to futter with eggs and the cooled, carbon-black pan. Jones came for more coffee. "Do you want some eggs?" I asked. He shook his head. "I thought I heard Bobbi."

"She went out. . .to wait for the sun, I reckon."

Flute picked at his trousers, yawned. Jones poked a thick forefinger into his shoulder, and Flute jumped up from the box like he'd been bitten. "You staying?" Jones asked him.

Flute moved away from us, toward the fireplace, one hand over his sunken chest. "I'm going down tomorrow."

73

"If you'd bring that *chick* up here, you'd save a lot of gasoline." Jones was laughing as he spoke, but Flute didn't seem to hear---he found his shirt, got it on, and went down the hall. Jones turned back to me, smiled, shrugged. "I guess you shouldn't deal with some people in the early morning," he said.

"You gotta perk up," I said, banging things on the stove. He rubbed his stomach, then held out his coffee cup. I poured it full.

"Claude, you're all right."

I put the pot down, reached for the lard, and with my hand in it, snuck a quick look at him. But his head was turned away. ". . . thank you," I said, for lack of anything else.

"That crew is coming at eight."

"I'll be ready," I said, wishing Bobbi would get back before we had to go to work.

Later, I went outside and watched the gloom that still huddled around the house; it was time for the fog to be past. Some fluke of the weather on this Monday morning. Someone had left Jones's chain saw on the porch boards near the stoop. The yellow casing was shiny with dew. Drops of water had gathered on the greased beak that shaped the chain. For something to do until the lumber crew came, I took the machine and went down behind the barn. I hefted the twelve pounds of saw, thrust it in front of me, pointing its stubby end at the back wall of the old barn, holding it by the grips like a machine gun yanked off its stand. Gas sloshed in the tank as I swung in a circle with my feet for a pivot, playing a silent game---shooting the fog to shreds with the saw, surely to reveal to my eyes Bobbi Love running for me in the sun. Things *were* perking up. I was spinning like a kid flying one of those wasp-buzz airplanes when I heard the sound of a heavy truck crossing the bridge over the stream, chugging up the road and into the yard on the other side of the barn. Not wanting to be the greeter, or listen to the talk, I squatted down against one of the woodpiles, still carrying the chain saw.

74

Thc screen door of the house slammed. Both doors of the truck banged shut. The barn blocked whatever words were getting said while I sat and fiddled the saw's gas primer button. Behind me the stream cut quietly through dirt and rock. The fog began to thin, no doubt about it. I was loosening up myself, ready to go to work, break a sweat.

I got up and walked around the front end of the barn with the saw hanging from one hand. A dusty red-orange flat-bed sat next to the weapons carrier in the yard. Most of its grimy bed was taken up by an old gas-powered buzz saw. I eased around the weapons carrier for a look at the men over by the pool, three of them, talking to Jones. Kate sat behind them on the porch, vague in the wispy fog. Three of them, all with their backs to me. One, shorter than the other two, wore a pair of greasy pants. Slouching, familiar, he hung back while Jones talked and pointed out over the brightening ridges, in the direction of the pile of young redwoods we'd cut down.

It was Piro. That short man, that hanging back man was Piro. I dropped the saw and crouched alongside the front wheel of the weapons carrier. It figures, goddammit, it figures. I kneeled in the grass with my head empty of plan, only remembering in a happy flash the feel of my knuckles pushing into his face, the bite of his tooth, the froth of blood at his yapping lips. In slow gray motion Jones was cupping his hands to his lips, calling out. The sound came across the spread of lawn like a queer low echo. "Claude, Claude!" And just as slowly, Piro turned and saw me rooted in the grass beside the screwy spotted truck—no barricade against the grin that surely came over his face.

I got up from my knees, wet knees, chilled backbone, and walked towards them, moving fast, thinking: I can handle this. *I am among friends. I am among friends.*

"Are you ready then?" Jones asked. I took a deep breath and nodded. "These guys will take care of the logs."

"Yessir."

"Yes sir, yourself," he said. "This is Bub Gant." He gestured but I kept looking at him. "And Joe Gant, and. . .what's your name?"

"Piro Webster."

Jones's gesturing hand stopped in mid-air. He cocked his head to one side. I stared at the still hand. "I see," he finally said, and let the hand fall. "You guys will have a lot to talk about, eh?"

Among friends, I thought, and turned to look at Piro. He was smiling, almost politely, standing in an easy slouch with his hands stuck in his back pockets. "Howdy, Claude."

"Piro," I said.

"You two know each other?" asked Bub or Joe.

"Yep," Piro said. Then came what my tangled guts had been waiting for: he giggled, with his chin sunk into the neck of his shirt.

But Jones cut him off, "Let's look at your equipment." He started for their truck and on his way past me he took hold of my elbow and squeezed hard. Bub and Joe followed him, Piro didn't move.

"Nice set-up," he said. His voice was low and rasping in his throat. He jerked his head at Kate on the porch. Stein was sitting with her now. "That the cunt over there?"

"Watch your mouth," I said, and stepped toward him. He laughed and started to walk away. I followed.

"You should've stayed, humhead."

"I like it here."

He stopped. "Have you got laid yet?"

"What do you want?"

76

"I wanna fuck you up," he said. "What is this, one of those free-cunt tribes? A man named Fikes is around Eureka saying his old place is crawling with Commies and freaks." He poked a fist at me. "You ain't hard to find, clown."

"I don't owe you anything," I said calmly, and walked past him to the truck where Jones and the other two were up on the bed fussing with the buzz saw. Piro came and stood away from me, next to the weapons carrier.

"I want ninety one by threes," Jones said. "In four and one half foot lengths."

Piro leaned on the front fender of the truck, pulling at his crotch. The chain saw lay just in front of him. He picked it up, gripped it with both hands. "This work?" he said into the gray air.

"Leave that be," Jones said from the truck bed.

Piro looked at me and giggled. "Oily little mother, isn't it?"

I started towards him. "Put it down."

He showed his tooth and did a queer dance away from me in the direction of the house. Somehow, with a quick blurred jerk of the pull-cord, he got the thing started. It sputtered, coughed once, then whined into tuned, well-oiled pitch.

"I said to leave it be!" Jones yelled.

"Hey Webster, quit dickin' around," came from Bub or Joe.

Piro got a good hold of the machine with both hands and began to spin around exactly the way I had behind the barn. The saw was alive and snarling in his hands. He spun in bigger and bigger circles toward the pool and house.

I started after him, hearing behind me Jones's grunt as he jumped from the truck and hit the ground, hearing then an awful moan, enough to make me stop and look back to see him laid flat on the ground, Bub and Joe gaping down on him from the truck bed.

Piro gave the saw full gas, it pitched and shrieked, and Kate rushed past me, crying, "His back, it's his goddamn back!" And she was by me, kneeling over him, while I stood stockstill there, looking from the flattened Jones to the crazy spinning Piro.

I went after him, my boots slipping and sliding on the grass. Close to the house, with his weapon flailing in the air, he stopped his wild turning and made straight for the porch. He thrust the saw out from him like a battering ram. And there was Stein, side-stepping along the length of the porch for an impossible inter-ception; Stein flowing down that porch like water. He leaped, and cleanly missed Piro. He fell and skidded on his chin in the grass. I stumbled on, my head whining like the engine.

Piro reached the porch and sheared through one solid redwood support post in the time it takes to spit. He sheared it once, and then again, higher up. A piece the length of a baseball bat spun to the ground just as I reached him. I leaped at Piro over the fallen Stein. But he was gone, on to the next post—the saw teeth clawed through the wood just like paper.

While I picked myself up and the screaming pitched even higher, the porch roof sagged loose in slow silent motion. It sagged, pulled slowly away from the front of the house, and fell or fluttered to the porch itself, where it split right down its center.

I was up and after him again, past someone—Flute—peering through the screen door at the remains of the roof.

Behind me Stein shouted, "What! What!"

And Piro reached the pool. He scuttled up on the diving board, holding the shrieking saw like a jackhammer. I hit the concrete siding just as he cut through the end bit of board and canvas slipguard. I hit the concrete full tilt, leaped to the back edge of the diving board, pushed hard and sailed into the air to meet the center of his crouching back with my own stunned head. Both of us went free and tumbling in the air. The engine coughed, gasped. We went down. The water cut to silence Piro's loud, final giggle.

# PART TWO

So.

It's a beginning. A *neat* beginning Kate might say. . . .

To declare: I, W.V. Flute, have spent nearly three months following my private and ambigious path to an epoxy moment in the air above one fogbound swimming pool, a color snapshot of which I have propped here in front of me this very Christmas moment. And how bold of me to call the shots of this suspended moment through eyes and ears other than my own, even if (for a change) I was very much present myself---in the peripheral role of comic porch lackey.

*Lackey.* It's like a word from one of the chiding scenes Kate was fond of initiating not so long ago. "Oh, you've written yourself out of lackey-hood," she might say. You see, Kate, at the end of my beginning, I am---like Sinbad---on the very top of the situation; like lying, virtuoso novelist (which I'm not) I am in control. Of course, I will admit to being conscious of the swarm of events about to be let loose, just as soon as my epoxied people come unstuck. But who can fault me for wanting to pause a moment before the swarm, to stop, to create a brief, garrulous silence? Momentarily, it will be lickety-split into the rural and urban course.

But, for now, please accept some frozen moments of another sort during New Hampshire's Christmas season.

Mr. and Mrs. Wolliam Victor Flute and their daughter Ann spent the season alone in their well-caulked home. Mr. Flute locked up his on-going project, ignored his papery reveries, bought through the mail a piece of soapstone Eskimo sculpture for his wife, and an oak rocking horse with marble eyes for his daughter. His freshening memory contrasted this with other Christmases past.

In Pasadena, the jaunty soybean factor would say, some December 25th mornings: "Yes, well, Mrs. Andy Flute, she wants us to go ahead with the presents, with this whole day in fact. She has a small headache, a chuckle in her chest." Flute's mother being vodka-smashed for Santa Claus.

At the great university. Flute, Ellen, young Bellamy, Mila, and others drove south to Big Sur, took a cabin, poached a tree, tinseled their heads with tablets of LSD---ah, that early sixties acid--- and ate fried eggs by the dozen.

## FEED YOUR HEAD!

Merry Christmas excess, while Flute's freshman consciousness expanded to include an unending coastal vision of the Point Sur Coast Guard Station.

Or New York City, the year after his graduation, stalking the fire-bomber Bettina Miller, Flute wore a spanking new three-quarter length suede coat: Christmas Profits. "Bettina," he phoned, "I'm in the Tombs and need a lawyer. I'd like to. . .uhh. . .be sprung for the holidays." She took him for plum pudding at Max's Kansas City. "Baby," she cried, tackling him in her vestibule, "there's no place for drug dealers come the Revolution!"

And yes, even this: California's Death Valley, three years ago. When Jones first spotted his future wife Linda Saint Thomas in the distorted perspective of the dunes, piled like snow drifts to infinity. . . .Well, *he* would never admit the Romantic Bullshit of that Christmas jaunt. But that's seven hundred and fifty dollars a month alimony, Mr. Claus.

And finally, sucked forward in time to the one and only *Eureka* Christmas, Flute balks. . .

So it's Christmas in New Hampshire, the here and now. Home, hearth, family.

Maudlin, Mr. Claus?

On Christmas morning, some long-buried psychic alarum struck me, about six a.m., into complete wakefulness, as if I had gone to bed with a snootful of methamphetamine only an hour before. I felt so *ready*, so clear, that I immediately thought to leap from our bed for a nude run through the snow pastures of the neighborhood. Instead of acting, I lay in the warm sinking field of the bed and reflected that I had had no cigarettes this recent Christmas Eve, no nicotine and no visions. . .while we quietly fucked the eve away.

Kate woke up.

Ann howled from her room below.

Kate offered me a rare morning smile, and I realized for perhaps the n-th time in this my one and only marriage that this woman would not be smiling at me, would not be smiling at all, had she not happily and successfully engaged in coitus six hours before. Instead of opening her eyes to the memory of it, they would open to nothing more than the yowling baby, a sound punctuated only by her dormant husband's fetid breathing. This kind of thinking, these realizations, I find very difficult to retain—like dreams—once I step from that funky bed. I should try harder. If I could only remember to be *here* at the right times, I thought (smugly) as Kate rolled out of the bed and ran into her icy clothes. She bent to pull her jeans the short distance of her legs. Her breasts hung pointed to the floor like two. . .lovely. . .beanbag. . .cones.

"Kate."

"What." She put on the damned mangy blue sweater, the same I think to throw away, unknown to her, every New Hampshire morning I live. "What! Am I supposed to listen to your lapses? The baby's crying."

"Merry Christmas, love," I said, gripping my morning balls, my early member.

"That's right." She ran a noncommital comb through her hair. But smiled again, a glint of orgasm in her eyes. "Are you getting up?"

"Are you kidding? I'm on my way."

We ate pancakes with maple syrup. I was well-shaved and wearing a red wool shirt with a green bowtie, for the sake of the day.

"Kate."

"Yes." She was bent over cleaning Ann's masterful breakfast mess off the high chair. If only I had done something to deserve this; I'd be dead and buried without her. She straightened up and gazed on me: lapsed again. "I think your, ahh. . .reinvigorated sex life is turning you into a *dolt*," she declared.

"Pardon me, I'm just. . .thinking. I mean, remembering a lot of things, little films in my head."

"Oh? Is this a sentimental breakthrough?"

"Be nice," I said. "In case you didn't know, I love you."

"Ha! Next thing, you'll be scribbling a light, first person memoir."

"Shit, give me some more pancakes."

"Anything for a man on top of the situation." And, though I fought it, Sinbad's gay monsters rose before my eyes as clearly as the new stack of pancakes. No matter what was biting her it was *me* who suddenly shuddered for my locked room where the gents still hung over the pool. "Eat," she said.


ACTION!

Of sorts. I sit now toying with a genuine document, a personal artifact, certainly the first evidence I might introduce to prove my boxes contain more than news clippings. I have a portion of a letter, a personal letter to Jones from Bobbi Love. It is written on four paper placemats which were originally the property of a now defunct coffee house called Saint Mikel's Alley in Palo Alto, California. Or perhaps it is complete. It's not signed. That it was written by Miss Love will be clear enough. As the letter itself will clearly be a device of mine to reach.

ACTION! A New Voice! An illuminated Robert Quell.

(I crab closer to the heart of the matter, believe me.)

Bobbi's handwriting is like a second grader's exercise in O's—loop'th'loop'th'loop:

85

*Dear Jones*

*I'm sorry. I was in a tree. You were always saying, before, that Claude was such a nice <u>KIND</u>, especially a gentle person. I guess he can be, but I saw what he did, a contradiction you would say. Not so nice and that's why I left. I'm sorry about stealing the car, and you can tell Flute that <u>his</u> car's okay. If you say so I'll come up there with Robert who's well now. If I am not being clear it is because of confusion. I had to leave when Claude did that to Piro (?). Maybe Claude couldn't help it, but it was terrible just the same. You had one idea that people up there wouldn't do bullshit things to each other, no hurting for one thing, but it sure didn't come out like that from my tree. Why does the past have to be such a big deal anyway? Claude <u>knew</u> something freaky was going to happen---he was nervy, like that, but I thought it was because of all the new people. Well, it was a good time to take a walk, so I had to see that guy with his nose cut off. It's not Robert Quell who's a lunatic---he doesn't go around cutting houses with saws, falling around like a stinking battlefield. I saw the water turn red, maybe you didn't, like blood. That man's face in shreds. . . .And HE DIDN'T HAVE ANY NOSE JONES!! You let that happen. You're supposed to be such a great spirit, but man you really screwed up. Everybody did, don't listen to me. Robert says. . . .*

Robert Quell is going for a Monday afternoon walk, remembering in flashes like blown out bulbs where he is supposed to be going. And in a single flash why he should be going to the foxtail grove where he might have hidden his intricate Mexican box. The box is like the wallet he would have if he could have one; only memory can open the secret compartment, which the whole box is: press the varnished square, push the lid with a thumb, anticipate the creak of the hinges, tremble.

Because Nurse Kelp issued him warnings, spilling like foul pearls from her lips. "Don't go beyond the Elliott Tree, Robert." "Don't sing to Lois again. Lois thought you were screaming." "Don't frighten people. Are you listening?"

But it is simple to go beyond the Elliott Tree, and on down to where the lawn ends and the courting bushes for the patients begin. Robert carefully wades the bushes, then stops to make sure the hills still exist. They do, at a distance over the green valley; he sees them as a crowd of soft girl shoulders, rounded, and tanned by the summer light. Of course, there is a reason for moving on to catch the first vanilla sight of the foxtail brushes along the river bank. At the Elliott Tree, Fred LaJolla gave Robert a square message, a message Fred made with brown crayon on a piece of drawing paper like silvery filmscreen across his lap. He folded it and offered it to Robert, who thought it might be a fine sketch of the bright brown hills. Thinking this, Robert left his hands much too long in his twill pockets. Because Fred dropped the folded square lightly on the lawn. "Pick it up, dopey. It's serious, ya know." Robert leaned down from his height and picked the white bit off the lawn with both hands, as if it were a delicate tray, or an electric flashbomb.

With the foxtails fully in view, Robert remembers with a tremble the note now in his back pocket -

A LITTLE GINCH GIRL, NOT A INMATE, WANTS YOU TO

COME DOWN TO THE RIVER & SEE HER

IT IS URGENT

He hurries on toward the river, his stride lengthening, as if he were hurrying for subways in New York City. But if he ran *there*, he remembers, the lights would become a bumble of fluorescent tubing and topple on his head. He hears the thump-thump-thump of his heavy cordovans on the California soil.

URGENT

But where is she? He holds his hands aloft and runs his palms over the furry foxtail tips as the ones in his path give way to his bulk.

The Mexican box is buried in a clearing about ten feet from the Russian River bank. Nearly there, he hears, just barely, words in *her* voice---they override the sound of rushing water like explosions from an air rifle. He stops, his arms still outspread beneath his large, cocked head. The words in the air multiply in his ears and come to some meaning at the exact flashing moment he knows that he already knew: BOBBI! She is calling from invisibility, "Robert, I hear you, I'm over here."

Now he's a gangling, flailing juggernaut, bashing through the foxtails those few feet to the clearing, seeing her before it is even possible. In his head he sees images of the girl in every posture of going and coming, and in a second they become multiexposures, revolving and jerking one atop the other until he stumbles into the clearing and finds himself on his knees at Bobbi Love's damp, bare feet.

W.V. Flute, vassal, novice draft-dodger, unwilling pursuer of stolen cars, is winnowing down California's Route No. 101, underneath him his crusted russet Morris, above and surrounding him a bright and clear mass of roiling air. On a complicated first Monday in July---winnowing through Garberville, past round hills fuzzy with sunburnt grass; on to Legett, Willits, Ukiah. The slight, moustached man in the moldy car is in hot pursuit of Bobbi Love.

In Ukiah he stops for gas and a telephone booth.

"Talmage? Three mile."

Flute approaches the booth, steps in, inserts a dime, ratchets the operator, and is put in connection with San Francisco---Molly Noel whispering from Jake Bogue's reception room, a direct connection. "Hullo," he says cheerfully, for he is cheerful, despite the excesses and reversals of the day, "I'm in Ukiah on a chase. . . . What?. . . .Yeah, I'll see you when I can. . . .Heavy scene up here this morning. . . .I don't care. Tell him to go analyze a mirror. . . . I'll see him at the end of the week. . . .Some guy wrecked hell out of Jones's house and D'Mambro cut off his nose and Bobbi Love stole one Margaret Pickel's car and winged it. . . .Yes, it's hilarious; this whole scene is a hell of a lot more involving than business. . . . Excuse me?. . I'm counting on her going to see her friend Quell. Bogue knows of him. . . .Got to go, see you. . . .No, I don't want to talk to him. . . .Bye."

Bobbi covers Robert's ears with her soft hands. There are sounds of laughing and crying fighting for breath in the air. With his eyes on the black wet dirt, and Bobbi's hands over his ears, Robert can't help but confuse the sea-roaring with all the other sounds, all the while worrying that it is not right, is never right for her to cry with him. Yet the laughter blurts over the sea-roar too; it flashes great orange and blue sprockets across his closed eyelids. Robert is crying. A corner of him is ashamed of stumbling, while the gay sprockets continue to wheel across his lids, directing a machine-like raising of his head from the dirt, the shaky soil-covering of his Mexican box.

She is laughing at her old friend, he can see, after the fantastic golden shock of opening his eyes. A whittled, glowing doll hovers above him in the foxtails, laughing, with shimmery drops falling from her eyes. That have been looking at him all this time.

Her hands continue to cup his ears, and now she uses them to ease him from his knees and into a squatting position, both of them completely out of sight in the foxtails. Robert is a big man, and the weight of his butt is warm on his thick calves. Bobbi kisses him on the end of his nose. The light weight of the kiss topples him on his side, like a tree falling to a snug fit with the earth, and he hears what Bobbi says, "Stop crying. Are you happy to see me? I'm on the lam, do you wanna come?" before the voice from the box in the ground, or from those mean places in his head, speaks:
*You were both on top of the mattress ticking, remember? Sure, you imagining those things to do to her, wanting them all to*

*happen before she went off to California, but being smart enough to keep your grubby dimwit hands to yourself. And she knew what you were thinking, and was kind enough to go away before you exploded. Bobbi left you in the city with Peter who was pretty sure why you wouldn't sleep on that particular scuzz of mattress ticking anymore.* Robert gets up from the ground.

Flute drives the Morris into the Mendocino State Hospital parking lot. Before his eyes the elegant patients stroll about in pairs and threesomes---over the clipped green grass, beneath landscaped oaks, near fat shrubs. They are dressed, men and women, in soft breezy costumes of their own choosing. An occasional nurse flicks by in white. "Where is Mr. Robert Quell, please?"

"By the tree, the one there, we call it the Elliott Tree. You be kind to that boy."

"He gives you trouble?"

"No, no trouble. Just that we lose him. He forgets so easily." Flute thanks the handsome nurse and strolls on to the tree. A man, not Robert, is sitting under the tree with a drawing pad set on his knees. "Hello. Where is Robert Quell?"

"Who?"

"The big blond guy who never says anything."

"Just who wants to know? Fuckin' crowd around here today."

"He's a friend of mine." Flute watches the man scribble quickly across his topmost white page, rip it from the pad, fold it carefully into quarters, scowl at it, and hand it up to him.

"Go away now. I don't have to truck with you, weirdo." Flute goes on by the Elliott Tree and stops to read.


YOUR FRIEND IS DOWN IN THE FOXTAILS

WITH HIS COCK IN THE MUD


"I came to get you, Robert," Bobbi says. "Come on, let's go." He smiles at the echo of her words in his head. "We'll get lost in San Francisco." He reaches down and touches her shoulder, sees the bright speckles of light in her blue eyes. But that yelling is like a bassoon blowing up in his ear.

"My wallet," he says, listening intently.

"I've got some money." He tumbles to the ground and furiously scoops thick gobs of dirt into the air. "Shit, here comes Flute." Her hand digs into his barren scalp, slips down for another hold on his ear, jerks him erect, a ruby sting of pain, and they are off along the riverbank with Robert still clutching a handful of the muggy dirt—it vibrates in his mammoth fist. "Come on, you lunk." Soon they are cutting away from the river and up the incline to the parking lot. She pushes him into an open one, into the back seat, and makes him squinch down among the newspapers and junk until it hurts and he cannot think anymore of what he might have forgotten. The machine makes grinding, spitting noises; by the time it comes to motion Robert Quell is moaning and crooning over the floorboards.

W.V. Flute witnesses his second automotive theft of the day. A-round him mill the handsome nurse, the man with the pad, and other patients in their wondrous smocks. They all watch the re-treat of Flute's Morris with wise and wizened grins.

"Ha Ha, Miss Kelp, there goes another one," says the pad man. "A willful release."

Flute carries his irritation to the car Bobbi has abandoned, happy only that Bobbi Love hadn't the slyness to take the keys with her on the second stage of her flight.

The patients breath with excitement behind him. "What d'ya think that dude will do now?" "He better take Robert's stuff cause that boy won't be back, for sure, he's a voluntary." The pad man dashes off and returns with a bundle of clothes which he hands to Flute in the car.

Flute drives off and soon turns north on Highway No. 101, back to *Eureka*, accompanied by the smell of the stolen car's interior--- stale patina of small Dutch cigar smoke. Moving north, encased in steel and the unmistakable aura of Margaret Pickel, he calculates along legal, moral and sexual lines. Because his thinking is three-dimensional tick-tack-toe (the key to his *worldly* success), the car automatically noses into the service station, dips its white snout just in front of the battered telephone booth he left less than forty minutes before. He calls the Honeydew number, connects with Stein, receives into his ear a collection of information neither pleasant nor alarming; in fact it is what he expected to hear. "I'll try to be there by seven," he promises by way of ending the conversation.

He next is given a line to San Francisco, and his humming tick-tack-toe game is slightly ruptured when he hears the voice not of Molly Noel, but of Jake Bogue, an eerie voice that burps through the wire like laughing gas -

Ah! Hello. Breathes there a man? I knew such was my fate. . .is why there is no secretary's voice to again welcome my patient with soft fleshy syllables as toothsome as a fresh and hairy clam. In other words, Flute, I set this up, sent Molly floating early into the streets after she told me of your most recent difficul-

94

ties. One can cohabit with one's employees and still not explain them many, many things. Eh. . .What's happening, my bullshit friend? Let me guess. Your hands are covered with a mixture of legal, sensual and violent gore; you are about to be inducted into the most efficient war machine on earth; and at the immediate moment you are listening to a man you do not know, love, or trust, whose *quirks* you perhaps take too much for granted, while in point of fact you continue to lay my sole reason for continuing to function upon this faulty earth. But let Molly pass. . . Shh!. . .I know who *you* are; I know the airy brain which is receiving the artful pulses that begin in my brain, pass my glottis as invisible orgasms of air and thus into this plastic telephone direct to YOU, Flute. Someday you will kill an individual with your empty silence, your nattering ambivalence, your *neuter* watchfulness. The ironic thing is how you misunderstand my instructions! If you'd only believe the enormity of what is really going on in this world, the disasters to come, you'd be driven up the wall. . . into an obsessed, neurotic fugue-silence, rather than this idiot vacuum you're in. You're a piece of glass into which light passes, is trapped, yea, and nevermore passeth out. . . .What do you want from me now? A lawyer? Some private dick with a diploma, a fellow to squirm ratlike for you over this loveless urban garbageheap, shitpile, gaschamber. Have I pegged it? I've pegged you, for sure. Molly's at home, I suppose. Call her there if you will. But I'm the one who will *act*, the man to put Phineas Clingsmythe on to the case of your missing children, so you remember that, remember me. . . .

Robert is upright in the front seat of the windy red machine, on the mad dash to San Francisco. His clipped head rises above the top of the windshield; he is afraid when the swooping gulls dive-bomb his unsheltered crown. A close fog ceiling is everywhere in his sight---except where the Mars orange spars of the Golden Gate bulge above the murky late afternoon traffic. He hopes the city will still be there when the fog clears, when they cross the bridge and someone turns on the lights and explodes the city into his eye-balls: bunched square shapes, powdered with fiery flour squatting behind the purple bay. Bobbi yells, flicking her fingers at the crowd of glassy machines pissing across the bridge, perhaps to fall off the earth together, forever.

Robert nods emphatically, not looking at the girl. He feels the motion of the car relax, and eases the muscles that have held him rigid in the seat. He watches the string of green, then red lights at the houses where they take the money. The blue man winks at him with his hand out and cupped near Bobbi's face. Moving off to speed, suddenly the bridge lights erupt through their thick len-ses, a series of diminishing after images sink through his eyeballs, and he realized that Bobbi is still talking, perhaps has never stopped. As if someone has thrown a switch, his ears turn on. He wonders where in the buzzing, crackling world the voice could be taking them.

Now headlights from the left lane. The voice goes on. She pokes a stiff something into his yielding hammy thigh, laughing over the wind. Perhaps she doesn't know the difficulty of listening when it doesn't matter much, words, when the lights are coming in his San Francisco city. He interrupts her, "I know what's happening," he says, turning his head and looking down at her, imagining it is the first time since they left the place for the incarceration of loonies.

With both hands on the wheel she guns into the speed lane. She is no thicker than the seat against which she sits. In front of the gumdrops of streaming light her hair is blown into beautiful gleamy spiderwebs.

They are in a tunnel of neon and oil smells. The tiles rush by them the color of piss and carbon farts. A yellow school bus creeps up to his shoulder; a midget leans out and gives him the finger with a happy smile. "I know what's happening," he shouts as they are propelled from the tunnel, and the bus pulls away from them in a cloud of foul gas.

". . .eat?" He nods up and down, as if to signal a person miles off his firm intention, which is to hold his friend's hand under a formica table in a Chinese place near his brother Peter's house. She points the car down a ramp, and they float into a wide and still street. His ears ping, and again hear the mutter of the engine, or his stomach.

Her hand feels like soft blue jeans under the formica table. He holds it carefully on top of his knee, a thing not to be let go.

Flute drives into the *Eureka* yard at dusk. The clear, high yellow light gives the wreckage an unnatural prominence---a sharp focus for his driving-tired eyes: the splintered diving board, the de-porched house. He sits in the deserted yard, watches the raw pink of the sunset grapple over the fog bank to the west. The Gant Lumber truck is gone and so is the weapons carrier. The only light in the house seems to come from the kitchen, a vague fire-orange light from the kitchen. In the creeping darkness he sits, *watching*. . . . . .

The savagery to the porch roof supports and the immediate collapse of the roof cut Flute off from the buzz of events. By the time he had gone out by the back door and come around the house, Stein was hauling the bloody Webster out of the pool, and Claude lay on the ground nearby in a fit of hyperventilation. Muttering and calm, Flute turned in the direction of the barn and trucks to see Kate kneeling over Jones, whose body on the ground appeared oddly wrenched. Above them, stockstill on the platform of their truck, stood the men from the lumber company.

It occurred to Flute that the entire tableau in the yard was now, without question, his responsibility. "The King is wasted, long live the pretender, Flute!" he heard trumpeted within his head; simultaneously another voice judged him a silly asshole; simultaneously he heard from space, Stein saying urgently, "Flute, how the hell do you put a tourniquet on someone's head?" And he saw, behind Kate and Jones and the truck, a white automobile poke its way into the yard and rock gently to a stop. It disgorged a single fat female figure.

At the precise moment, thin buckskinned Flute wished he might become absolutely neutral---just a camera lens, incapable of either judgment or action.

What is this advancing blimp?

98

She stalked into the center of the yard behind a full paunch of matronly bosom swathed in thick red wool, and stood, hands to trousered hips, while she surveyed the carnage through a pair of hornrim glasses thick as an index finger. "I'm here to welcome you people," she boomed. "I'm Margaret Pickel." She turned slowly on her booted feet, got her bearings. "I'd like to know what the hell is going on here. What the *hell* is going on here?"

With a jittery glance for the pool (where sanguine events had frozen once again: Stein held Webster's head over the rose water, like a raccoon caught with a less than tasty morsel), Flute strode to within a foot of the woman, and politely but delibertely blocked at least part of her view---slender weed fronting her polar bulk. A scatter of noises broke the momentary quiet. Webster yelled, cursed obscenely. Behind her thick glasses Margaret Pickel's eyes magnified, distorted---startled blue beetles, Flute thought. In the distance, Kate cooed over Jones, and over all, the harsh symphony of D'Mambro's poolside breathing.

Flute wished for bedlam, chattering, screams, movement, anything to distract this Pickel woman, and allow him to retreat. He stared at her pebbled wattles, remembering some forgotten maxim: *You can deal with anyone if you'll be what they need you to be.* But he, Flute, was not responsible. Damn Jones for his immobility!

"Are you going to speak to me, sonny?"

A glib, informative reply took form, but before he could speak he sensed, then saw, a quick movement in the distant background of the scene he was unwillingly the center of---a small white figure streaked from the trees beyond the pool to his left, formally entered his vision as it passed behind the No. 1 dome platform, and made straight for Margaret Pickel's virgin automobile. Flute calmly watched Bobbi Love flash into the driver's seat, heard the engine grind and erupt, and before M. Pickel could wrench her amazon bulk aboutface, her car jolted into reverse, stopped, then pounced forward into a tight curve that sent it out of the yard and on to the humped dirt road.

Flute stood mute, unwilling to force the situation any further than the simple, delightful act of watching the car theft. "How do you do, Mrs. Pickel?" he said.

The morning of January First.

Last night we had Guy Lombardo on the radio, a fire, a dance with Ann on the hearth, a fifth of California *brut* (a vintage bubbly, 197__, that interrupted vintage), and---rare nostalgia---a thin joint made of what little marijuana remains from the older days. And celebrated what is to be NEW, this new year, atop the brass bed beginning no later than 12:15 a.m.

Happily, I flew no unreal airplane, swooped through no choking fogs, and was at no time visited by my looming Point Sur Rock; indeed, in keeping with this entire Holiday Season, Jones and Company remained shackled in my room below, this room, while Kate and I rocked our pleasure to the hollow silence of a new year beginning. Afterwards, Kate switched on the table lamp and craned over me with a sharp but pleasant enough look---at me, winded upon my back.

"You're coming along okay," she said. "I mean your being here is more than a temporary fluke, isn't it?"

"Ummm."

"You feel familiar." She touched me lightly. "I guess you're not lost."

I rolled towards her. "You look like a scallop," I suggested, laying hands on her.

"I was in your room yesterday," she pursued, yet she approached me with her thighs.

101

"So?"

"I gotta ask you. . ."

"What?" I spoke with my mouth enveloping her ear.

"When you're going to quit writing about yourself in the third person?" I kept quiet. "What is it you're trying to avoid? Yourself?"

"Right." I gave her poor eardrum a gigantic exhale.

But she retreated from me in order to continue this midnight tack. "I was there too," she said. "In actual fact. Do you forget?"

"Sure. Otherwise you wouldn't be here."

"But if I wrote it down or talked about it I know I'd be more than a. . .a character. I'd commit myself directly to my own voice, no matter how unpleasant, and ALL of my feelings, not just my slick neutrality."

". . ."

"I'm supposed to believe that you know what you're doing, though. Bolster your husband, and all that stuff." I tried to interrupt, pull her towards me, but the resistance was now a matter of muscle. "You won't say anything now, but you'll. . ."

"Go and scribble it all down. . ."

"To prove how clever you are." She kept her fierceness for a second more, then laughed.

I kissed her, and we fell asleep. Nothing new.

The First of January.

After breakfast I came into this room, and from the least disturbed banana box I took a film tin, that kind that has a screw top and is designed for 35mm color film. This tin was wrapped in adhesive tape, gone gray with handling, moving, packing, hiding--- yes, an artifact of stash days, when drugs were ordinary in my luggage. Yes. I fooled early with dope, and entered into its commercial maw as easily as my urbane father mastered the vagaries of the commodities market. While Jones was in Paraguay and later, Nova Scotia, I casually became (as Bobbi Love conjectured) one of the top four or five drug dealers in San Francisco. Yes, ambidextrous me: urbane, gregarious, facile. I was, unbelievably, friend and vassal to both the straight Jones *and* the insane genius King Christopher Owl.

With some difficulty I unwound the soiled tape, exposing the bright metal underneath.

This drug history that I am finally claiming, if not advocating, goes back ten years to high school---a precise, recordable progression forward in time, like jobs I never held:

LIQUID ADRENALIN

BENZEDRINE CAPSULES

MODEL AIRPLANE GLUE

DEXEDRINE TABLETS

GROUND PEYOTE BUTTONS

MARIJUANA

CODEINE ELIXIRS

PULVERIZED MORNING GLORY SEEDS

AMYL NITRATE POPPERS

NITROUS OXIDE

METHAMPHETAMINE

PHENOBARBITAL

DMT

HASHISH

MESCALINE

ROSE HIPS

LSD

I held the film tin to the feeble morning light, appreciating the precise knowledge of what it contained, wondering if I felt as sure of the positive qualities of the experience as I had in the old days. How would it be in this particular place and time? Would I remain in control? On top of all my situations? In making my way through the list I was unable to remember one unpleasant experience, one bad trip; the various substances remain a decade's series of simple experiments---just a little peripheral toying with my perceptions. Drugs are good for some.

So I sat this morning with a shiny metal can that contained, as I remembered it, one fat tablet, smaller than an asprin, which had originated with the very King Owl two or three years before: the pure stuff---no artificial stimulants added: a tablet of Lysergic Acid Dyethylamide. An approximate dosage of one thousand micrograms. And, in those days, you could believe whatever Master Chemist Owl, or his lieutenants, claimed. But the Owl is dead, along with other of the high priests, low bus jockeys, and assorted friends not worth mentioning.

Because *I* am not dead. . .

Because it is the first day of a new year. . .

Because the single tablet *existed*. . .

Or because it will heighten what I already know, and prove to Kate that in fact I am committed to my own voice, that the illusion of "neutrality" is necessary to my method, and that I am in control of my problem, my voices, and doubts be damned. (My god! THIS has always been the exact opposite of neutrality.) I took a spiffy new razor blade, taped one end, sliced the fat tablet into four roughly equal parts, swallowed one with a glass of neat well water, and because I envision no further use for drugs in this life I flushed the remaining three fourths straightaway down the toilet.

I am here and must report: A certain dryness to the rear of my throat; a tension in the stomach; a white brilliance, with few contrasts, pouring in through the window; and everywhere, over everything I see, a transparent scarlet shimmer.

I'll order tea, hot.

No, a pot of hot water, a portable electric hob, a canister of exotic teabags, a bowl of roughcut sugar, two spoons, my wastebasket here for the used tea bags, discardable. Kate brings what I wish, and I make a big earthen mug of sweet tea.

No one is ever stoned unless he speaks of it. I do not speak it, merely murmur my thanks, perhaps a word of affection to let Kate know the day is New, somewhere the year is just beginning.

This elation.

This joy.

My tea tastes like some shaky jell.

And there is *Sinbad the Sailor* askew upon my cratered wall. I am staring; the tones at the top of the picture are dark, the tones at the bottom are bright joy. Sinbad, who stands in a small boat, may not be a part of the darker top tone but it is clear to me that he is *of* it, whilst the sea dragons with whom he is fighting, and bloodying with his warped staff, are a definite part of the joy, i.e. all three are imposed upon joyful designs of blue and are illuminated by a shaft of light which thrusts up from the ocean deeps in order to enlighten the gaping and bloody jaws of the monsters, a light that also indicates very delicately that Sinbad himself is thrusting out of the dark, into the light.

ME!

Light billowing in my head, a sign of something more around the eyes than what normally is there---as if the periphery has been sabotaged in favor of some greater scheme of things, but still shaky, out of focus. Closing my eyes brings only more scarlet and a greater consciousness of the page in front of me, while my fingers continue to operate this typewriter, as if they belonged to another.

A sweet ache in my kidneys.

I see, sticking from my tea like a pair of silver and absurd oars, a brace of spoons.

*Invention is the bastard child of neurosis.*

I must direct myself. What is needed? Music! A stereo set and a collection of. . . .Who were they? THE ROLLING STONES!

*Acid rock?*

What man was it who danced with his wife and daughter to the drones of Guy Lombardo this late night passed. Surely not the fancyman of exaggerated moustache, silken shirts, voluptuous Molly Noel, and bright, untold California murder. Is this he, horrid multi-fancier, sitting here with the clear ping---each and every note---of his typing machine? Which is which is which? I cannot *now* be the same man, and yet Kate accuses me of just this. How do you describe the "involvement" of imagination? I am unable to concentrate; sentences begin in my head, like straight lines, but before they are complete there are offshoots, deviations, detours. . .a spiderweb of fables and facts. . .fifty cul-de-sacs.

*Focus!*

Ah-ha, nomenclature, jargon: the safety, if temporarily, of the specific. Film terminology lies in a corner of my brain like a stack of ancient black and chrome equipment---dusty lenses winking in the pink snowlight that surrounds me. I, Wolliam Victor Flute made three films before quitting the profession: *The Great Rug Robbery; Fellows;* and the unfinished *Men, Women and Children First.* They all reflect the multi-druple nature of that medium, not to mention Me---a *smatterer* at work.

*Focus, please!*

Well, I say it's all a shambles of people, places and cataclysmic events I may or may not have witnessed. It's a redhot shambles in my head, I say. And no amount of rotten film making could deal with this current, personal shambles.

*Yes, but the purpose of writing things down is to bring order to the shambles, spoke the old saw.*

What a lie, I say.

The purpose of putting matters down is to clarify. . .just how you have managed to *come to terms* with this lunatic world. So you freeze all your bits and lies and facts and pieces in a linear fashion;

gleefully, tragically, inevitably aware that the shambles, cataclysms, whatever, must and will remain just exactly as they were.

Back to *focus,* huh?

If you would be so kind.

I'm a'hum, an exaggerated hum. Ping, ping ping. . .to it! High or no, this so-called arbitrary business must continue.

From the air I pick a spot. It's not even necessary to close my eyes and squeeze the difficult draughts of invention. I will play at being a lap dissolve machine; in film parley, this is a means of fading out one image and simultaneously bringing up the next. At one brief point in time, the two images should double-expose quite nicely. So, over this most recent *Eureka* tableau, containing the victimized Margaret Pickel, and the just-unfrozen Flute (among others); its colors: the red, white and blue of Mrs. Pickel's wool shirt, the pale rosé of the stained swimming pool, I impose my most recent establishing sequence. We see a day image of San Francisco, long shot, approaching the city from on high---a swoop over the Golden Gate and eastward to the white decks of the city, subtitled "mid-July," a clear day. Zoom in fast for a panoramic look at the warren that used to be called Pacific Heights---its collection of roofs with their various constructions of glass and wood roof coop is a kind of shanty penthouse, really a three-sided shelter, mostly glass, which contains a seedy collection of lawn furniture. The rest of the roof is gravelled over. A tin hood covering the stairwell entrance sits next to an octagon clothesline. A canvas-covered tent platform serves as a sunbathing area. See all this in a milli-second; as the roof image passes swiftly through the double exposure stage (in my head the *Eureka* tableau fades) the scene becomes one of the most crucial detail, focused to a T, steady as a rock.

Click, ping, it's gone. I'm returned to this room. Far away, eons away, Ann is crying; muffled music.

There are no curtains in this room. Kate will not block the view. We have only glass, very polished and clear, between us and the outside. What is outside is of course snow---foot after foot of it, with terrible spire-like shadows over its purity. All of this is in front of me, Ann cries somewhere behind the walls, and yet I am desperate to recover the roof image long enough to dissect the sunbather, that warm July day.

It is Molly Noel on Flute's (my) roof.

It is Molly Noel.

Molly Noel.

I begin to circle her from above, a lyrical descent, the circles growing smaller and smaller until we are so close to her that a mere throat swallow is sufficient reaction to her soft flesh craters, one to either side of the base of her nude spine. The dark blue of her bathing suit underlines these two points. A clear drop of sweat appears from the area of her muffled shoulder blades and tracks down until it comes to rest in the left skin crater, where it mixes with the sheen of lanolin. The roof shimmers white, white pebbles of gravel, heat convecting in vertical squiggles.

From the metallic hood over the stairwell I materialize, incorporate. I wade through the heat shimmer of the roof, seemingly cut off at the knee, wearing finely striped pants of blue and white and a full-elbowed blouse the color of fresh cream. My face is grim behind the apricot moustache. I stride across the roof to meet the glistening Molly Noel. She turns on her side in time to see me advancing over the roof gravel. She flicks off a buzzing radio and squints in the heat and light.

What do I say?

My face, the V at my neck, my hands---an albino next to Molly's sunstained flesh.

I say, "Bogue is downstairs."

"Oh?" Her languid response! I seem irritated, and thrust my hands into the front pockets of my pinstripes, meanwhile watching the delicate push of her stomach as she folds into a sitting position.

"Jake is downstairs in the apartment, and very agitated." I punctuate the last word with an upnod of my head. Swatches of my hair jump and swirl in the glittering air.

She shades her eyes with one palm. "What's he want?"

"It's hard to say, Molly. Perhaps he's come to say good-bye, or perhaps to do us violence." I see that I am clipping my words sharply, propelling them like gobs of spit with my lips, all the while not quite looking at her; staring off at the purple bay, at the sea beyond the Golden Gate. A coal gray aircraft carrier slithers under the bridge, its tiny superstructure sticking rigidly into the sky.

She interrupts, "Well, did you tell him I was up here?"

I refocus---her breasts just barely sit in the brief blue cups of her costume. "No. . .no, he's talking on the phone. I said I was going to check the mail, but surely he knows you're here, your sly boss."

Molly pinches the bridge of her nose, digests the information while I apparently return to the real imposition of the carrier into the bay. "Relax," she says. I jerk my hands from my pockets and quickly recapture them in my trickling armpits. "Maybe he comes bearing fantastical comfort for the inductee."

"Fanatical comfort," I correct. "Anyway, he's onto more worldly matters at the moment; he's talking to this Phineas Clingsmythe person, and Phineas is with Bobbi Love."

"Fortuitous," Molly says, inscrutable mistress of my organs.

"I hope he gets my damned car back."

"He will, he's very efficient."

"Well, then, you can all tell me what the hell I'm supposed to do with little Miss Love and that. . .that cock-in-the-mud while I'm trying to grow insane enough to avoid the draft." My hands escape to paddle wildly in the currents of heat that seem to radiate directly from Molly Noel.

"I don't know," she says, using both hands to shade her eyes.

"All things must pass. Is Jake wearing a suit?"

"What the fuck! This is getting perverse."

She laughs, this vaulted lute. "I want to know; it's a key to his. . .state."

I sound the higher ranges of sarcasm, "It's an Italian number with plaid checks, in lovely tones of gray and green. I also noted a faintly purple shirt, buttoned at the collar. No tie."

"Working clothes," she concludes, assuming a half-lotus position, compressing her lips. Can I really lust for each microgram of this flesh, even though I appear so clipped, brittle and more agitated than Bogue below? Is she more than she seems, this handmaiden to my convoluted shrink?

The aircraft carrier is abreast of Alcatraz before Molly chooses to speak again. "Go down and tell him I'm here." I look haughty. But I go down. As I disappear into the maw of the stairwell, she shouts after, "Take care, my love!"

Here, in my room, I am winning this struggle to remain elsewhere for the necessary time. . .though now my heart sits panting on my chest like a marvelous mechanical carbuncle. I become increasingly aware of these present physical matters as Molly and the roof fade and give way to the brilliance of the snow outside my window.

I thrust a Camel cigarette into the butt mountain of my ash tray, take a fresh teabag from the canister, note that my body ends at my waist, and that I am one with the Prague chair, its every contour. I rip the white tea packet and place the scrim bag in my empty mug---watch fascinated as the oval of waterbundles falls into the mug with a musical splashing and filling sound. Layers of reverberating water notes smash into my ears. I seize one of my spoons, hold it over the liquid and lift the saturated teabag into it. With the bag's string I wring hell out of the bag itself, using the spoon as a fulcrum, shelf, brace. I see each fragrant mote of misting steam as it rises from the cup. Three shovels of raw sugar fall into the cup like sand into a bag. Unerringly, I calculate that two hours and thirty-five minutes have passed since I swallowed the quarter-tablet.

What is it that keeps me in this room? Perhaps it is Kate, and the knowledge that for her the door is not locked. At any minute during the course of a day she could walk in, dump me from my chair, tear up these pages, berate or love me in a number of ways. Why is she so tolerant of my buried aberrations? Couldn't I simply take the easy out, rejoin both Kate and Ann in their real world, and forget this other for good; these strenuous replays of the messy past?

Self-conscious, eh Mr. *Jones?*

Just plain *Jones.*

The syllable of his name sputters in my head. Suddenly, and without warning, I am sitting on a circular, treeless plain. I am surrounded by the now-familiar Joy. Yet I am so large in my sitting that I may, if I choose, lean a bit in any of three hundred and sixty degrees of direction, and peer over the edge of the plain and into a bottomless moat. I feel clever, tense, joyful in this knowledge. But, at the pit of me, I know that if I gaze over the edge at

112

any one point I will be absolutely terrified by what I see. How simple it is, though, to avoid the fissure, smile at the horror below. I mean, all it is is an honest mirror of the miseries within my delighted self. I think I am laughing. I open my eyes. Kate is in the room.

She has said something. I drag it from my memory---a small distant cupboard with psychedelic shelves. "Excuse me?" I inquire politely (still not seeing her), remembering just then that she has asked about lunch. I put down my cigarette and take a sweet sip of the tea, hold the heavy liquid at the back of my throat in order to order my thoughts. "Might snow again," I observe, and the window changes to a perfect snowflake as I keep track of the oscillations of Kate's body somewhere on my left flank. "Perfect," I say, hearing the word as an echo a few moments later. "What?"

"Stop typing a minute," she yells. I stop.

She was at my shoulder like a dark shifting cloud. "Sure," I said, and raised my left hand to my face, repeatedly pulled its palm from my nose down to my chin in a steady rhythm. I recall I was in the process of containing an irrepressible grin. It seemed quite funny that she should be kept unaware of the fanciful matters in which I was involved, although what possible difference could it make if my wife knew she was addressing a dope fiend who had just hallucinated himself on a plain surrounded by every yapping horror he'd created for himself since the murder of their friend? "What's the matter?" I asked.

"Matter?" she replied, and her smooth mouth promptly froze into an O that flew towards me and swallowed my head. I continued to participate in the conversation through all her mucous membranes. "Nothing is the matter," she gurgled. "Do you want lunch?" There's some cottage cheese." I immediately fell from her mouth and into a bowl of fat white curds, swimming, and momentarily I bumped smack against a green pickle, lovely and opaque.

"Are there cucumber chips here?" I asked, or yelled, from beneath the surface of the cottage cheese.

"Yes!" she hollered down at me from the rim of the bowl.

"Okay, lay it on me."

"Why are you shouting?"

"Never mind," I shouted, and frog-kicked to a greater depth.

Have I lost track, control or thread? Nope. For instance, rooted here, I know that a lake of cottage cheese is on its way, disguised as my lunch. For respite, I have, until it appears, decided to forswear tea, and also images, voices, lies, though the harsh blessing of cigarettes will continue uninterrupted. The crucial proof of my continuing powers of control and impeccable neatness is that I can list the unresolved pits that hand in the thick treacle of my brain, but there is no need for such a list, no need to catalogue specific moments in plotted space. Were I not master of myself I would need a wall-sized chart to keep these events properly ordered in relation to one another. Yet now, stoned out of my gourd, I can make the flat statement: The mere pits are meaningless; what counts is that I have not lost track, thread or control. No matter how I order them; no matter when I produce them, soon all will come clear.

Ergo: the arrogance of my ergot. (The first pun of the New Year—the appalling latter years of this hollow century.)

> The next earthquake to hit the San Francisco Bay area is already outlined in a scenario compiled by the FOEP. The conjecture goes this way: the quake will be a Richter 8.3 and will begin deep beneath the surface of the San Andreas Fault about eighty miles south of San Francisco. Shifts in the earth will have overcome the elasticity of rocks locked along the

114

*fault line. To relieve strain the rocks will snap
and hurtle past each other, sending out giant
shock waves and creating surface ruptures as
wide as twenty feet. . . .All major routes into
the city will be cut off, including Highway 101
north of the Golden Gate, where a landslide will
occur, and Highway 1, where the Devil's slide
area will crumble into the Pacific. . .Experts indicate that in San Francisco itself many buildings
collapse, their facings dropping off, burying
downtown streets in rubble. The Embarcadero
Freeway will be knocked out, homes wrenched
from their foundations, railroad yards wrecked,
and fires started across the city. Hardest hit
areas will include portions of downtown, Fish-
erman's Warf, the Mission, Sunset, Ingleside,
and Marina districts, with sections of Potrero,
Bayview and Presidio badly crippled.*

Ah-ha! Just by reaching into the leading banana box, I've snapped
and hurtled myself into it again. I must credit the moribund prose
of the defunct magazine called ESQUIRE, page 191, December,
1968, illustrated. The quotation is freely adapted, like everything
else I am about. Freely adapted now, in this most paradoxical
of binds: Expanded Consciousness. Or is it *focused* conscious-
ness---certainly a desirable state for me---that expands, intensifies
and exaggerates to the point of. . .insight? clarity? obsession? Or
(I slip the mood a notch) is historical consciousness all bunk?
Perhaps I might give up this whole effort, and turn to the truth of
dreams and fabulation.

I descend the dark and narrow stairwells of the Green Street building, encounter Jake Bogue in my kitchen. Sleek Bogue is standing
near the stove about to end a phone conversation, speaking and
apparently staring into my face. His own face hangs blank and pale
beneath heavy-framed dark glasses.

Outside the window behind him leaves droop in the July sun.

Molly on the rookery in her fleshy half lotus is the latent image lurking on the periphery of my irises. I hear Bogue's breath whistle into the diaphragm of the pearly telephone.

"Call me later, Phineas," he says loudly before replacing the instrument in its wall cradle. He leans against the stove, crosses tailored arms over his chest and continues to have at me from behind the shadowy circles of his eyeglasses.

"It's simply amazing," Bogue says, nearly to himself. "You can see I'm still functioning; I've just talked on this telephone in a very organized manner, manhandling your asinine detective problems. This morning I rose at the usual hour, performed the usual rituals, went off promptly to my office, where I spent the morning talking with intelligence and wit to a succession of people who imagine themselves bad, unlovable, incapable of giving something important to others. Perhaps ironically, I maintained my balance, held my perspective, kept my cool---with each *sucker* I projected the necessary and proper image. My secretary wasn't there, but I managed well without her.

"I remain efficient. But panic is running through me in rich currents. Can you tell? Haha. If I took off these glasses you'd find me bug-eyed. Can't you tell, Flute?"

I raised my knobby shoulders in a shrug.

The spell breaks again. Here at my desk, I sense my lunch flooding thick and silent across the doorjamb. Some sort of Gregorian chant numbs my left ear; a cigarette burns my stained fingers.

To masturbate now would be the ultimate in private, god-like control: Yes, he has mastered the situations and they are His. But

116

then, diluting this remote lust, it occurs to me that such an act would be a solo perversion of Sinbad's battle against the sleek sea monsters; it would be a low, guilty desecration of his bent and orange staff.

Mercifully, the Green Street kitchen comes up again; Bogue goes on and on, saving me the temptations of this fractured present.

"Pay attention to me, you silly asshole," he intones. "This city we're standing on is doomed. They all say it will happen, but immediately *think* it won't happen here. All of them blind, pig-gish, ignorant." Heavy sarcasm invades Bogue's rising voice. "What about you, Flute? You're no different. No. Oh, your intelligence and luck, not to mention my help, will prevent you from the draft, but then what? Escape to the privileged community groove of your cocksure friends? Ha! You can't even get past the over-ture without a bust, a catastrophe, a fuck-up. What your boy Jones is doing represents faulty, disastrous thinking because all you people are no different from the rest. . . .confusion, selfish-ness, envy, violence! It's all human and all things human go bad-ly. . .Moles!

"You, Flute, creeping in your private tunnel, creeping into furry Molly, insulting me with your insubstantial life." He is screaming. "You refuse to acknowledge my advice, my insight, my self, I give you the truth, I give you Molly, and you insist on treating me like a creature in a bubble, you hairy little fart! Think you're so clever about using me, but the earth will open and swallow your. . ."

"Molly's on the roof, Jake."

"Oh goddamn, of course she is." Beneath the glasses his patrician face sags in all its parts.

From here I am able to see Bogue's face clump together like discolored curds of cottage cheese, just as I am *un*able to keep this magical lunch out of my ruptured head. The door to my room slushes open, compelled by the flood of my arriving food---inevitably, thickly, it rises above my ankles.

Kate places a turquoise bowl at my bent typer's elbow. I cast one eye leftward and note the skinny line of electrical force shimmering about the bowl, colorless but quite real. "Want a beer?" She is staring at this paper, breathing small zephyrs into my hair. "See!" A chill pops between my shoulder blades, jolts me from the enveloping Prague chair in such a way as to start the lunch bowl a'sliding down the slight incline of the desk. She's yelling, "You're no better than a tape machine with a two second lag!" Neat and smooth, the bowl reaches the waxed edge of the desk, and without so much as a teeter. . .flips.

Now I must go quickly, keep this acidic report flowing lest I drown or burst or both. An hour has passed since the splattering failure of my innocently anticipated lunch. Physically, I've been away from this darkening room; mentally, a fabulous thing has happened. I went into the bathroom. Suddenly nude in the mirror, alone with the grotesque pink tiles, unruly shower curtain, hissing water in the sink. I spotted the nude in the mirror again and again, like a stranger rounding a corner---the bones of a stranger. I approached the mirror to catalogue a naked face: its lips were thickening, they approximated the texture of porcelain with a Chinese Red glaze; these lips seemed to pump like bright lungs beneath a monstrous space where the moustache once was; I could not see the nose, only a narrow glistening line which pointed to a pair of eyes dilated, bulging, like opaque blue olives thumbed into the skull. I *saw* the actual noise of a zither haloing my head, and immediately sat down on the toilet to let away all the thick dross of my imbecilic body. Purged, free, I was swatted by the phenomenon of literary tunnel vision. I rushed down this startling black and white tunnel, made of paper and print, all of it; and I soon encountered, in a total state of JOY, an unfettered, irrelevant and linear parable, which I had not one qualm about performing the act of reading upon, and now copy true off my tunnel's graffitied walls:

*Jilly was a man who no longer had a sense of people. He had lost that delicate, keen perceptiveness which enables us to imagine quite starkly the putrid whiteness of a human face kept too long in captivity, let alone the foul odors that might lurk beneath that face. Jilly's imagination long ago learned to change people into animals. He was accustomed to thinking of massed humanity in terms like herd, gaggle or drove. When he heard a war report of people laid about in the streets dead, Jilly immediately saw crumpled rows of sooty geese neatly entangled in green military canvas. Jilly was in tune with the times. Jilly got up one morning and spoke a true word. "Crap," he said. "Don't make your foul temperament any glossier with words like that," said his wife Pooch. Without reply, Jilly went to the lavatory and shaved off his elaborate curling moustache. Then he put on a neat pair of tan pants and marched out of the bedroom, past his wife who merely groaned and turned her machinery to 'appliances.' Jilly woke his son Neville, who screamed when he saw his father minus his moustache. Not wishing to hear a similar screech from his daughter, Jilly went into the kitchen and prepared his usual breakfast of soft egg and whetina. He washed this down with great draughts of the instant juice that comes from a jar of golden beads. Jilly was ready for his morning. At nine, the postman rang a sharp tattoo on the front buzzer.*

*Jilly was momentarily seized with terror; his ima-
gination had immediately offered him the picture
of a dying swan cradling an expired koala on his
front stoop. "Rotten day, eh, Mr. Neville?" the
postman observed. "Stunning," replied the shaken
Jilly. The postman touched his cap sardonically
and stepped off into the haze. Jilly was left holding a smallish brown parcel crossed with velvet
twine. Ahh, thought Jilly who was quite fond of
inanimate objects; ahh, this must be it. He went
back into his kitchen, placed his parcel carefully
atop the counter next to the bottle of golden
beads, and ate one of the radishes Pooch kept in a
studiously irregular wooden bowl. He firmly believed that a man was not meant to encounter any
Moment in Life without his mouth being singularly
tart and fresh to the tongue's touch. Dropping the
limp tailend of the radish into the disposal, Jilly
said to the kitchen, "It has arrived." "Huh," qua-
vered a tiny voice from beneath the counter. Jilly
fought back the picture of a crudely feathered
wren slumped at his feet, and bent his head for a
wry look at his son Neville, who sat on the floor in
flannel pajamas and bare feet. Neville blanched at
the full force of his father's newly shorn face, but
did not, thankfully, scream. Jilly, making a valiant
effort to look benevolent and fatherly, shooed his
son from the kitchen with absurd skatting noises.
He watched Neville's retreat into the bowels of the
house, where the other hid from him, and he could
not help chuckling at the healthy extent of his do-
main. But he immediately crosscut this thought
with an even vaster chuckle at what he, Jilly, now
has in his possession. "It has arrived," he said. The
azure wall telephone tinkled shyla. Pooch despised
loud, insistent noises. "Is that J. Neville? Mr. J.*

Neville?" "Yes, it is," Jilly replied. "Is it true that this morning, 8:30 sharp, you spoke a true word?" "How do you mean?" "*Crap*, Mr. Neville, CRAP!" "Who are you to say?" Jilly asked, gathering force. "An answer please, Neville, otherwise. . ." "Yes," Jilly said. "Yes I did, but. . ." "Thank you, Neville. Consider yourself one of us." Bewildered but vaguely triumphant, Jilly replaced the phone in its bed and, as an afterthought, reached under it and pushed the lever to 'loud.' Then, at sea in his thoughts, he floundered back to the counter and ate another radish. He felt refreshed and much more comfortable with his thoughts when he heard the distinct, moist crunch of his teeth destroying the innocent radish. He inhaled loudly and was pleased by the ripe tingle in his nostrils. One of us, am I, he thought, and filled his healthy lungs yet another time. No man to question or agonize over any of the events in his exterior life, Jilly took sweet pleasure in the fact that **someone** had chosen to single him out for such an odd phone call. He paced about his narrow kitchen and every so often eyed the smallish brown parcel. He clasped his hands at the small of his back and rubbed the ball of his left thumb rhythmically. He paused in his pacing long enough to brush some imagined crumb from his neat tan trousers. He looked at the ceiling, sighed, and paced on, trying valiantly to keep his rebellious imagination in check. Out of fear of parcel and sender, call and caller, Jilly fought with wildebeests and hedgehogs, boar and shrew. They loomed large in his head and behind them he could see acres more of the brightly colored devilments. With sweating, knitted brow he kept them all at bay---gnashing behind the thinnest

121

*of veils. In short, Jilly won. Now, at his leisure, he could open the parcel. He took out some pinking shears and made efficient slits in the free air about his head. Flushed, he went to the counter and neatly parted one of the velvet grids on the tiny parcel. The two ends lay like long purple larvae on the cross-hatched surface of the paper. "Ah-ha," Jilly said, and made a similar cut further along on the velvet twine. He picked up the parcel, and the severed velvet fell onto the counter in a soft heap. With the pinking shears Jilly made a slit in the heavy brown paper. His breathing upped two or three beats, but the thin veil at the rear of his head held fast. After three right hand turns with the shears, he realized that he* **had** *a door into the parcel. He peered. Inside was a shiny new moustache, special adhesive included.*

The Lesson for this moment of January the First:

ACID IS A FABULOUS PARABOLIST

Robert Quell sits in his favorite peninsula city-place, Palo Alto's Saint Mikel's Alley, watching dust flakes in the sunbeams which splay through the front windows of the coffee house. The Alley is like a cave today; the sun sends bright darts into the mouth of his cave. They bring him a fresh tongue sandwich and a tall thin glass of milk. Others are singing to him, the glowing plastic machine somewhere behind him -

*I HUNGER FOR YOUR PORPOISE MOUTH*
*AND. . .STAND ERECT FOR LOVE*

Slow, breathing notes of Country Joe's music enter Robert's body through the soles of his feet, peacefully electrocute him before they exit through his fingertips. His mouth works at the soft tongue. With the music and the dancing yellow dust, he cannot hear what the others around the table are saying. It is enough that Bobbi's hand is on his knee, hidden beneath the table. The music ends with an easy electrical twang. ". . .hear me, Mr. Quell?"

With his mouth cram full of tongue and bread and lettuce, Robert turns to stare curiously at the slight man who has spoken. "Don't call me mister, my name is Robert," he intends and tries to say as pink and green and white scraps tumble from his mouth to the plate, even splashing into his glass of milk.

Frowning, the man pushes his suited body a few inches from the edge of the table. Bobbi gives Robert's knee a gentle squeeze---no embarrassment here, my friend. "All right, Robert it will be," he says as if to a child, and Robert knows well that snotgreen tone. The man goes on, "I'm simply trying to discover if you understand what we're talking about." He raises a waxy forefinger, prepared, it looks like, to talk of many things: one, two, three.

"Excuse me, Mr. Clingsmythe," Robert says, and leaves the table

123

as what remains of his last sandwich bite bobbles down his throat in the direction of his stomach. His face glides through the agitated light, and suddenly he is into the high ceiling shadows at the back of the room, by the kitchen. A fat bald man in an apron looks up from his sandwich board and winks. "Hiya, Peebo," Robert greets, and passes into a hallway. The walls are covered with nubbly red stuff like velvet; he runs his fingertips along both walls, which remind him of the texture of his own crewcut skull. On past the phone, an icebox, to the door of the MEN room, outside of which all the smells of the place gather and ricochet in his nose: damp concrete, frayed lettuce, cinammon, stale farts, fresh-cut bread, tokes of beery breath, cold meat, and disinfectant. The best city-place smells lurk for him.

The MEN door creaks him inside, where he closes his eyes against the buzzing fluorescent flare of the lightbar above the mirror, closes them also against the sight of the drawings and words struck onto the pale green walls.

Bubbles of red and green light bounce and shatter across the bottom line of his closed, squinched eyelids. He turns, by memory, to the lavatory, and fumbles at the button fly of the new Levi's pants that Bobbi bought for him in San Francisco a couple of days before. The buttons (stubby metal mushrooms---he can imagine them, gray and written-on) don't want to come free of their blue holes; he has to undo his eyelids and peek. And zap! By the time he gets his eyes closed again, one of the wall drawings is embedded behind his lids, dancing before the bubbling red and green lights.

While the water falls out of him, he screws up his eyes even more, in a half-hearted, sad effort not to see the stickman on the wall shoving his enormous tool. . . . *You'd still like it to happen, wouldn't you, loony?* Robert's surprise vanishes the stickfigures; the baiting voice has somehow got out of his box under the dirt in the hospital foxtails. He feels betrayed, but by a friend who at least knows all about him. So he resigns himself---his voice is back to stay. . . . *How did you really feel, that first night out of the booby hatch, when you guys broke into Flute's apartment? Were you sorry your brother Peter was gone from his house, so you and Bobbi had to be alone? You waited in the dark wishing like a demon that she would hurry. . . .For what? She came with a stub of a candle, and instead of laying down on the quilt she sat cross-legged on the floor and told you a bunch of things you didn't want to hear. Holding her hand, too, while you tried to forget what you wanted and knew you didn't deserve. You were flatout there, listening to all her junk about someone called Claude and all the others, with your silly eyes open wide to the flickery lemon light, and meanwhile that thing is swelled up to bust your hospital twill. Right?. . . .*

Shut up! Robert says outloud, and blindly leans forward to grope the flusher with one hand, madly cramming his fly with the other. Over the sound of the swirling, foamy water he hears, through the fan vent, the over and over crashing of a dishwasher, and even above this, and closer, a dime falls into a telephone. . . .*That's Peter calling up the state hospital again, buddy. Don't forget to wash up.* . . .Still fumbling with his buttons, Robert turns around, his shoulders brushing the walls, the drawings, the words, and bends to the sink he refuses to see. The numbers are clicking on the phone while the warm water splashes over his palms and wrists. He sees a sharp TV picture of Peter bent over the telephone with his hair frazzled out from his head like burnt out sparklers. But the voice that comes through the bathroom wall belongs to Phineas Clingsmythe. . . .*He'd do it to Bobbi in five seconds, that lawyer, and he'd let you watch too, bet on it!.* . .The dishwasher crashes down and hisses wet and hot. "What's 'sa matter, Jake. . . . Really! Well, the earth is very stable down here, precisely one mile from your San Andreas Fault. . . ." Robert stops the flow of water and dries his hands on the thighs of his pants, then decides to wait until Clingsmythe is finished with his phoning; he doesn't want to have to pass close to the man, who looks like a sharp skinny bird and smells like ozone. ". . .Jake, I have these ludicrous people here. . . .No, the girl is very nice, cooperative, and they *did* stay at Mr. Flute's house, and they still have his car. . . ." Hearing this, Robert reaches for the door knob, busts his knuckles a good one on the jamb. "I just told her that no one was going to press any charges, that Flute was cool about his car. . . .Yes, she seems

125

convinced, but this Quell ought to go back to Mendocino, he acts like an addict. . . ." Robert pushes through the door, swings left, and stops up short just in front of Clingsmythe.

"I'm not a junkie," Robert declares, and stalks past the twittering man, into the sunlight and fresh music -

*HER HEELS RISE FOR ME. . .*

God's blood! Please, just a moment's relief from my fractured brain; it's as if I have not been able to catch a true breath since early this morning when I embarked on this chemical journey. Perhaps I might grab a breath with a trueblue scrap of *reality* from my ugly banana boxes.

PAINTED DRAFTEE
IS TURNED DOWN,
FLUTE AND ALL

*SYRACUSE, N.Y., June 6*
*(AP) - Ronald T. Ashford, 23, report-*
*ed for his draft physical as ordered*
*Friday, but the Army turned him*
*down, at least temporarily.*

*Ashford showed up wearing only a*
*flimsy red orange toga and playing a*
*flute. An officer at the induction cen-*
*ter told police the man's Selective Serv-*
*ice number was painted on his body*
*and his toes were painted blue and*
*white.*

*Police charged Ashford with ob-*
*structing government procedure, pub-*
*lic lewdness and loitering after he re-*
*fused to leave the center.*

Or would it be more apropos to reveal a dreamed letter from my former President, dreamed this very second?

Mr. Wolliam Victor Flute
6869 Green Street
San Francisco, California

GREETING! YOU ARE HEREBY ORDERED
FOR INDUCTION INTO THE ARMED FORCES
OF THE UNITED STATES, AND TO REPORT
OAKLAND ARMY TERMINAL (PLACE OF RE-
PORTING), ON JULY __, 197__, AT 8:00 A.M.,
FOR INDUCTION PHYSICAL EXAMINATION
AND EVENTUAL FORWARDING TO BASIC
TRAINING CENTER, FORT ORD, CALIFOR-
NIA, LEAVE YOUR PRESENT HOME WITH
YOUR AFFAIRS INTACT AND A MINIMUM OF
CIVILIAN PARAPHERNALIA, FOR NOW, SIR,
BARRING ACTS OF GOD, YOU BELONG TO
YOUR COUNTRY, THE LAND OF THE BRAVE,
THE HOME OF THE FREE.

YOUR-COMMANDER-IN-CHIEF

On Green Street, 4 A.M., a dark slice of San Francisco July, it was as quiet as cotton. Outside No. 6869, the Morris sat a foot from the curb with its passenger door wide open. Sections of green winds escaped from the Presidio forest at the end of the block, and drifted to the pavement underneath the decapitated car. Inside the building, on the second floor, W.V. Flute stood alone in his dim bathroom. For two days he had been preparing for one of the major events of his various life, and now he had four hours to complete this particular job of work, four hours to the Oakland Army Terminal.

Without sleep for the past forty-eight hours, he leaned his crotch into the sink and calculated the aches and stings spreadout over his body. Fits of almost alcoholic giddiness swept between his ears as he regarded himself in the speckled, yellowing mirror. Flute's face and bare torso were covered with a thin, spotty, but quite obvious layer of grease and soot. In the Southern Pacific yards the afternoon before, he had spent a good gritty hour wallowing in the fruit of the railroad. There were streaks of black grime running from his high forehead back through his tangled mess of reddish hair, and his eyeballs stood out of his face like swollen pistachio nuts. Gloating over himself, he carefully washed clean his apricot moustache, rubbing it hard with a stained washcloth. He performed this early morning ablution with an occasional chuckle, a backward sway or two, and a certain floating sensation in his brain---the brain in loose but firm grip on matters immediately at hand. He did not dwell on the morning to come.

He finished scrubbing the moustache and took up a warped wooden bowl of shaving soap and an expensive badger brush with an

129

ivory handle. Adding steamy water from the tap, he commenced to create a powerful thick lather, a brushful of which he carefully spread over his moustache. Aha! He stepped back to admire the effect---the horizontal bush of pure white in dead contrast to the filthy rest of him---and nearly fell with dizziness into the bathtub behind. Recovering, he went on ha-ha-ing to himself and seized a pearl-handled straight razor from the shelf above the sink. This next was not going to be easy. He fumbled the razor in his left hand, managed it open, and allowed its inverted V to rest gently on his trembling fingers---a wicked gleaming instrument he had never learned to use properly. Yet rituals such as this deserved the best machinery available. The Solingen shaving engine, for example. He twitched his nose several times, stood up straight, his body centered perfectly in the mirror's dimness. With slow, careful motions he entered into the process of scraping off the left half of his magnificient four-year-old moustache. He found it as difficult and painful as pulling nosehair out by the roots. But the act was done quickly and, he thought, symmetrically. At mid-upper lip, half-way across the vertical groove beneath his nose, the hairs left off and startling white skin began. On this stark patch of white he sprinkled an absurd and stinging amount of witch hazel. The act of patting the tender skin sent him reeling back from the mirror in a fit of laughter.

He recovered, seized solemnity as tightly as the dry towel with which he further spread the grime over his face, though he carefully preserved the integrity of his absent half-moustache. Then he took up a stiff and sticky blue workshirt from the toilet back.

A soft knock at the bathroom door caused Flute a paroxysm of inaccurate shirt buttoning. "Yes?" he said, and since no answer carried through the door, he groped for the knob and swung the door violently into the hall, knocking Robert Quell directly against the W.C. Fields poster hung on the opposite wall. "Pardon me," Flute said, confusing for a moment the two faces he made out in the shadows. The alive and sleepy Quell advanced a step and stared at shaven Flute, who suddenly had a vision of himself embraced and suffocated by an enormous and gentle panda with a bristling crewcut. Quell smiled.

And said, enunciating each syllable, "You look good."

"I do?"

"Yes." Quell continued to smile in the bathroom doorway.

Flute performed a useless shrug, trying to telegraph his massive preoccupations. "Is Bobbi asleep?" he asked with an unintention-al, deranged leer.

Quell, from his height, blinked. "She's tired." His voice rose and boomed oddly in the hallway.

Automatically, Flute put a hand to his left shirt pocket for a cigarette. Finding none, he nervously insisted that the hand keep traveling in the air until it reached the resting place of the pearly razor, still flecked with soap. He picked it off the shelf and fiddled it closed, watched Quell watch him do it. "I know what's happen-ing to you today," Quell offered.

"Then you know I'm not exactly prepared. . .to talk. In fact, I can hardly see you."

"Okay." Quell smiled more than ever.

And Flute decided the escaped-lunatic game was hardly worth playing, especially considering the self he could still make out in the ancient mirror. He discovered he had dropped the razor to the floor, that Quell was bending his length to retrieve it. "Here," he said.

"Just. . .do something," Flute said. Quell was now in the bath-room, right next to him. He stooped and regarded Flute's spectre face with a serious, intent gaze.

"You've made a good start, you'll do all right. You'll blow their eyeballs."

131

"I will?"

"I know those kinda people."

"Yes."

"But I still need to ask you. . ." Quell pressed.

"In the living room, later, how about that?"

"Sure," Quell said cheerfully. "But don't wake her up. You're not all as bad as she says," he pronounced, and went away.

Flute stepped lightly into his living room, darkened since midnight when Robert and Bobbi had arrived to take up residence on his floor. He switched on a soft light near the boxed books, and saw Bobbi was still folded into his reading chair. Barefoot, dressed in the murky white jumpsuit, she began to snore lightly when he approached. He bent over the chair, swaying, not clear as to what he was doing or why, but he accurately recorded the furrows of strain at the edges of her mouth and eyes, even in sleep. He stared; and in his wadded and preoccupied brain saw the bright, still delightful image of the small girl whipping Margaret Pickel's car out of the Eureka yard, a shocked and shocking theft in the aftermath of quick, bloody, noseless violence.

Dizzy, shaved, exhausted, vaguely lusting for the sleeping girl, Flute sank to the floor in front of the chair, and decided, or suddenly knew that he must see that Bobbi and Robert Quell, together, were safely and gently transported north to *Eureka* no matter what the cost---to Claude D'Mambro's abruptly abandoned sensibilities, to the lurking forces of law and order representing Mrs. Pickel, or whatever. Despite his present stupor, he had finally made at least a fantasy leap in his concerns, beyond whatever the coming morning at the Oakland Army Terminal might have to offer him. And so, on the floor, he kept staring at Bobbi, delirium waving through his brain, watching. . .watching his own curious *feelings* warp and whirl. . .hearing D'Mambro's fists battering the wooden table over and again.

In the creeping *Eureka* darkness Flute got out of Mrs. Pickel's car and walked stiffly, with twitches of unease, toward the battered house, toward the vague fireglow of the kitchen window, past someone's half-hearted attempt to reorganize the remains of the shattered porch roof, and around to the back door, from which he had emerged into a frame of frozen chaos not quite ten hours before.

Some beginning.

Flute went inside.

D'Mambro was in the kitchen, sitting at the table just as he had been that morning (Flute, hadn't he said, I will make you some eggs). On the floor near the fire Stein sat hairy, crosslegged, with a pad of white paper balanced on his knees. Whatever he was drawing was small and furry.

Twisting to look at Flute in the doorway, D'Mambro's burnt swollen face fought a small battle with itself, a tiff for control of the dislocated mechanisms.
"Isn't she with you?" he blurted. His face lost the struggle.

"No." Flute suddenly felt weary as an old tire. He avoided D'Mambro's eyes and carefully watched Stein lay down his drawing pen and squint through his glasses at the unwilling messenger in the doorway.

"Tell it quick, Flute," Stein said. "The man is anxious."

Flute told them without moving from the shadowy doorway; the descriptions, conjecture, interpretation he directed to the sullen D'Mambro. Stein had quickly returned to the belaboring of his drawing, but his pen stopped moving when Flute began to describe the turn of events at the state hospital. He could almost see Stein's ears flapping from his head to embrace the physical information.

D'Mambro devoted his attentions to a tin fork on a table in front of him, caressing it, tapping the tines on the worn wood.

When Flute said, by way of summing up, "I thought I wouldn't chase them from there. I had the woman's car and decided to return it," D'Mambro slowly bent the fork into a soup ladle shape.

"Prudent," Stein said, and forefingered his rimless eyeglasses back to contact with his thick black brows.

Flute moved to the table and sat down across from D'Mambro, prepared to see the man drive the bent fork tines into the table, or perhaps his own hand.

Flute said, "Some people I know in the city will find them. Bobbi's upset, man. Give her time."

D'Mambro said nothing, kept on with the fork.

"Your turn, Stein," Flute suggested.

Stein did not look up. "Jones is okay. His vertebrae came unstuck a little after you left." He was calmly erasing some detail of his paper animal. "He was up before the fuzz and the ambulance came."

D'Mambro broke the fork and sat still while the separated piece flew past Flute and into a dark corner of the room. Flute, for safety, stood pat on the side of rational information.

"Fuzz?"

134

"Sure. The very kind and very puzzled highway patrol. How do you get some de-nosed fella serviced out here in the sticks without involving such people?"

Flute saw it. "Right, but what. . ."

"Shit, let Jones tell it in that special way of his, little cosmic glow on the entire proceedings."

"Where is he?"

"He and Kate took that rotund woman to her place. She only lives about three miles, Upper Mattole. I think Jones got her to believe she *gave* Bobbi her car."

"Good for him," Flute said, preoccupied and aware that D'Mambro had raised pale and rattled eyes at him. At that moment Flute was quite sure he didn't want or deserve involvment with this man's ragged anxiety over a frightened, whimsy girl, and an unknown cipher called Robert Quell.

D'Mambro shouted, "I thought you were going to bring her back! Jones said you'd bring her back!"

Stein jumped up, dumping his pad to the floor. "Dammit, Claude, Flute's explained all that. Just cool it!"

D'Mambro blinked several times, eyes still fixed on Flute. His eyes brightened in the firelight. He raised his fists and brought them down once, twice, on the table top. And Flute thought: I am going to get the fuck out of this whole business.

It was Claude D'Mambro who left. He stared at his knuckles for several seconds, then he got up and walked out of the house.

Whose eyes? The blinking chocolate eyes were Molly's for a moment, Kate's, until in the dimness of his living room Flute recognized he was being stared at by Bobbi Love. Had she spoken? He ducked his head, embarrassed that he was discovered, and saw his knees like fat stumps; he noticed he was kneeling and immediately thought to rise up. He managed to regain some height in the room, only to discover that, erect, his legs would not support his racked body. From the distant rear of his head came a great woosh of numbness, and he flopped backwards with the grace of a man stood too long on his head. As he fell he caught a blurred glimpse of Bobbi Love's startled eyes, then Robert Quell's bulk entering the room, hands outstretched in some out-of-focus offer of help.

He woke up in his bedroom and immediately said to Molly Noel, who sat astride both him and the army cot, walloping his face with a clout of frigid wet towel, "Stop!"

She dismounted and watched him through narrowed eyes.

"Are *they* still here?" he asked, an airy but aching nothing beneath the checkered quilt.

"They're sleeping."

"Ahh, after putting their maggoty host to bed."

"No doubt," Molly said. She was wearing some dark green trench coat, belted and epauletted, and a black felt slouch hat bent to shade her eyes from Flute's intrusion; he decided she looked dramatic and quite silly, but kept the startling revelation to himself because his predicament hardly merited such observations.

"They arrived last night," he said instead. She waited for him to go on, and suddenly he knew she had just come from the bed of Doctor Jacob Maven Bogue, as surely as if he had managed to hear the merry ting of Bogue's sperm dropping to his (Flute's) hardwood floor beneath her trenchcoat. "It's early, "he observed.

She tapped her foot. "It's six forty-five."

Flute supposed such a lovely, abandoned *Fuck* might be shared in cities all over the world. In the face of such a delicious flesh machine, what difference did it make that she and Bogue had him marked as pawn in some convoluted and private game? Then he compromised this induction morning epiphany with the thought that this delicate queen's body in front of him was probably itself an unknowing pawn in Bogue's mis-wired brain. He sat up on the cot, swept the quilt to the floor, swiveled his legs sideways, and stood up before her: bony, limp, filthy man. "Molly, I must say it's been a real pleasure laying you." And he began a lively two-step on the cold, sperm-laden floor. "Jake Bogue has excellent taste. . . .He takes superb care of his patients. . . .At least this wretch. . . ."

She smiled. He watched the stretching of the tiny chap marks on her pale, bloodless lips---a tolerant smile; she thinks she's a spectator at my induction rehersal, he thought. Doesn't she know that I know that *fanatics* can only be cuckolded by their own choice? "Out-of-whack Flute," she said tolerantly, and while Flute was choosing to ignore the patronizing lilt of her voice, the familiar words, Molly brushed his nude penis with the expensive stuff of her coat, and moved to the bedroom door. He began to hum an old tune, unsung lyrics his final gift to her -

*SHE COMES IN COLORS EVERYWHERE*

- over and over while he dressed in the clothes his undresser (Robert? Bobbi?) had left at the foot of the cot. "Thank you, Mick Jagger. Thank you, Molly Noel. Fuck you, Jake Bogue. Thank you one and all. . .dum-dee-dum."

137

From the bedroom door she coolly oversaw and overheard his sly, inane punctuations. "Jake's wondering if you have any plans," she said, perhaps by way of acknowledging all that had passed through *his* head since it came awake.

"You've seen him then?" he confirmed, jerking the stiff buckskin trousers over his drooping part.

"Of course." She laughed. "On Sunday he was as quick as silver."

"Good one, Molly." Flute went barefooted to the door. She reach-ed up and touched the bare patch under his nose. He shied. "It was very painful," he said.

"Subtle," she observed wryly.

"I'm simply following directions, sticking to a pattern. Aren't your instructions roughly the same?. . .The Doktor prescribes."

She raised an eyebrow, said nothing, and he followed her into the kitchen, where she began to rummage in the icebox for the elixir she had prepared the afternoon before. "Seriously, Flute, we want to know your plans."

"Oui. We? Personally, I plan to change my whole life."

"Well, Jake likes you very much. He'd like to get to know you and your friends better. If you wouldn't treat him so lightly."

"And you?" he asked as she approached him with a tumbler full of cloudy liquid, leering regally.

"You're an interesting case," she murmured.

"Yeah, very very interesting." He was beginning to lose track, hardly seemed to be in the room. "What's the use of plans at this point? Nothing is ever over. Today is just an event along the line, a knot on the string. Why don't you and your boss come up to Jones's place and watch me change into a worthy human being?

We'll watch the world crack-up together."

"Maybe we will. Drink this. It's an external fact and should cause your poor, addled brain a few more tremors."

He stopped listening, fed up with the arranged pattern that he seemed to be a part of, sick of her feigned aloofness, weak with trying to keep himself in some kind of functioning order---practical and future fantasies seemed impossible now. What was, was immediate. In the middle of the kitchen, in front of his eyes, Molly appeared to perform a nude, lascivious jig, in the midst of which she produced from her blonde wedge a pink pill in the shape of a valentine heart. He accepted the amphetamine and swallowed it with the tumbler of straight onion juice.

By the time he had finished banging back and forth from the ice box to the stove, his vision of Molly was gone and her clothing had reappeared. She took him by the neck in order to rub a mixture of kipper and sardine oil through his already stained and massacred hair. He began to perk up, took ten deep breaths. There was no time to *consider* just what was going on---who was responsible for what action, motive, or Flute-plan: Things simply got done, or undone, on one's Induction Day.

She rubbed his face with a dish towel, spread the grime. "Keep your mouth shut. You forgot the tee shirt."

He had enough physical presence to remove the workshirt and don the tee shirt she offered from a trench coat pocket. He replaced the other without buttoning it, and gazed down at the white cotton stretched over his cratered chest, the easy sand trap where its center caved in; and stupidly regarded the inverted letters done in red across the tee shirt's front -

KILL FOR PEACE!

139

Molly Noel guided the Morris through Oakland's dead gray factory streets, 7:30 Monday morning. Flute slumped in the back seat, out of sight of the city's morning work crowd.

Occasionally, as they cut through the streets beneath an unmoving fog, his head bounced loosely on his neck and thudded into the cracked plastic of the seat covers. He counted his heart beats, and took note of his blood as it reversed direction at the end of his toes.

Molly stopped for a light, tapped her fingernails on the steering wheel, while the radio -

> (*Today the President ruined the Quality of Life, and agonized over Withdrawal; meanwhile Order jived Law. "It's a whole new ballgame, my Fellow Americans," he declared. "I am responsible. . ."*)

- might have spoken far outside the current range of Flute's ears, though he definitely heard Molly say, as they moved off from the light, "I said, you smell worse than baby crap," and laughter hummed in his ears, barely dented his elevated brain---even with the top down. As she jerked into second gear his chin bobbled on his chest, and he noticed---for the first time since leaving the apartment---that he was wearing a bright yellow and blatantly spotless nylon windbreaker of the type common (he reflected) to professional golfers and uncounted San Francisco homosexuals. And further on, past the buckskin pants which had made the foul journey to the Southern Pacific yards, he saw his own feet encased in yachting sneakers so virgin the laces seemed to have been tied by machine. "Psychiatric splendor," he mumbled, and fell back into a reverie involving his racing heart and the sewage pit squatting in his mouth.

Molly brought the Morris to a bucking halt just around the corner from the Oakland Army Terminal.

140

"Umm, yes," Flute muttered, attempting to coax some liquid up into his mouth with a tongue as dry as last year's leaves. The weak morning sun hazed through the fog, raped his starting eyes. "I can't see," he moaned. "I mean I *can* see, but it can't be what I'm supposed to be seeing." She reached back and handed him a pair of sunglasses with mirror lenses like two silver dollars. He put them on and suddenly felt as if he were in some dark, binocular film. "Is it time? Where do I go, for Christ's sake, what do I do?"

"Stop blabbering for a start. Do what Jake told you to do."

"Haha. I think I'll self-destruct. . . .Do what comes to mind." He ran his hands quickly over his soiled face, through his reeking hair. "Eeech," he said, and resisted the impulse to sully the mysterious windbreaker. "The death of a dude," he moaned.

"If you get out of this," Molly was saying efficiently, "call me at the office."

"If!" He bulled erect in the back seat. "Where is Bogue anyway? Where is that bloody fugue-ist now that I'm about to put my body on the line?"

"There's no knowing these days."

"You're such a lovely cunt when you're lying. They've probably got a letter from him in there says I'm sane and straight as a deacon."

"No, my love, I typed it myself." She turned and offered him a full, disconcerting smile. "It says that in most capacities you're unable to deal with other human beings on any realistic level."

"Gee, it *sounds good*," he blithered. "Am I up to it?" He climbed from the car without opening the door. A man in a white plastic helmet walked by on the sidewalk, stared. Flute smiled at him, all of a sudden feeling clear as a bell chime. The hard hat sneered and clumped on by. Flute bent to Molly's inviting ear. "Tell Bogue

141

that if there's an earthquake today, after all this, I'll personally crawl from the wreckage and wring his rabid neck." Molly ducked her head away from him, started his car. He placed a speckled hand over one of her breasts and smiled---an idiot bidding fare-well---as she wielded the Morris away from the curb, leaving his cupped, trembling hand suspended in the factory air.

"Hey, fella, don't go in there."

In front of the squatting terminal stood four officers of the law: immaculate blues, white crash helmets with plastic visors raised. Four pair of steely eyes stared not at the approaching Flute but at a bedraggled huddle of sign-bearing youths. In range, Flute stopped near the entrance, a few feet away from the officers and their charges.

"Hey freak. . ."

"Hell NO!" someone shouted.

Under the impression he was invisible, Flute read signs -

STEP FORWARD & DIE

PEACE IS ORGASM

THE U.S. ARMY SUCKS

Flute ambled for the stairs. Stony policemen, like library lions. One stepped toward him. "Where do you think you're going?" Flute hesitated---all sounds filtered through the steady rushing in his ears. "Hey!" The cop laid a gloved hand on Flute's immaculate jacket.

"Sir." He spoke directly into the man's ruddy face and was pleased to see him take a step to the rear, baring his teeth. "I'm going in here to be or not to be inducted. . . .Okay?"

142

"Good god, go right ahead."

Flute proceeded up the stairs.

"That man's a fuckin' cesspool," the cop said to his immobile fellows.

Flute came to the room indicated---the size of a basketball court, high-ceilinged, murky. He walked quickly toward a group of inductees, perhaps fifty youths grouped together, but lost in the spaces of the room. He stood on their fringe wearing his mirror glasses, ignoring the examinations of those peers closest to him.

Over the loudspeakers spaced high on the walls came a voice echoing, rattling, feeding back upon itself, a jaggery voice accustomed to addressing great masses.

"All right!" it said. The group stirred, looked forward, but Flute was unable to see the source of the electric voice. "All right, shut up and answer up loud and quick when I call your name."

The silent, sad bunch got ready, the voice cleaving into their heads from every direction. "Shut up, shut up, quiet!"

"Alpe. . .David Berry."

"YES."

"Chambers. . .Peter Clug."

"CHALMERS, SIR."

"Shut up! Duggan. . .William."

"HERE."

"Fiker. . .Louis Emery."

"SIR, HERE."

"Flanagan. . .Alexander Dubrovnik."

"YO."

"Flute. . .William Victor."

". . . ."

"Flute!"

In the silence the several loudspeakers began to yawn and ping.

"Flew-ute!"

"I AM RIGHT HERE," he shouted from the pit of his chest, only to hear his own voice crack and burble as it issued from his failed larynx.

He felt them begin to turn on him, and he knew in the deadcenter of his flowing head that he had committed himself irrevocably to a most public course, and one that Bogue had not advised.

The staring inductees on the fringes of the pack appeared to move even farther away from him after his throaty shout, crowding their fellows toward the unseen man and his microphone. With his hands stuck in the back pockets of his oily pants---smelling, smelled---he was quite alone.

"What's going on back there? Shut up! What the hell is going on back there?"

The pack in front of him began to split and soon he was able to watch the progress toward him of one stiff green figure, one mannikin in fatigues, one efficient corporal bearing down.

"What's this?" the corporal said.

Flute felt sure the cotton fluff in his mouth was ballooning between his lips. From his berserk heart, small triphammer pulses

144

shot out over his body. The short, rigid man thrust his face into Flute's---in front of Molly's mirror glasses, a silly foreshortening occurred, as if the man's face were too close to a wide-angle lens.

The crowd was hushed behind the corporal.

"Good morning, sir," Flute said thickly. The man blinked and twiddled the dotty muscles along his extended jawline. His nose was a tanned slab of lard stuck willy-nilly on his face. "My name is Woll. . ."

"You. . .are. . .repulsive."

The bunch tittered. Flute, Molly had often observed, I love your balls. Yes, he needed some protection from the horror flic happening in front of the mirror glasses.

"What's your name, fellow?" Flute jumped. Lemon balls, she was fond of saying. "Hey! You answer up." The inductees pushed closer, into the thick of the stench.

Suddenly recalling the value of inconsistency, Flute snapped his fingers just under the corporal's nose.

The stuff of his brain continued to feed him: Molly whispered, Yes, look they slide around the way brown sugar does when you push your finger in. This was how to maintain *inner* dignity at least; Flute was grateful to her for the memory.

The corporal was busily flushing blood through his cheeks, apparently trying to hold his breath and talk at the same time. "Wise ass," he said. "We'll bust the fuck out of you!"

Then she might also say, See your cock, a helmeted knight in the bush. And Flute felt his knight's cock stir beneath the buckskin. His vision zoomed in and out on the poor corporal's nose. His head was an immense echo chamber of several and various parts.

He said, "Sir, I am ready," and he said it slowly and with much

145

respect glowing in his voice. The corporal shook his head violently.

"I'm getting you out of here," he said. "You come with me, mister."

They were in a hall, galloping along. Cool green tiles skipped under Flute's feet as he followed the panting, wheezing corporal up some stairs, along another corridor, a door, series of rooms full of apoplexy faces over a background of weary green. All the while the corporal muttered and attempted to hold his breath.

In a room crowded with slivery wooden benches, hooks rammed into the walls, Flute stood, though his body was still in rushing motion. The corporal threw him a vicious glance and began to shout through a nearby door. "Dikelen, hey! Run this guy here through before the rest get up. . .Dikelen!"

A voice acknowledged it was being spoken at.

"Yeah, well, he's one'a those." The man turned on Flute. "Strip to your shorts. Hang your clothes on the hooks provided. Your valuables will be safe, but you may take your wallets if you wish to."

"I am invaluable," Flute said, removing his yellow windbreaker and hanging it on a hook.

"What?" The corporal eyed him, had his fists half-cocked.

"I said I appreciate this."

Flute unbuttoned the workshirt.

"A bath and a shave and I'd have you eating shit, buddy."

"I believe you." He removed the workshirt.

When the corporal caught sight of the tee shirt, its scarlet lettering, his eyes bulged, the fists finished cocking -


KILL FOR PEACE!

- he advanced. "Take off them glasses! you dirty faggot sa'versive!"

Flute did as he was asked, turned his back in order to put the glasses in the pocket of the windbreaker. And in a quick motion undid his belt and twitched the buckskin down to expose his nude hindquarters. "Look here, where's your underwear? You gotta have underwear here."

The corporal's voice had risen a fair two octaves. Flute bent over, pants at knee level, and removed the spotless tennis shoes. Then he turned to face the corporal again, sat on a bench, and finished taking off his pants. He stood up, delicately took the hem of the tee shirt in both hands, and stretched it down over his private parts. "Will this do, sir?" he asked, resisting the temptation to flounce and curtsy. The corporal gagged on his own impulses. Flute snapped to attention, taut pink leg flesh, knobbed knees. "Wolliam Victor Flute, number 41-9-41-208, brought here by special executive order, by order of our Chief." Flute winked. "Here I am, do what you will, corporal."

"Yeah," the man muttered. He wheeled, shouted, "Dikelen! Never mind all the other shit. Get the shrink up here NOW, and file on this. . .Flute,W., 41-9-41-208. Right, buddy?"

Flute, feeling that he had passed the rehearsal test, allowed himself a brief prayer, *Please keep me together; I've come too far to let words get in the way.*

But the corporal wasn't finished, "You know what, slime, they're gonna commit you, your crappy tricks won't work on Uncle Sam, no sir. We'll cut your cock and throw it to the sharks, people like you, shitheaps, you're all gonna get it, boy, let me tell you, guys

147

like you, break your goddamn heads all over the street---lock you up and throw the key away!"

"Yes, thank you," Flute said, saluting. The corporal---a hippo--- blew the remainder of his air and left the room, just as another man in green appeared at the door to beckon Flute his way.

Night. New Hampshire night; I am a closet in its stellar sphere, locked up totally alone in this most private and lonely universe of shifting, nubbled walls in the single ray of my tensor lamp; at precisely thirteen hours into my prolonged rush: A thirteen hour orgasm of nearly linear words that mask the shame coming in my heart. At least this darkness is suitable cover for my personal debris. . .drying gobs of cottage cheese scattered willy-nilly over my floor and even to the detritus of my banana boxes. Yet I am isolated, suspended like a glowing pit in the ink of this timeless cell. . .and ready, I shakily suspect, to follow my mind and cock through black space to an end I have no way of predicting or intending. . .

Here is a pink, orange, and white medical mind-man bulging my strained optic nerve. "Come in, Wolliam Victor Flute," he demands, leaning easily against (what is it?). . . .a metal desk in the middle of an institutional room otherwise as barren as a dungeon. Beneath a thick, pressed wad of orange hair, he wears a taut mask of bubblegum flesh stretched over a nearly round foundation of facial bones. His slouched body is draped in a lengthy white technician's coat with a deep bulging pocket at either hip. One of his opaque hands delves into a pocket and, clutching a wad of green tissue, leaps to his nose. Wheet! To cover this genteel nasal snort he snaps shut the file he is holding, places the rectangle on the barren desk surface, and repockets the tissue. "Come in," he repeats in a high-pitched but firm voice, though he has yet to glance at the modest tee shirt in the doorway. "I said come in."

148

Flute steps reluctantly into the room and sidles against one blank wall, exactly the physical attitude that Bogue was wont to suggest: Dissociation, an attitude of true romantic funk, snakepit variety. Yet, already Flute is beginning to sense that it will not work--neither Molly's artful filth nor Bogue's pedagogish funk; that perhaps nothing in this private interview will work but instinct, following his own ambidextrous nose.

The psychiatrist points to the folding metal chair on which one of his rubberized feet is resting. "Sit down." Finally, he looks up at Flute and, betraying not a twitch of reaction, says, "Good," his circular pink face rising and falling in once-over. Flute hesitates, willing to cooperate, unwilling to deal with the social problem of the doctor's foot. "Here you are." The chair, propelled, moves nearer to Flute, its seat now free to receive his skinny ass. "My name is Job." Job unslouches and assumes a youthful, crosslegged position on top of the desk. Flute shuffles away from his wall and takes the chair, careful to see to the modest arrangement of his tee shirt. In tones of reflection, the shrink says, "Now why? Why why why?"

"Doctor Job?" Flute tries to keep his voice level but incredulous.

"Ummm." Job yawns, fingers his clogged nose, looks briefly at Flute's crotch, where the tucked shirt makes a feminine bathing suit V. "Why are they *all* unpleasant? You, Mr. Flute, are really unpleasant. I'm sick of you already."

"Are you really, Doctor Job?"

"Oh please, forget the banter," is the reply. "It's a long day."

"All right," Flute is abuzz, chilly, but queerly relaxed.

"Are you willing to answer my questions, or has your uhh. . . *Doctor* Bogue advised against it? I can tell you something, I used to know Jake. In fact, I worked *on* him once. . . .Well, *with* him. Do you think he's strange?"

149

"Do you?"

Doctor Job smiles like the man in the moon. "Does the penis seek the vagina?"

"Rhetorically," Flute says, winking at the man.

"Good *ploy*, Mr. Flute! Shall I now suspect you of *less* than hetero-sexuality? Would you please tell me your age."

"Twenty-six."

"You're getting on." Job mocks the barren room with a simper of picket-fence teeth. "That's a bit old for here."

"You're baiting me," Flute accuses.

"Not at all, not at all. . .Well, these petitions of yours." Tut-tuting, Job lays a finger on the file. "I'd forgotten. You know how institutions are, always out to *get* someone. I wonder why they pick on a fellow like you," says the coy government psychiatrist.

"Pasadena," Flute declares, twitching one knee on top of the other, exposing his entire thigh to the Doctor, all the way to the meatless left buttock. Job looks quizzical. "My draft board is there, right there in that most fascist of counties."

"So?"

"It's my neighbors, you know, the fellows on the board; as you say, they're out to *get* me."

"Why?"

Flute opts for the sudden, high-pitched scream: *"I'M A FUCKING COMMIE FAGGOT PORNOGRAPHIC UNAMERICAN WISEASS PUNK!"*

In the midst of which his knees detach, fall apart; the tee shirt rises to his navel from the force of his scream, and the freshly nonplussed headshrinker lights his colorless eyes on a most flaccid part, and pair of shy balls.

Just as quickly, the two men are composed as before, though Flute, covered again, now sees a red fuzz on the periphery of his vision.

Job purses his pale lips, looks beyond Flute to the open door, waits several beats before saying, "I see," and then asks, "Your family lives in Pasadena then?"

"Correct. They do live there."

A rivulet of sweat escapes his left armpit, drops to his waist and visibly courses his exposed, dimpled buttock. "That is," he continues, "my father is alive there. My mother is dead. Andrew remarried, has three or four new children."

"I see. Andrew is your father. What's he like?"

"He's a bigtime bust."

"Really?"

"Yes sir, he's a real cocksucker. He's a motherfucker, Doctor."

"You hate him, I suppose."

"No. I admire the hell out of him. Even though he's a shit and a loser, he's the most consistent, unhypocritical son-of-a-bitch I ever knew."

"What do you think he'd say if he saw you now?"

"He'd laugh his head off, calculate the odds, then go cry in some bar. I don't know. What would *you* say if your son got drafted?"

151

"That's irrelevant."

"You said it, Doctor." Flute feels himself skirting some exotic and loony state of mind where anything is possible---and Bogue's vaguely remembered instructions can certainly be all but cast away unused, in favor of instincts that he feels to be operating flawlessly. "Have you really taken a good look at my file?"

Job uncrosses his legs, allows them to hang over the edge of the desk, and picks up the file with a newfound smirk. "You see this blue tag? Very few of these folders have them."

"Yes."

"How long have you been seeing Jake Bogue?"

"Three or four months. You know very well."

"Enough time to get a good *dose*," says Job, cryptically. "Any other psychiatric. . .excuse me, psychological care?"

"You know that too."

Job regards him for a moment. "Let's be specific, Flute. You're quite alert for someone who's supposed to have such difculty coming up against the harsher edges of reality, if I may paraphrase your distinguished charlatan. Oh sure, you're hairy and weird, and you stink like a submarine's air filter, but you seem so. . .straight. I can't fathom what Bogue is treating you for."

Flute shrugs. "Anxiety. . .mild schizophrenia. . .a little *angst*. . . alienation from society. . .hostility. . .normal stuff like that."

"Not to mention a fanatical urge to avoid serving your country."

"You mean to avoid my country."

Wheet! Job performs on the green tissue once again. Flute's impulse is to leap for the swollen pink face and stuff the entire green

152

tissue slowly up his baby nostrils.

"Do you have any friends?" Job asks, leering now. "What about this man you work for, Smith. . .what's his name?"

"Look it up."

"You are employed? I know Bogue doesn't do charity work."

"I get by."

"And this felony charge, possession of dangerous drugs, the state of New York magically decided to drop?"

Moment of panic, close secret---some file. "It cost me seven thousand good American dollars! What's *your* price, Job?"

"Careful! In this building you are no free man, I guarantee you that." The doctor is leaning at Flute, tight-lipped, breathing very distinctly.

Flute gets hit again: "THAT'S PRECISELY IT, I'M NOT A FREE MAN!"

"Good Lord, get away from me, would you please. Any more yelling like that and I'll have the military police in here."

"Forgive me, I suddenly felt a little anxious. *You* know how it is."

"Yes." Job is gazing at Flute's midsection. "Cover yourself, man." Flute regains modesty, but very slowly. Can that be sweat on Job's smooth brow? "Where was I? Any homosexual experiences?"

"Bogue goes down on me at the end of every session. And then I rush right into his secretary, who also happens to be his mistress. What would you call that?"

"I'm not. . ."

"I mean," Flute interrupts in a flash of eagerness, "Imagine the convolutions here: me doing a job on Bogue's middle-aged mouth while he's manipulating *his* cock some short distance away, that which has probably the night before been dipping quite quickly into *hers*, to which very thing I rush fresh from *his*. Think of it!" Flute snaps up from his chair. "Look at it, Job!" Indeed, the front hem of the tee shirt begins to rise magnificently. Job remains frozen upon the desk; his neuter eyes fixed on the phenomenon.

Flute watches him coldly, yet smiling broadly. The Doctor's head seems to swell out just above either ear. Job seizes the folder, blindly rolls it into a tube, a weapon. The papers crackle and explode onto Flute's boosted eardrums. From outside the room, echoing through the corridors, comes an indistinct roar---the approach of the first inductees.

Flute crosses his arms, fingers the hem of the now-distended tee shirt at either thigh, quickly snakes it up his torso -


KILL FOR PEACE!


- and over his head. Wadding the shirt he throws it in Job's face; it slides off the baby skin, down the white coat, and falls like a shroud over the doctor's roll of incomplete and lying records, which Job begins to wave frantically in the air---pathetic flag.

Flute is off into a whirling frenzy about the office proper, holding his part like a livid bat before his nothing belly: he leaps into a monstrous buck&wing, now holding himself with both grimy hands, pointing it straight at Job's heart as his heels come together in the air with a thwack. Then, in one graceful motion, he abandons his grip and falls to the floor for a quick series of charged pushups, seemingly on a fulcrum of his own making, pushups which miraculously blur into four crotch-wide knee bends. He stands on his head, frontside to the Doctor, sees the man approaching with the rolled records outstretched, and manages to call up a monumental rent of a fart, foul tribute to the rotten and exhausted condition of his innards. This before he tumbles toward the floor in a fit of dizziness---in falling his feet whack neatly on Job's shoulders, rest there. And the two fall straightaway to the floor in an obscene unit: barefeet to pinkish head; half-moustached face to rubberized feet, and into the doorway steps the first inductee.

It is the evening of January Second. I am down, no longer high; my body is a peaceful, empty space. . . .This post-chemical deception of my senses! In truth, I am sick at heart, only my heart has been artificially, temporarily *quashed* by the acid's wretched dross. Much to explain, gentlemen (and Kate), but first I must order my wizened accomplishments.

I see that the fussy, 19th Century temptations of the third person became the ironic vehicle by which I, W.V. Flute, was able to belie the tone of that brief but crucial (to *my* life's zany progress) unpleasantness at the Oakland Army Terminal eighteen months ago; an agonizing event, by any standard, and incredibly distant from this New Hampshire room. . . .At least until the chemical trigger brought it all home, right up to the very present. My gratitude, then, to LSD for its prime mover power of Total Recall of *actual* events, for the part it played in the irrational eruptions of my parabolic (fabulous?) fancy, e.g. the mythical *Jilly*.

But, gentlemen, there is more to it, a darkness beyond this momentary peace and gratitude. . . .

(Incidentally, I was on the sunny Oakland streets, with a 1-Y deferment, by 9:30 that July morning. For all I know, disgraced Dr. Job fled through those same streets by 10:00. I thank him now. I do. Would that he could hear this clown's sentimental hindsight; but Job will never know how his misery of suspect embarrassment affected my life. Had he not scrawled those two letters---1-Y--- somewhere in my battered folder, why Kate would not presently be my wife, Ann my daughter, and *perhaps* Jones would not be dead. Certainly I would not be sitting in this chair feeling nothing.)

If Kate screams at this unsubstantial, fleeting, parenthetical denouement, I shall call it fanciful revenge for this morning's Family Outing.

But, sirs, there is yet this matter of a darker fancy, another sordid revelation from the blind artificer. . . .

At 5:00 this morning I recorded that final, compromising arrangement of the limbs of Doctor Job and Inductee-Interruptus Flute. The *spell* broke: my pulsing high intensity lamp took this occasion to die, and I was left alone in the dark with the dregs of the acid--disoriented, surrounded by papers and other personal muck, all the disorder of a journey of astounding length. Fiddling for the lamp switch, I knocked my earthen tea mug to the floor and heard its shards join with the sticky, aging mess of cottage cheese, pickles and corn relish. The tragic crunch of pottery. . .and then I myself climbed down to the floor and crawled into a reverie among the tea pools and gobs and painful chunks of mug.

This mindless reverie I attribute to the appalling erection that I had sustained (maintained) since entry into the vision of my past self's lascivious dance for Job; it was a real and marble-still problem for my trousers there on the floor, and not even a false dawn outside the windows to light the way to some resolvement of my state. I found myself stuck with the physical result of fantasizing a past event I had thought my mind's eye was finished with. But it is even more convoluted than this. For how was it possible, in the first place, to create and maintain an erection in circumstances so threatening, so opposite of sexual, so basically unhealthy as those in Job's military closet? I am not, and was not then, a faggot, though I will admit to manhandling an adolescent dick or two, screwing a ewe, and (during my 13th year) providing onanistic thrills for at least one grateful Golden Retriever. No, I thought, I had directed no latent brain buggery at Doctor Job. The feat was more ordinary. . .and there on the black floor my uncooperative brain continued to replay the reconstituted, heterosexual fantasies I had called up at the Oakland Army Terminal. To say: female persons in triple and quadruple exposure continued to flit and reel

157

through my head in an orgy of flickering images taken from *The True and Accurate Sex Life Participles of W.V.F.*, who, lying rigid in his New Hampshire refuge, understood truly the stupendous mental achievements of the Great Masturbators of the world.

Stop it! I yelled, principally to the forest of technicolor vaginas, thighs, mouths and nipples. . .which were distended in every possible and livid way. An exact reprise of what happened immediately following my words to Job, "I go down on Bogue every. . .," when I began to receive (and certainly force) the mainstream of flesh images which were snipped from an historical line stretching its way from Molly Noel on back to that very first young lady's rubbery 14 year old clitoris---and when all of this sweaty lineage came close to becoming simultaneous. And these remembered parts were very soon cross-cut---fantasy-memory interlocking pure-fantasy---by freeze-frames from graphic scenarios involving those ladies seen but never *known*. I refer to females of my then recent environment: Bobbi Love, Kate Ximines (Yes!), and even the briefly glimpsed Nurse Kelp; I found all of them suddenly mounted upon my priapic bandwagon, their shorthairs eagerly glimmering in the dowdy institutional light of Job's examining room. Each and every female conscripted to the cause of stirring a frightened penis to an altitude that would---hopefully---be useful to a Greater Purpose, that of avoiding the draft of the United States of America.

So this morning, eighteen months later, these images, thanks to the unkind drug, came crowding back to me, and with the same elevated result.

Phenomenology, gentlemen.

I lay on the cold floor, my former selves being sucked, nibbled, licked, pressed, fucked; and when, as it had to happen, my stiff member began to erupt of its own will, I must truthfully record that I also spilled a joyful chuckle, a perverse salute to all the lively female shades who at that exact moment were getting a good psychic jolt, a ghostly wad from Flute there alone in his dark---

quite enough for everyone. And I wondered, too, if Kate sleeping above had any inkling that her husband, shooting off in his pants, was in direct fantastical connection with the hasty moment in the Oakland Army Terminal when he first saw *her* not as Jones's, but as his.

This then is how to create and maintain. . . .No! This is how to get it up---and keep it up---in the worst of times.

Should I also label it the darker, the perverse, the shameful side of the fanciful coin? This acid exaggeration that has led me to the masturbator's *extreme* self-involvement: led me to make fantasy *objects* of my women. . .my wife.

There I was, floored in my private room.

Unaccountable time passed.

The sun rose. Ann cried.

My door opened a crack. "Flute."

I heard, but my eyes were closed to this non-agressive invasion by my present life; I felt placid, uncomfortable, cold, suspended in the colorful, onanistic fluids between my past and present. Perhaps, thinking I was asleep, she would go away and leave me to mop up my own room's wreckage.

"Flute." The door swung full-open behind me. "Hey!"

I knew immediately what she was seeing, and rushed to my own defence, but she was upon me before I could muster any explanation. She laid a hand on my shoulder, shook me gently. "Are you all right? Are you there?" I opened my eyes to the awful bright of the morning sun; her fresh face interposed, frowning, concerned, my partner of healthy skin, white teeth, sweet brown hair that even now brushed my soiled cheek. "You couldn't make it upstairs?" she asked with just a touch of censure, and no knowledge of the pun that smashed me between the eyes.

My unused voice erupted in a fit of falsetto croaks. "The light went. . .out," I managed to say. She gazed around at the debris, the dark puddles on the polished floor. "I got clumsy in the. . . wee hours."

"Ahh," she said, "You're all right then?" I nodded vigorously and tried to get up from the floor, but my body would obey no such orders. Finally, I held out a hand, which she took, and by leaning back she was at least able to bring my torso erect. "Come on," she urged, "get all the way up. I've got to feed the baby. Why don't you go to bed?"

"Can't. . . .I can't do that."

"Okay, then clean up this mess and come and get some breakfast. We're going out today, all of us."

"OUT!"

She was halfway to the door, and most precise, "That's right. This entire family, of which you are a non-practicing member, is going to leave this house together, and you've got nothing to say about it. You haven't been anywhere with us since we bought this god-damn house."

"Kate, I can't. . ."

"Why not?" She slammed the door, was gone.

At noon I found myself alone in the polar strangeness of the garage, a shanty structure across the road I had not so much as put foot to since the bank allowed us possession of our new property exactly four months before. I mounted the amber Jeep, my aging Universal with its salt-scourged canvas top---once white but now

160

gone speckled gray, a veteran of half a winter's trips to grocery stores, doctors, wherever Kate travels with Ann. Pummeling the engine alive, I sat in an invisible fog of exhaust fumes, and while the heater whined I seized the memory of this vehicle as a slick new piece of machinery. . .in California, before we made the slow journey from chaos to our life of tranquility in the undisturbed Northeast woods. Now the bucket seat seemed no less crisp and leathery than it had on the day I laid out three thousand dollars in cash for its formed cushion and all the metal that went with it, a seat that had suffered little from the weight of my narrow ass; nor had I even fingered the gear shift lever of the transfer case, or "put in" the Warn Hubs---specially ordered---that Jones would surely have recommended had he been more than a name on a recently probated will. I never punched that transfer case into some fantastically compounded low gear in the midst of one of our mammoth snowings. For a minute, as the heater finally began to spray hot air over my legs, I hated and regretted the recluse life I had been living since September: the self-pity of the foolish indoorsman!

But the giddy, arrogant aftermath of the acid prevailed (as it still does at the end of this long day). I could never have come even this miserably short distance in my dubious ancient history, I thought there among the heat and exhaust fumes, without locking myself up, miserable but eager prisoner of this public document of what I have done and not-done. Without this oblique record I would be *nothing, nowhere, buried---the misery in the closet, the lunatic in the attic;* certainly no man of machinery and the great outdoors, as I was pretending to be now.

I reversed the Jeep out of the garage, extra power necessary to hump over Kate's latest job of shoveling the driveway, and stopped. On the passenger side the metal doorstop flipped up, the canvas and plexiglass door burst open, and in climbed my wife and child. Their faces were cheery from the cold, both bodies bulging with winter clothing. Ann smiled. In her yellow parka Kate looked determined, resolved, anxious to hit the road. She sat on the seat with Ann in her lap and gazed straight on, not saying a word, apparently expecting me to assume the guide's role and wheel them

161

immediately to their destination.

Which I didn't know. How could I be any more than a menial cipher, a follower of orders given by the woman who only this morning had discovered me on my floor in a pool of sun and terrible debris? I give thanks now, as I gave thanks then, that the dried *evidence* of my expanded morning consciousness was well concealed by dark blue Levi dye. "Let's go," Kate said, with evident impatience and nary a glance for me.

"But where?" I tried to sound unconcerned, cool about the whole tortuous business of this unlikely departure from my private if not safe roost.

She continued to look as if I might be driving us all to some tropical island that very instant. "Well, love," she toned with what motive I could not guess, "California is not so far," and then she smiled into the bright stuff of Ann's hood.

"Umm," I said, with poking dollops of snow beginning to melt inside my boots. *Going* is all that matters to her, I thought, and rolled the car on back over the remainder of the driveway onto the road, pointing us in the direction of the store and gas station which make up the town centre of W————. Like a novice I stumbled over the combination of clutch, accelerator and gear shift, but we did then go forward and even to second gear, with a lurch and a spectacular surge of V-8 speed, while I swung the wheel in futile attempts to avoid the frost heaves which bloomed everywhere like warts in the road and the bounce into third jarred everyone's bones.

"Slow. . .down!"

"I'm getting it," I yelled, just as we hit another frost heave, and they rose very near the roof. We swept down the treacherous road and soon enough came to the store/gas station, where an unshaven man---coatless in the two degree weather---crouched to fill the tank of a colorless pickup truck.

"There's old Bill," said Kate, waving and fluttering Ann's mittened hands. Did the old coot grimace as we skimmed by? Did he spy the no-account ghost of a husband at the wheel of little Kate's Jeep? 'eh-yeh, he was out with her'n the kid just today, I saw 'em go right by, sixty mile an hour, all three.'

On the slick main road at sixty-five, cold air poured through the airy spaces around the clutch and brake sticks, got into the tops of my boots and surely began to freeze the snowmelt already there. The heater whined between us, and I was happy to be going, wherever; high on this rush of speed, perhaps ready to disconnect from the earth and somehow regain the sweaty exaltation of the single flying lesson I took with Jones.

"You're not going back now," Kate cried over the laughing, humming car sounds.

"This is true." A funny elation stuck like a bubble in my craw. "My toes are frost bit. I am at odds with this machine, we may go into a snowbank, but fuckin-A lady, I am NOT going back!"

And my daughter gazed at me with her entire fist stuck into her mouth.

"Go faster!"

I poked the pedal. "Where?"

"Does it matter, dear fellow?"

Seventy-five, eighty miles per hour, until the heaps of roadside snow began to blur, and I held to the black steering wheel for sweet life.

"Pass!" Ann waved her arms cheerfully. I shoved the pedal all the way to the floor and watched in fascination as we curved into the left lane and slid past a cranberry sedan full of youths---brief plexiglass caricatures. Ninety miles per hour and the tires were

163

stuttering on the frozen pavement, and my brain began to move beyond the speed, to ignore the mechanical process it controlled; in fact, I did---for one long lovely instant---feel *one* with the machine, with Kate, with this present life, enough so that when we came to the outer limits of Antrim it was near to a physical pain to back my foot off the accelerator for a compromising and dullish coast through that town. "OH! that was fine," Kate said, smiling now, whispering into Ann's shrouded ear.

### PETERBOROUGH 13

Out of town, regaining a sedate sixty, we swept south past leveled snowfields, tumbled barns, a choked Monadnock River, and not a person in sight. . .until we backed-down into Peterborough, and Kate declared, "We shall eat at the People's Diner, all of us peoples."

I giggled, parked, continued to travel in my head, recalling California freeways, Bloody Bayshore: the Morris carrying me every direction under the only slightly besmogged sun.

"You going to buy me a hambooger?"

"What?"

She leaned across the gap and put her face in mine. "Hey! We're here, come on." And inside she ordered us hamburgers, potato salad, milk, and successfully used a ketchup bottle to occupy Ann in a distant corner of our booth.

I floated on the dark founded ceiling of the diner, appreciating the quiet cooking beneath my nose in this neat legitimate place. We all ate an amount of delicious food. Ann knocked over Kate's milk and smiled as it made its liquid way over the table and dripped into my lap---a gay if sickening reminder which I tried to ignore.

164

A bit mockingly, Kate asked, "Aren't you glad to be *out?*"

"I think so, yes." And although my queer high spirit was beginning to receive nervous twitterings, I was able to look seriously into her left eye. "You're a lovely woman, Kate."

She gaped, frowned, ducked her head. "Do you want some ice cream? Is something the matter?"

"No."

"You're just bemused, sort of vaguely charming," she said, "you left your major preoccupations at home, right?"

"But of course. What you've got here in front of you is a simplified Flute." But I experienced a private wince at this misleading statement.

"Then clean up the milk, dope, and tell me how you've been."

I put white napkins on the still liquid. "I just did a job on Job. I'm coming along," I said, and noticed another wince.

"Job?"

"My United States Army psychiatrist."

"Ahh. . .the poor guy." Three neat vertical wrinkles appeared between her dark eyebrows. "Why don't you save your *jobs* for Jacob Bogue. *You* used Job, but all of us got used by that Bogue."

"I'm getting to him. But understand that I have to concentrate on a single moment at a time. . .in all that ragout."

"Maybe you concentrate too much, love," she said.

"Come on."

"Don't wail at me, you *concentrator.*"

"You're being an asshole," I suggested.

"Don't you call me that!"

"I'm sorry, I haven't been to sleep."

She was glaring, nodding. "Right."

"Like Jones," I injected softly.

"What!" Her eyes flashed, already recognizing my weak ploy, but I continued to talk at her angry face.

"You know," I said, "he was nocturnal, a night man."

She softened, as I knew she would. "Yeah, among other things."

"Yeah," I echoed stupidly, and realized in quickening panic that Jones's habits were exactly what I wished to avoid, had been avoiding ever since the beginning of his (my) roundabout resurrection.

Kate was staring at the table. "You're sloughing him off, Flute," she said quietly.

". . ."

"It just seems to me that the very first thing to do is acknowledge responsibility; if it weren't for Jones, my lover and your friend, we wouldn't be sitting here, would we? In the People's Diner. . . Peterborough, New Hampshire. . .Mr. and Mrs. W.V. Flute and their daughter. . .the atomic family."

Tears jumped into the lower rims of my eyes. The neglected lady reappears, I thought; marriage remains always in the present tense. Once again I had forgotten, and now she was rocking my boat, chivvying poor Sinbad's delicate skiff. Please, sweet lady, stand off a bit, allow me to approach these monsters at my own speed, without your damnably correct opinions. Heat rose in my brain and threatened to make cascades of my floating eyes.

166

"I'll get to the center," I said weakly.

"There's nothing at the center, love. Are you crying?"

"No!"

"Take it easy then." She leaned toward me. "Flute, you're so hard. You push me out. And you don't even know this baby. You come along once in a while, love me at night, and tell yourself you've done your duty. It just doesn't work."

"I don't believe you," I snapped, stiff and dry in the lips.

"Come off it! For you it amounts to avoiding the present."

"I know, Kate. . .but. . ."

"Just say you understand what I'm saying."

But I could only look at her. I began to feel threatened by a melodrama; in fact I felt in great danger of snapping out of the scene and hovering near the diner's ceiling a second time, a new surge of acid dissociation. And she stared back, calmly, as she must have regarded all of them: Jones, Moody, Flute.

"I ask you to leave me alone!" I exclaimed, and immediately knew how ridiculous I was, the true man of melodrama. But I was caught in my own idiot mechanisms.

"Take it easy," she said again, a hint of anger now behind the words.

I took a deep, rattling breath, finished my milk, fumbled for a cigarette, and with instant logic, accompanied by horrendous images, thought: This is a lousy way to compensate for a cold, spermy morning on the floor---my wife is taking a lot of shit. "Okay," I said in a proper voice, trying to smile through the smoke, which was diabolically stinging my eyes to more tears,

167

"I'm sorry I'm so pissy. Sometimes I literally don't know where I am."

"What do you mean?" Worried, she cradled Ann, kissed her face.

Kate's small victory; she was sucking confession to my surfaces like some blotched monkeybite. "Something happened this morning," I blurted. "My light blew out, I ended up on the floor. . .I thought I actually *was* at that damn physical. . .other places where I certainly wasn't." And I came very close to telling her about the LSD, the fantasy females, the willed masturbation, all the various symptoms of what is frightening me. But I could not admit, in speech at least, that these suppurated weaknesses were real---no matter how much they help me in what I am doing.

When we got home she put me to bed. Suspended, weightless, I thanked her; inadequate syllables for the complications I felt even in the luxury of the bed and the bubble gum of my brain. At some point she told me that although my education in women was less than rudimentary, and that she sometimes felt more a fantasy of mine than flesh and blood, she loved me, and didn't care whether I heard a word she said as long as I remembered the presence of her flesh and blood in this house.

Or perhaps this Outing was a rude figment.

Wouldn't that be an easy out? A way of denying that *Wolliam Victor Flute* escorted *Kate Ximines Flute* to a diner in Peterborough, New Hampshire, accompanied by their daughter *Ann Arden Flute*, and there, in the presence of other human beings, discussed themselves.

But now, back in my ordered room, rested, undoped, I desire some peaceful state, and so how much easier it would be if I *had* made it up.

How much easier if all the rest of it had not happened. . .

# PART THREE

Robert Quell strides the *Eureka* meadows to the big house, a green glowing afternoon in the middle of August. The sun pesters his scalp. When he spies the No. 1 dome-house he detours, as is his custom, to avoid the place where Bobbi Love now lives with Claude D'Mambro. It is Robert's courtesy, this deviation; he knows he is not all of her life, and by his own choice he is no pain in the ass---even though at this moment Claude and Bobbi are probably not even there. He melts into a stand of the giant red trees.

Of all the people on this *Eureka* land, Robert is now thinking of his friend and roommate Julius Stein, a man who loves odd animals and talks every night in his sleep about giraffes, koalas, elephants and most especially the kangaroo. Over his cot in their dome-house Stein keeps an exploding photograph of what he says is a Great Gray Boomer, and every night he sings like a happy prayer:


*HEAVEN GIVE GRACE TO GREGARIOUS KANGAROOS*


He then winks at Robert's pleasure from behind eyeglasses that shine in the lantern light of their domed space on the cliffs above the erupting Pacific Ocean.

Continuing his dogleg way east, Robert approaches the chocolate barn and the magical yellow and black machine parked near it; the weapons carrier is his baby, his to wax and to feel. "Take care of it," Jones told him soon after Robert and Bobbi arrived from San Francisco. "I want some high visibility. . .some shine." And Robert took to the truck as if it were a legitimate replacement for the secret box he'd left in the foxtails somewhere. Other, duller machines are nearby the barn: Flute's squatting Morris; a black motorcycle leaned against the barnside; the big-butted gray Caddy belonging to Dr. Bogue or Mr. Clingsmythe, the newly-arrived persons who peer at Robert from room corners. But the spiffy weapons carrier sits in the sun like a crazy map. He touches one winking taillight where maybe a halfmoon of gray dust mars the bumpy red glass.

Claude D'Mambro steps from the blackhole entrance to the barn, and through the upside down V of the man's stained fatigue pants Robert has a sharpened vision of Bobbi Love's white cloth legs. While his body is still connected by a dangling finger to the weapons carrier circuit, Robert's old voice starts up: *I bet you think Claude D'Mambro's been rubbing small Bobbi on those sacks in the barn loft, poking her in the shadows, sniffing her perfect skin.* Robert continues to rub the machine, but his head is bursting with the solid presence of these two in the barn's doorway.

"Hey," she calls. "Robert!" She's out, soaked in light, but he's unable to look directly at what he loves. "Do you know where Jones is?" Now she's a foot away, her bare feet in the corner of his splashing left eye.

"Come on with us, Robert." Row-bert, D'Mambro says. "That thing is clean enough for a parade."

The near world seems washed over with red dye as Robert rises from his stoop to face them; Bobbi reaching to his chest, D'Mambro's glaring white forehead to his shoulders. "I wish I had a dog," Robert says, out of the blue. "I'd have a Collie like ginger ale." Bobbi smiles straight up to him while the other man pokes his boot in the soil. "My friend George had a Lab named Clap." *Hey, loon, you reckon they do it the way dogs do?* "Stein likes dogs and so does Miss Kate."

D'Mambro is clumping up the grass with his boot. "There's plenty of dogs," he says. "Plenty of dogs here. Jones has Zero, and old lady Pickel has a Corgi named Brutus."

"I haven't seen 'em," Robert declares.

"Zero's sick in Palo Alto."

171

"It's an old dog," Bobbi says. "Let's go." She is no longer smiling, and Robert knows he's interfered again.

He follows them across the yard to the pool and house; the pool electric with ripples from small winds and---for all Robert knows---gentle movements within the earth. *The trouble with you, friend, is you'd like Bobbi to be your dog.*

"It isn't cool to tell Jones," Bobbi is saying to D'Mambro as the three of them come to the repaired porch where the old trouble happened; Robert's clearest fantasy-picture is of a Highway Patrolman standing by the pool with a plastic baggie containing a nose and streaks of scarlet gore---the very reason Bobbi met him in the foxtails not so long ago.

"Whatever happened to that Piro?" Robert inquires, but the other two go on up the porch steps without appearing to hear his question. "Did he die?"

"Goddammit, Bobbi," D'Mambro says in a low voice that carries from the porch, "Jones *told* me to tell him. I work here, I work for him. . .not you."

"Jesus!"

Robert decides to remain on the soft grass while they barge into the house, but they stay and their harsh voices continue to violate the peaceful afternoon.

"I'm responsible for who comes on this property," D'Mambro barks.

"But you said you liked her, she's a harmless old lady."

"With field glasses and a rifle? Sure, Bobbi."

Robert, patiently waiting, sees the sky rushing bluely by in the jumpy pool water. *Listen, bonehead, they sound like old married people.*

"What?" Bobbi asks, and then she looks over D'Mambro's shoulder at Robert. "What's she up to then, smarty?"

"She lays around and watches us."

"Margaret Pickel!"

"Don't be so nice. She was the one at the beach after you jumped out of that airplane."

"So? She's not much different from you, I guess. Old peeper." And Bobbi Love presents Robert with a quick but definite wink. *Watch out!*

"All I know is it's Jones's place, and she's a trespasser, I'm gonna tell him."

"He'll laugh."

Then Jones's voice comes in volume from the inside of the house. "Claude, quit jawboning and tell *me* whatever it is." D'Mambro bangs through the screen door without Bobbi, who steps toward Robert and smiles enough to jolt his grassy stance, return his eyes to their fix on the trembling pool. *What a laugh, you wanting to trust that winking girl.*

"Hey," she calls out, "you my friend?"

Robert's eyes don't move. *She's putting you on, boy.* Voices drift outside from the kitchen, impossible to make out the words. Miss Kate laughs like a bell.

Later, with the sun dead and gone, he is building a fire for the main house. Wind coos in the chimney, having sprung up at nightfall and made chilly the end of their noisy supper. . .when Jones said, "Would you build a fire, Robert." And Jones smiled across the long table, out of his big square face, which was a beacon for Robert in the midst of all the contradicting faces of the assembled

173

people. Jones made it seem that a fire in his fireplace would soothe the whole bunch, like a gooey dessert to stick in their overworked throats and keep them quiet for a while. So Robert went out the door to D'Mambro's woodpile, where he strong-armed a few pieces of kindling and some thick, spongy logs about as wide as his chest.

He makes a ditch through the old ashes in the fireplace, a breathing tunnel for air. Behind him he hears D'Mambro set coffee mugs on the table. Clumps of unhinged words rise from the people, mix and mash together, only to peter out in the chill air, one by one. . .

*"But this paranoia. . ."*

*". . .the sperm-laden ocean. . ."*

*"I'm not befuddled. . ."*

*"Let's see, one hundred and sixty-eight oyster beds now irrevocably polluted. . ."*

*"Flute's an excellent example of. . ."*

*"I don't wish to speak of the law as an abstraction. . ."*

*"Zowie, America sure is a. . ."*

*". . .power resides with. . ."*

*"Pass the cream, you nit."*

*". . .nor does a black like this Sandor Moody. . ."*

*"I didn't bring it, Jake. . ."*

*". . .is probably a catastrophe. . ."*

*"It's too cold to live up here. . ."*

. . .while Robert wads newspaper into balls and crowds his air tunnel with them. He lays kindling over the newspaper, and places two of the logs atop the pile. "How's the fire coming over there?"

". . .or someone like this Mrs. Pickel, her very bones are made of fear."

"Oyd Fikes is no slouch. . ."

"Far out, but you're mistaken, sir. . ."

"Robert. . .here." The box of matches arcs from Jones and tumbles by luck into his startled hand as he hunkers beside the fireplace. The first match crumbles when he rubs it along the side of the box. The second bursts orange in his fingers. Carefully, he holds it to a corner of newspaper, watches the flame creep the length of his tunnel. Grabbing a thick magazine, Robert rolls an air-bat and with it fans the flames until the kindling begins to crackle, and he can sense the people at the table turning to stare at what he has made.

"The fire is before us," Jones says.

Silence.

Still on his haunches, Robert turns away from the heat into the fire-stares of Bobbi, Jones, Miss Kate, and the older one. . .the peering Dr. Bogue. D'Mambro is back by the stove, while the others at the table seem for a moment to be not much more than jawing shadows.

"And where will you go now, Jacob?" Jones asks.

"After meeting you, I assure you I don't know," the doctor answers. "Molly and Phineas and I have very much enjoyed. . ."

Now the heat of the fire drives Robert toward the table, his neck stinging like sunburn. He takes a seat between Stein and Miss Kate, who offers him her cup of coffee. He accepts the mug and is about to lift it to his face when Bobbi leans across the table with a mounded spoonful of sugar and dumps it into the firespeckled liquid. "Thank you," he says. "Thank you," and is suddenly content. Bobbi has come from the shadows to take care of him---for now, D'Mambro might as well be burning in the fire, shriveling among the logs, leaking a harmless, bubbling paste into the ashes. But D'Mambro, finished in the kitchen, arrives at the humming table with a new batch of coffee. Robert can see the fire behind him reflected dully on the surface of the pot: cherry metal going soft in D'Mambro's Bobbi-touching hands. *You jealous mother.*

Miss Kate is looking at Robert and whispering, "I think that Bogue person is made out of wax," and when Robert gazes down the table he finds that Dr. Bogue is regarding him with eyes that are like tar buttons in his whittled face. Robert nods and shivers and wishes he were as deaf and dumb as a gutted log. *You know, there are people in this room who think you're nuts. Are they right? Don't you know what's happening?*

Robert tunes in the nattering people once again. . .

". . .Molly will confirm that Flute. . ."

I do know a few things, Robert says to himself.

*"And where will you go now, Dr. Bogue?"*

*"Robert and I are going to build a fantastic giraffe with. . ."*

*". . .uhh. . ."*

*"Now look, Kate is asleep in her chair. . ."*

"I know all that matters is what you do while you're walking around," Robert declares in a loud voice.

*"Eureka!"*

*"The rains come very soon. . ."*

*". . .and then Moody said martial law was. . ."*

*". . .in the north I am waiting for the earth to speak."*

*"Well, marijuana is scarce up here. . ."*

*"That's not quite as precise as. . ."*

. . .and Robert Quell understands that no one is talking in turn, that each of the people might as well be alone---at least until Jones himself decides to open his own magician's mouth; until then it is as if they all sit still in order to worship what Robert decides is nonsense. The pretty, jumpy sounds they make, words dovetailing like millions of TV dots that make a picture Robert can perhaps see, but then not-see for sunlight, ghosts, and a now-sure knowledge that it is what you DO, not the TV dots that bubble from your mouth.

Be a Watcher.

Robert burns his lips with dark steamy coffee.

With an orange pillow tucked under her, Bobbi Love handles the weapons carrier through the fog wisps of this late August morning. Patches of blue sky hang like bright amoebas in front of the windshield. Beside her Robert is happy to be making the mail and grocery run to the village of Honeydew---though for days now her eyes have come nowhere near his. *Bet she's got something up her sleeve, some sly maneuver, some royal screwing for you.*

The dashboard gauges push their trembling needles at him, glass winks in the stray rays of sunshine that enter the truck's cab. He hasn't been on a trip with Bobbi since they came up from the city with the never-there Flute. *You're a Simple Simon if you think this trip will have any kind of happy ending.*

Ahh, shut up.

"What?" She touches his knee, he shakes his head.

In Honeydew Bobbi pumps the machine to a halt in front of a gray and drooping frame house.

## GOOCH BROS. STORE

### United States Post Office

When she switches off the key, the engine keeps on chugging. *Maybe she'll have you stamped and sent off to your brother Peter, C.O.D.* The truck gives a final gasp, dies, and the two of them dismount. Robert hears the Mattole River beating its wings across the road, and the sun, as it comes into its own above the redwood trees beyond the river, warms his head. "You coming in?"

Goods everywhere, even suspended from the ceiling. Canoe paddles. Like a little gold jail cell at the back of the store, the Post Office window---a fat lady floats in front of the bars, dealing with her mail.

"Help you folks?" There's a cash register like a haunted house, and behind it a man with a face the color of salami. He's frowning at Bobbi, who is saying good morning just as she would to any human being in the wide world.

"Help you?"

"May I have a basket, please?" she says.

"No baskets."

"But. . ."

"You just bring the things on up to the counter." The man smiles without opening his mouth, or lightening his kerosene eyes. "That'll keep your hands occupied, little girl."

Bobbi's shoulders hunch under the white stuff of her jacket. "Okay, Mr. Gooch, whatever you say." She sends Robert after milk and eggs, pointing to a glass front icebox next to the Post Office cell.

*Does the door slide or pull, looneybird?* His reflection in the glass is covered over with a gray steam, but through it he can see the fat lady's reflection; she has pulled away from the gold bars and is giving him the eye. The icebox door slides, and out comes a smell like dying wood---from the storage locker behind the display of chilly goods.

Three half-gallons of milk under one arm, a fourth in the same arm's hand, and four dozens of eggs held against his body by the other forearm. "Sonny, don't leave the cooler open, you'll *spoil* everything." Robert turns back, loaded down, and stares into the glasses worn by the fat lady, who is a sausage below him, wearing a shirt the colors of the American flag---tiny patches dancing over her ballooned chest.

A bald head presses against the other side of the P.O. windowbars. "What's the trouble, Margaret?" he shouts into the vastness of the store.

Robert gestures helplessly at the open icebox door. Like a thick jar of softly moving flesh that fat lady, Margaret, takes a step toward him. "Please," he finally says.

"Oh, all right," she mutters and turns to slide the door shut.

Robert attempts a smile, sure that the dealing has been successfully concluded. "Thanks a lot, ma'am."

The angry postmaster grunts and draws back into his dark office, and Robert returns to the cash register and places the milk and

179

eggs beside other cans and boxes on the counter. Bobbi is not in sight. The salami clerk smirks, leans over the top of his register and looks carefully at Robert's pants pockets, sniffs like a hound dog, and slowly sinks back to his stool. "You from down there too?" he inquires.

Robert shuffles a little, smiles, shrugs, wishes Bobbi would get the hell up there---his friend lost among the stacked and hanging goods. "Yeah," the clerk goes on in a voice that seems to squeeze from his nose, "I see that crazy truck out there. The little girl is in here a lot, or the pale fellow, what's his name? Claude. He's friendly, shoots the breeze some. . .Shall I total up this stuff?"

"Sir?"

"The groceries." The clerk---Mr. Gooch---points to the assembled shapes.

"Please." *Where is she? Swallowed up? Your so-called friend has flown the coop.*

"We don't see the big gun."

"The what?"

"The fellow that bought Fikes's. This Jones." Robert nods, several times. "You had some trouble in July." No comment from Robert Quell. "Well, whatever you say or don't say, I *saw* that Webster boy when they brought him out. Oww!" Robert tries another smile, but Gooch glares at him. "What do you people do down there? You got lot'sa women, right? Haha. . .is that why you're grinning like a rag doll? You'll need plenty women when winter comes, colder'n a witch's nip." Robert shrugs, Gooch leers. "Shee-it. . .plastic houses," he grumbles.

The register twangs, and Robert decides it's safe to go and look for Bobbi, but there she is, behind him with an armful of goods, and a frown on her mouth like an awful cloud. As she sets the things down, Gooch snickers. "Can you add this up while we get the mail?"

"I'm doin' it, girl."

In the back of the store the swollen jar lady is once again pressed up against the barred window, but when they arrive she withdraws and right away begins to speak. "Hello, dearie. Frank you know Bobbi, of course, and your name is?"

"This is Robert Quell, Mrs. Pickel."

"Howdy."

"Hi."

"How are you people doing?"

"Groovy. Is there any mail, Mr. Gooch?"

"Good," says Mrs. Pickel. "I see Claude D'Mambro from time to time."

"I know," Bobbi says.

". . .and he says everyone is just doing fine."

"What?"

Margaret Pickel forms her red lips into a quick smile. "Well, you know, that Mr. Jones has recovered from his back ailment, and that you built all those cute little houses."

"You should know." Bobbi is trying to get past the woman's bright weight in order to pick up a packet of letters waiting on the worn brass shelf.

"I beg your pardon!" A kind of shriek in the jar lady's voice.

181

Bobbi sweeps up the mail, and turning, smiles sweetly. "Nothing. Claude gets around the place a lot."

"Of course. . ."

"He probably sees more of you than you see of him."

"Young lady, what are you trying to say?"

"Trespassing is against the law. Let's go, Robert." They turn up the aisle, leaving Margaret Pickel with her mouth open like a red bulls-eye. Bobbi pays. Robert hefts the boxed goods. Mr. Gooch grins at them like a dirty joke.

Out the door. Bobbi leads, muttering all the way to the weapons carrier, "Asshole. . .Claude's right. . ." Robert loads the box into the back of the truck.

The door of the grocery store bangs open; Mrs. Pickel's there on the porch above them, eyeglasses flashing like sparklers in the sun. "Now just hold on there."

"Something wrong?" Bobbi asks, about to climb into the cab.

Sputtering lady, her great chest heaving. "This was a decent community!" The words fly like buzzing rockets.

"Yes."

"Keep a civil tongue there!" She is waving her thick fingers at them. "You better believe I know all about your activities. . .and MaryJane Fikes, bless her, she knows too. . . .Your lewd beach activities, we know. . .bunch of perverted ragamuffins!"

"Nice to see you, Margaret," Bobbi calls out, turns her head to smile at Robert, and climbs into the truck.

"You lar. . .larcenous trollop, your sweet-talking Jones won't get

182

you off next time you steal from me." The words slammed out by the truck's doors. Robert can see the salami clerk as he peers out the window behind Mrs. Pickel and steams the glass with his breath. Robert rolls the vehicle's windows up tight, and as Bobbi backs up they see the jar woman batting her lips like a strangling fish, her face as red as the checks of her wooly shirt.

South of Honeydew, clear out of town, Bobbi pulls off the road and onto the grasses of the Mattole riverbank. "Shit," she says, shutting off the engine. "That's some neat people there. She was pretty mad."

Bobbi laughs. "I should be more careful whose car I steal next time I decide to leave." But her laugh tells Robert she doesn't mean her words. He calmly watches her pull the packet of letters out of her jacket pocket and shuffle them in her hands.

"So she's the one Claude sees?" Robert asks, hearing the badgering voice even before he gets all the words out: *Christ, birdbrain, if you're to be such a jimdandy Watcher, don't ask these stupid questions.*

"Yeah, except Jones doesn't seem to care much. . . .Look, here's a letter from your brother."

*Ha!* "Jones is funny," Robert hurries to say, his throat sticking together. "He. . ." She gives him the envelope

> Master Robert Quell
> c/o Jones & Co
> Gen Deliv
> Honeydew, California 95545

*Look out, chump, people are busy busy busy over you.*

"He's what? I bet you know."

"He's like my friend George; he's always talking, but. . .but he's never talking to somebody."

She smiles, points to the envelope. "Why don't you open it?"

"Why should I open this stupid letter?"

"Hey. . ."

"Bobbi," he shouts, "why was that lady so ugly!"

"Maggots. . .I don't know, maggots in her brain."

"Jones. . ." he's going on, hurling the words from his finally unstuck throat, "Bobbi, these people up here don't *fit.*"

"Shh," she breathes, and through the haze of his excitement he sees that her eyes are too bright, like shards of brown bottle-glass. "People are different, you know that. That's what the world is."

"Dr. Bogue has a gun."

Her mouth screws up in disgust. "He's something else. Besides, those people don't belong with us, and they've been gone for a week."

"They'll come back, that Molly said so. They *look* at me."

"Oh man. I thought you were over that stuff. So what if everyone's a little flipped? You like Stein and Kate. . .and me. Isn't that enough?"

"Are you going to stay here with Claude?" he asks in a voice that has fallen back into the quiet bottom of his throat. *You're going*

184

*to hear it now, baby.*

"It's not so bad." She is not looking at him. "The rainy time is coming, the cold. Hey, see what Peter says, is he back in San Francisco?"

*She knows damn well where he is.* Robert works his thumb under the envelope's flap, the whole whiteness of it splotched with oily fingerprints that only Peter could have put there. He rips it open, and picks out a tightly folded sheet of school notebook paper. Blue lines. And then lots of rounded pencil writing that reminds him in a flash of Peter and New York City and dirty snow. Whatever it says, whatever happens, he's sure now that Bobbi doesn't know all the things that he knows. *That's it, take her easy and you'll survive.*

Her hand settles easily on his knee. "Will you read it to me?"

He holds the notebook paper up to the bright windshield and speaks the letter in a halting voice: " 'Dear guy, how are you liking the country? Did Stein obtain a giraffe? Do you have elegance there? Mimi and me are glad you split from the hospital, and Bobbi says. . .' " Robert stops, looks right at her.

"I sent him a letter a couple weeks ago."

*See, they PLAN you like a little kid.* " 'Bobbi says you know what's up and do high quality work around the place. In the east I saw George, who possesses a beard, he says to tell you to come see him when the time is pro-pit-ious, okay? Mimi is pregnant and we are in S.F. til Christmas. You can come down here with us for a while if you'll stay around and not go tripping off. All of us folks got to be careful now, there's a lot of heat. What do you say?. . . Want to see you, love to everybody, your brother. . .Peter.' "

The cab is chock-full of their breathing. "You *are* going to stay here," he says flatly. "You and Claude." He watches her hand as it rises from his knee to his face, disappears past his ear, then lands

185

softly against his bristly neck.

"Yup," she says. "We're going to look after things." She laughs. "Keep that old biddy away." Her hand squeezes, shakes him slightly, like a puppy. "You know what I'm talking about, so don't be sad. We're friends, best friends, for keeps, no matter what happens." Now the hand is like a soft, loving animal on his neck. "You're okay now, everybody knows it."

He looks. She's smiling, or at least the corners of her mouth rise without strain, the clear pink lips, the up-and-down lines etched on them. "Yes," he says, and leans to touch his own lips to hers, quickly, firmly.

"You're a beautiful man, Robert. Go see what's happening in the nasty city, then come back up here. For Christmas, a Christmas goose for the entire freaky group, okay?"

*Sucker!*

OH, BLOW IT OUT YOUR ASS! And just then Robert Quell knows sure that she is saying things that are true, that there isn't an ounce of lying in her; that he knows what's what.

"Okay," he says, "okay. That sounds okay to me."

Bobbi starts the weapons carrier; they're smiling at each other like kids. The truck is vibrating, vibrating happily on the earth. Robert knows it.

186

At high noon: Molly Noel laid out upon *Eureka's* beach sand. From a vantage point on the seacliffs, W.V. Flute regarded his old flame. She alone violated the curve of sand, its intimacy with the August sea---an indigo blue cap for most of the earth Flute was able to see. Spread nude on the sand, Molly would not blend. He saw her as he might have seen an infernal chromium machine set in the crown of a two hundred foot redwood. Her pubic hair, a dark V smudge at the very center of the beach, left him fair to cold; like some flamboyant technician, he studied the environment's minor flaw. Yes, Flute was a man living becalmed within his skin while he observed a naked woman on the beach a hundred feet below.

If he chose, he could shout, "Go away! You don't belong here." She would hear him, roll over casually in order that the sand might entertain those curling hairs. Perhaps she would arch that efficient back so as to position her head for gazing at him, a grin distorting her features about the time he would notice her giving him the finger---a perfect fingernail raised to the heavens. But Flute kept quiet. He was really not much interested in losing the simple, visual perfection of her body's shell. What use provoking further demonstration that inside the shell resided his former psychologist's clever moll?

Flute lighted a cigarette with the brushed metal lighter given to him by Kate Ximines that morning---a startling gift, no comment or thanks permitted ("I've quit," she said). In fact, she frowned, hardly met his eyes until he made to leave, and then he saw the clearest eyes he had ever seen on a human being. Why? he thought with a tremor, sucking the windy, tasteless cigarette.

Molly rose from the sand and strolled to the water. Her familar butt rode like an inverted valentine heart at the base of her narrow back. She reached up and unpinned her hair, threw away the pins, and then commenced an erotic job through the early surf, soon disappearing in  water no deeper than her comely thighs.

187

Despite the self-image, that of a dude dressed in buckskin and bright cotton smoking a cigarette on the Pacific Cliffs, Flute found himself at sea. Serious doubts about Molly flitted through his brain, this woman now suspended beneath the Pacific water; this secretary and ally to Jacob Maven Bogue---unreliable architect (false draftsman?) of Flute's recent extrication from the Government's Armed Service maw. Had Molly been no more than another of Bogue's absurd psychological tools? A whore-assistant to a master pimp? Yet Flute's calm kept returning to drive away all his flitting conjecture. Who cares? he mused. While they're visiting here they're just people; different, queer, but no more suspicious or dissembling than anyone else. And is it not one of my charming talents, indeed part of my job, to deal with the differences between people without making judgments? So did his mind leap: mercurial, ambidextrous bastard!

Waiting for Molly to surface, Flute glanced inland, his eyes drawn immediately to the dome where Stein made his humorous attempt at living with the non-sequiturs of Robert Quell. Each dark triangle of the structure mimicked that *thing* on Molly he still could not help but admire. Perhaps, if I look to the sea again, it will have swallowed her up without a trace; goodbye Molly, goodbye my urban whore. Brief thought, the moment before he actually did twist his head westward, to discover an occupied beach.

Jake Bogue, dressed entirely in navy blue, was carrying his elegant head at a steady pace along the wet sand just above the reach of the surf. He carefully avoided piles of green bulbous seaweed, scattering sandpipers this way and that; the birds fled from him, this narrow blue fright. Bogue came abreast of Molly, now surfaced---Flute nearly shuddered to see---her head a dark china cup on the water's glassine surface. Bogue raised a hand, beckoning like a king, a patriarch. Molly's head appeared to toss, to throw words at the lithe and dry man on the shore, who crossed his arms at the waist, snaked his shirt up his torso and over his head.

Again, Flute's impulse was to shout, to be heard, to rape their *couple's* privacy. And again he kept quiet. He flipped his cigarette toward the beach in order to demonstrate that he was not hidden, not skulking. No innocent voyeur, Flute.

Molly's head moved slowly through the water toward Bogue. Flute glanced south, almost expecting to discover Bogue's fey shadow, Phineas Clingsmythe, standing in the shade of a sea-grooved boulder with a towel or a legal brief in his hand, ready to perform any service for his master, the Duke of Mind, the Shaman of Bullshit. No, Phineas was not there, was more likely closeted in the main house with a tawdry manuscript advocating government repression of certain actions that tend to destroy civic freedom: the Rule of Law. Flute reprimanded himself for his eighteenth uncharitable thought of the day; he didn't really know a damn thing about the obsequious lawyer, or much care. He refocused on the two figures on the beach. Molly had returned to shallower water, was half emerged, proudly carrying the two dots of her nipples to Bogue on the shore.

"By Christ," Flute said aloud, unconsciously, as he watched Bogue stretch his arms to the west, a welcome for the coming female. Molly trailed her hands, taking her time, lifting her knees on high. Her crotch glimmered in the sunlight. Perhaps her eyes caught Flute's obvious shape on the bluff; if so, there was no sign. By Christ, if she lays that old fart in front of my eyes. . . .

Bogue, still shaped in his expansive gesture of welcome, took two steps backward in the sand, and Flute imagined the soft shoes of blue suede sinking richly into the billions of quartz particles. Molly left the water behind, and came to kneel in front of Bogue, her torso erect, her eyes more than likely on an absolute level with his forty-three year old genitals. But Flute could not see any more than his pipestem legs and Molly's fleshy outline behind them. The psychologist lowered his arms until they appeared to be resting on her shoulders; the scene began to remind Flute of every anthropology film he had ever witnessed, and he fully expected the chief's shoulders to sprout ceremonial feathers of blue, green, and red. Molly was closer to Bogue now---had she walked on her knees? Sections of her dark thighs looked to be seamed to the blue stuff

189

of Bogue's pants. His head swiveled down until the nape of his neck pointed to the sky. And yes, there was no doubt about it, Molly Noel was blowing him for all the sea to see, and sandpipers were pecking at her lax feet.

"Let's take the O out of Orgasm!" Flute jumped, and turned to see that somehow hairy Stein, large-pored Julius Stein was sitting next to him, squatting on the very same rock. "Jinkies, will you lookee there," he exclaimed again.

Flute searched his bubbly, embarrassed brain for some kind of flippant observation as he watched this owlish Stein. Nothing. Stein thrust a half-moon of charcoal-clogged fingernail into his meaty nose. As intended, Flute relaxed, yet remained speechless. Stein always knows exactly what he's doing, Flute thought, The finger searched---distorted the end of the man's nose like a goiter--- then withdrew, rose to the bridge of the nose where it gave the center of his glasses a familar push: everything straight. "Dadgum, such fellatio has got to be one lonely affair, you know, Wolly?" This last delivered with much forlorn eloquence, as Stein had recently been informed of the imminent demise of all the earth- worms in the world.

On the beach the tableau continued in deliberate unconscious motion. Flute was now truly immobilized; over and over, his mind commanded a gesture, a shrug---at least a palm stretched out to the silly outrage below. But nothing obtained for W.V. Flute.

Stein squinted here and there, twiddled his thumbs in his lap, and finally, lugubriously, said, "Now those people will *always* be with us, so you wanna come over my house and play?" Which created, low in Flute's belly, laughter as unstoppable as a rushing belch. Sounds made rents in his chest, ruptured his mouth, until he was roaring there on the seacliff, laughter he had never known, the kind to bring hiccups, spittle, wheezing, tears. The two of them arose from the rock and made for Stein's dome, leaving the hap- pening on the beach unresolved, the outcome unseen, but their laughter a surefire victory for Flute. Goodbye, Molly Noel.

190

W.V. Flute offered Kate Ximines a bowl of string beans, which she accepted. Above her ear the brown, highlighted hair ran a delightful upsidedown French curve to the tortoise shell barrette perched at the back of her head. Flute held the white porcelain bowl while she spooned a clump of the beans onto her plate.

Jacob Bogue, on Flute's left, mumbled as he haphazardly offered Flute a small plate arun with this Sunday's butter. Jones, at the head of the table, was solemnly carving a portly leg of lamb.

"Thank you," Kate said, taking the bowl from Flute's drooping hand as he fumbled the butter from Bogue.

Stein waved a pitcher of ice tea. "Who wants the bugjuice?" he shouted, while looking directly at Molly Noel—teasing this out-of-place *girley* in a Shantung silk robe the color of new green leaves.

"No, thank you," said Molly.

"I do, please," Bobbi Love said, and when the pitcher reached her she poured full the glasses of both Claude and Robert Quell.

Phineas Clingsmythe observed the carving of the lamb. "That knife is not as sharp as it might be," he said to Jones.

"Is that so?" Jones replied, with a serious and attentive glance for the feathery lawyer, and carved on—neatly parting the meat from the bone, careful slice after careful slice. "It seems sharp enough. Kate, an end piece?"

Stein delivered the grace, "Lord Jesus Christ have mercy on our souls." Scattered, nervous laughter followed, though Kate kept silent.

"Jacob," Jones said, "you're a walker, I see."

Flute heard Bogue swallow his mouthful of lamb.

"I'm fond of purity," Bogue intoned neutrally, pompously.

Stein guffawed, as if he had choked on a morsel, and Bobbi Love pounded his back with great thumps.

"There's nothing pure about land itself," Jones observed. "Perhaps people can purify themselves *on* it."

"In it," Kate murmured, for Flute's ears only? He sensed that for some reason her table energies were directed only at him.

Impatient with his own and the table's vague tensions, Flute consulted a mental schedule and declared to the lot of them, "Sandor Moody will arrive tomorrow morning."

"Yeah," said Stein, "and where's he gonna stay, this Sandor Moody?"

"He's escaped," Kate mentioned quietly. Jones ceased chewing and looked directly at her bowed head. "He's a fugitive," she said.

"He's on the lamb," Stein said. Jones grinned; Bogue chuckled into his glass of tea. "So now we're an underground railroad," Stein went on. "I don't understand what's happening around here. The place has gone mad, and the less said the better."

Now Jones was laughing outright. "Stein," he said, "your own state of mind is generally unfitting."

"Shit, sir. Gimme some more of that redundant red meat if you please."

Bogue thrust forward his ignoble head. "What *does* one do with a revolutionary in these parts?" he asked, deadpan.

"Parts," Stein mocked.

"I would send him to school," said Phineas Clingsmythe mournfully, his face scaled with terrible concentration.

"O boom," Stein crowed. "I'd remand him to a very small island in the company of Oyd and MaryJane Fikes."

Next to Flute, Kate flushed, and across the way Molly Noel's face went hard about its queenly edges. "All they need is an excuse," Molly said. "Then bang! slam! and you'll have to go to old films to see a black face. *All* of it is very practical."

"Guess you can't come to my dinner," Stein inserted, drawing frowns here and there.

Robert Quell revolved his burr head toward Jones. "Who is Sandor Moody?" he asked in a voice that struck Flute as not quite coming from his mouth.

"Robert," Kate called out the length of the table, "He's a friend of mine who's in trouble."

"To put it mildly," Phineas said.

Suddenly Bogue struck the table with his waxen fist, nearly causing Phineas to spear himself with his fork. "It's damned inconsequential," he shouted. "It's all spittle on the real issues. . .black men, white men, red men! We need solidarity against. . ."

"Jake!" Molly made as if to toss her glass of tea in Bogue's flushed face.

"Excuse me." He calmed, effortlessly. "Is there another endpiece?"

Jones regarded him. "No, Doctor, there is not. Why are you shouting in my house? Why are you polluting us?"

"I?" Jacob Bogue, for the first time in Flute's experience, appeared honestly shocked.

"If you have to be in the city tomorrow," Jones said, "perhaps you and your friends should leave very soon. It's a long drive."

"But I have no wish to go there. . . .I have *left* the city."

"Then you have some other destination."

"Well, actually, no. We had hoped to stay a while with you good people. Flute has told me that you. . ."

"Come back another time." Jones's interruption was firm, level.

"Ahh, thank you for that," said the graceful psychologist. There was a long pause down the table. Then he said slyly, "We'll regret missing the famous Sandor Moody."

"He should be so lucky," Stein opined.

At that moment Flute lost his bearings; Kate's left hand had come to rest on his buckskinned knee. A mild electric shock traveled the space of his bowels as he glanced---casually---at this woman, and found himself looking directly into those clearest of brown eyes. Why in the name of Christ was her face so open to him? for all the disappeared world to see? She was speaking, whispering, "How many lives, how many lives do you have, Flute?" He could say nothing. Let her ask Jones. He looked away from Kate Ximines, broke the contact.

And Stein went on, "Will Moody arrive in a hay wagon, buried in the straw? Do we stash him in a root cellar, huh?"

"He'll stay in the barn," Jones said quietly, and no expression crossed his face as he lifted the remaining end piece from the platter with his fork and flourished it toward Bogue's pointy nose.

W.V. Flute surfaces. After three underwater pool lengths his cre-
vassed chest heaves, and his mouth sucks madly for brisk September air. He is, this afternoon, in the midst of his final *Eureka* dip.

Sandor Moody sits a few feet away on the porch, mulling things
over in a rocking chair. Next to the barn, Robert Quell polishes
the weapons carrier, and fifty yards behind Flute, D'Mambro and
Stein are disassembling Dome No. 1. In the kitchen, Flute knows,
Kate and Bobbi are washing lunch dishes. As for Jones. . .the distant burping of his chain saw probably means that he is cutting
winter wood in a clearing a quarter mile away---wood for Bobbi
and D'Mambro through their long caretaking Fall. But at this
moment Flute doesn't really give a hoot about placement or ar-
rangements; his private fantasy of things is complete enough: *it's
Kate he wants.* His lungs catch up with themselves. He blows a
stream of air up through his now-recovered moustache, and droplets of water fly gracefully before his eyes. Stein's voice, as always
punctures the air, "Shit fire'n save matches!"

Sandor Moody rocks on.

Kate comes out on the porch and hands Moody a beer. Wearing an
apron, a blue sweater with the sleeves pushed to her elbows, she
looks small but solid as she stands there not quite looking at Flute
in the pool, holding out the beer to Moody. Who finally, very
slowly, takes it. "Thanks."

"Nobody ever explained this to me," Kate says to the yard in
general. "There's no music here." The last few words rise in volume. She goes back inside, pronouncement made; perhaps it is a
coded message for the soaking Flute. Jones is tone deaf.

Moody rocks, sips his beer, while Flute folds his gooseflesh arms
on the pool curb and lowers his chin to rest. Awake this morning
in his room, quite alone, but a wall away from Kate and Jones, his
brain had produced the two horrific sentences that now stick
with him like an entrenched tune, a kind of prayer: *The hell
with friendship. It's Kate I want.* When the sentences first intro-
duced themselves, he was startled, disbelieving, appalled. . .but

195

then something in his mind had clicked off, so completely that he felt like laughing. He had proceeded then to rise and walk through the *sharpest* day he could remember. Those two declarative sentences had produced a reason, a simple and happy motive, if not for everything he *had* done, then for everything he would now do. No matter that he knew not what Kate was about.

"And what will you do now?" he asks of his elbows; part of his mind intends the question for the black man on the porch---whom he is afraid of and likes.

"Me?" The chair creaks on. Moody's handsome face is probably buried in shadow.

"Why not?" Flute looks up and is surprised that he can see the man so clearly. In the sunlight his face is a brilliant caramel color. "What's it going to be?"

Moody smiles. His hands rest on his black-trousered knees. He speaks in an educated, expensive voice. "I am the recipient of plenty of advice on this subject." Coming from a fugitive, an escaped convict, the voice is an on-going but absurd surprise. The steel-wool hair frames the man's head like an opened paper fan--- a black dome that extends at least six inches in one hundred and eighty degrees of direction. "Plenty," he repeats.

"Tabletalk is wholesale here," Flute observes politely.

"I hear you, man."

Flute laughs. "The Chairman says 'beware the motley intellectuals.' "

Moody is gracious enough to offer a tolerant chuckle in reply to Flute's inaccurate and probably patronizing quotation. " 'But seek refuge among them when expedient,' " Moody amends.

Now the both of them laugh. Sandor Moody: the name is typed on one, two, maybe three Federal Arrest Warrants. "We're learning it's not so remote here," Flute offers.

"The woods are full of fools." Moody's face is pleasant, composed, but totally without any expression that Flute can read.

"Fat women and maybe jug-eared ex-ranchers, to be specific."

"Dangerous folks, righteous folks."

"If you stay here with Claude and Bobbi when we leave. . .you ought to be goddamn careful."

"I will, bet your ass," Moody says, a slight frost in his voice. Flute kicks himself, an amateur advising a professional. He scrambles out of the pool, grabs his towel from the edge of the porch and runs it quickly, self-consciously over his frail, alabaster body. "I sure will be careful, Mr. Flute."

"No, I just meant. . .shit, I'm sorry, I don't know what I meant."

"Well, I appreciate your concern, but I don't think I'll stay around much longer." Moody stops the rocking of the chair and stretches leather-covered arms at the roof of the porch. "Sure is nice here, you know. The trees are out'a sight." Flute hoists himself up on the side of the porch, his towel draped over his shoulders; he is shivering even in the direct rays of the sun. Moody goes on, "Katie has herself a set-up, indeed."

"Does she?"

The man's catarrh eyes shoot into Flute's brain. *It's Kate, Kate!* "But she's been telling me things, Kate."

"What do you mean?" A helpless quaver invades his voice.

"What's the trouble, boy?" Moody's voice is cultured but cruel. "She tells me of this Bogue dude who got you out of the United States Army."

197

"Well. . ."

The rocking chair starts up again. "It sounds like a nifty cadre."

"Excuse me?" Flute has heard him perfectly well.

"The threesome. Katie speaks of the beautiful chick [he snickers], the mouthpiece-man, and this tilted psychologist, who is a source of devil-power, you see."

"Bogue is an old fart."

"No. You miss what I say, Wolliam, you do. In bent times like these we should be most wary of his kind. . .visionaries---professional idealists---black or white, no matter. They're driving for something, and what is it, Mr. Flute? It's simple. It's power."

"The man's harmless. He's a fanatic, but harmless."

"Sheeit." Moody slaps his knee, hard. "Don't be naive, Flute. People like him believe in chaos and ruin. They *create* it, because no matter how or when it comes, he and his people have got it all figured out how to use it. Your quack Bogue doesn't intend to be any bedraggled, vindicated prophet wandering through the ruins, with his cunt on one arm and his shyster on the other, no sir. He wants to *run* the shitstorm, and what comes after."

"You don't even know him."

"Oh but I do, Flute baby." Moody says in his controlled, precise voice. "But you go ahead and think of him as just another deluded paranoid. Maybe it would suit your concepts better to let this big cat Jones play the visionary fool in your never-never-land."

Kate walks out onto the porch. Moody picks up his abandoned beer and takes a long swig. "Katie," he says in high humour, "you have got intimate with a right smart passel." And Sandor Moody laughs so loud and long that Robert Quell, over at the barn, quits his rubbing to know what might be going on.

198

March. Beginning again. Outside, the snow melts, threatening to expose my grass. The trees on the other side of my window are grease pencil lines badly sketched on a harsh blue background. In New Hampshire, March is a grimy month, a nothing month, a trickling in-between time that in California we never knew. But April follows. Rising sap! The anniversary of this. . .*thing*; and I for one expect to be finished with it during New Hampshire's April slough. I expect to be freed. I expect to wake up on April 14th and laugh my ass off. On that date I hope to recapture a free breath, and perhaps my dormant self-respect.

"Quit it, these coy, self-conscious interruptions from faraway New Hampshire."

Does Kate think this? as she and Ann pass by my windows, walking to and fro, sometimes beckoning to me, calling my attention to the fact that the snow is slowly retreating, that the old stone well is no longer a lonely, unreachable hump on a field of white, that its stones may soon shine against the chartreuse, poking grass.

Inside, among this papery mess on my tilting table, I believe I have the new confidence to be brief. My boring banana boxes sit barely touched; tapped for a clipping here, a letter there, an anonymous date.

"So?"

Are not facts, records, notations, dates and biographies patently irrelevant to the lying novelist's higher *truth*? Isn't all that really matters is what is happening in my current brain? The swift, nervous, yes-unbalanced TIME MACHINE possessed by Wolliam Victor (Irony!) Flute, New Hampshire's circling wonder-boy.

"Well, there's the strong magnet of the narrative, but you keep up this obnoxious habit of invading the field, deflecting the *power* of your presumably guilty vision," Kate probably wouldn't say, though it might be her opinion of my interruptive instants. . . .

But Holy Moses! Kate. Don't you see that I must continually, frequently prove that I'm not losing my grip? And the proof that I have a grip, I suggest, lies in my ability to deal directly with my past selves, to deal directly with things I have done and been of my own free will, no matter how painful or horrible the results.

"Words."

Then allow me a demonstration:

> *("I casually became one of the top four or five dope dealers in San Francisco.")*

> *("The gross business matters of living having passed from my control. . . .")*

> *("My husband has a guaranteed income of eight hundred and twenty-five dollars a month for the rest of his life.")*

> *("Before, I was a great one for handling such rituals, legal and illegal. . . .W.V. Flute has inaugurated a deed search or two, delicately and discreetly handled large sums of money, and with fine skill manipulated bank officials, judges and bureaucrats. . .from Pasadena to Eureka.")*

"But what's the IT of all this?"

All right, attend the goddamn PLOT:

I left *Eureka* in early September.

*("It's Kate I want.")*

I went to see Lucius Pei in Berkeley. At that time, Pei was a wholesale drug dealer who received most of his operating capital or "upfront" money from various professional people in the Bay area. His general trade route led from Berkeley to Mazatlan, Mexico, then back north to Ensenada, to San Diego, and finally to a San Francisco warehouse where the goods would come to rest. Marijuana transportation methods used by Lucius Pei included the automobile, the airplane, and the fast sloop. This trade route of his was not personally unfamiliar to me; like Pei, I got my commercial start with the Kind Owl—archetypal baron, master of all routes and territory. In Berkeley, I presented Pei with a check for two thousand, six hundred dollars, a check drawn on Jones's account at the Palo Alto Bean Bank. The expected return on such an investment was approximately five thousand dollars, within three weeks of the original transaction. $2400 for immoral capitalist pig, W.V. Flute.

I then disappeared in the Pasadena-San Diego regions.

"Are you *afraid* to write down the motive for all this?"

No: I then disappeared in full possession of the false dream that money equalled freedom, and freedom (from Jones) just might equal Kate.

"What, you're buying me?"

Listen. How could I have *you* and still be bound to Jones? I required a stake for our new life.

"You bought me. . .unknown chattel."

It's not so fucking simple.

Selecting the PROOF: I reach behind me into a banana box, a

201

purely random selection, like drawing straws. And come up with a wad of newsprint and foolscap which may or may not have to do with the conception of my daughter Ann, the cloudy transfer of bank funds, the cockroaches of Ensenada. Nothing for me but to reach, unfold, separate. . .and record whatever comes up. No risky perusal.

I hesitate.

"As you always have, as you always have."

I've nothing to fear from these goddamn factual boxes. I willed their contents.


1) Letter to the Editor:

Dear People-of-California:

Please listen. I and my colleagues strongly urge all of you to move inland as soon as possible and no later than 197__. You will soon find out what we mean when heavy earth tremors strike California. . . .But the real disaster, which almost wipes out your state, will be in about two years. In resettling, look to the geological formation called the "Canadian Shield." Good luck and good bye.

Bert Pape
Sidney, Australia


2) Facsimile

A badly reproduced copy of a Palo Alto, California bank check, the *Palo Alto Bean Bank*, dated September 17, 197__: Pay Lucius Pei, Jr.

the sum of Two thousand & six hundred &
00/100 dollars. Signed: A.R. Jones, per W.V.
Flute.


3) Telegram:

PALO ALTO, CA
1/OCT/7-
CODE 489


W.V. FLUT
C/O A.E. FLUT
2 SEPULVADA BLVD
S. PASADENA, CA


EXPLAIN MANY THINGS. WHERE ARE YOU? WHERE
IS KATE? WHEREABOUTS OF MONIES? I WONDER,
THEREFORE I AM, ACKNOWLEDGE

JONES


4) Letter (carbon):

Pasadena
Oct 10


*Dear Jones,*
*I received yr telegram today, have been in San*
*Diego, other places before that, & I don't under-*
*stand the urgency you express. Isn't K in Red-*
*ding? with you? should I know? As for the mon-*
*ey, you'll find the account is now filled to the*
*mark. I needed cash and thought our agreement*
*included such unexpected allowances. What I*
*wonder about is trust. . .sir.*

*I was arrested twice in San Diego, apparently
stopped because of the way I look, and I might
have to serve time in S.F. for, yes, parking vio-
lations. I am a Scofflaw with 36 unpaid tickets.
Now that may be humor, but the second time
I was stopped, the "make" the cop ran on me
produced---on a kind of computer readout---
draft information, credit rating (!), elementary
school grades, and sexual preferences. The cop,
about 22, said to me: "I'd like to blow your
brains out, shitface."*

*My old man Andrew seems to believe he is har-
boring a criminal in his house and the step-moth-
er refuses to feed me. In Pasadena "they" spit
at you on the street. There's been a curfew for
black and white young since the Bank of America was dynamited to nothing. I hope Sandor
M. has moved on.*

*I'll be at Green St soon. Will we spend Christmas
at Eureka? Yr taxes fall next month, I will take
care of that and whatever else is required.*

*Sorry to have caused your brain any bother,
yet I still don't understand the urgency of your
telegram. Hasta luego.*

> *Yr friend
> in the bonds,*

*(signed)    Flute*


5) Headline

## SAN ANDREAS SIDESLIPS THREE INCHES
## SINCE MAY, RICHTER EXPERTS
## POO-POO PANIC

*SAN DIEGO, Oct. 14. Treasury Dept. officials today impounded the sloop "Elvira." Seized were two thousand cigarettes in neat packs of twenty, four glass jars containing No. 5 capsules filled with a reddish powder, and three one-pound cellophane bags of white powder the consistency of sand.*

*The master of the "Elvira," Lucius Zed Pei, Jr., was taken into custody following a desperate sea chase which culminated in his surrender to the superior aquatic power of the Federal forces. The impounded cigarette packages allegedly contain machine-rolled marijuana. Each package carries the word "Kite" printed over a script-slogan: "Genuine Fool's Gold."*

*The reddish powder was identified as "pure L.S.D." by T-Man A.P. Flatly, who also claimed that the sandy white substance "wouldn't test as snuff, you can bet your a--." The bedraggled Captain Pei, 32, stepped ashore at San Diego and was heard to exclaim, "My backers won't dig this at all. Modern capitalism, as we know it, is being hounded to death."*

7) Quote (Kate Ximines Flute):

"I see you've dipped into the morgue."

8) Transistion (San Francisco weather report, October 16):

LIGHT FOG BREAKING EARLY INTO SCATTERED SUNSHINE.

Driving to San Francisco from the south, I made a stop in Palo Alto at the Jones family home: a futile effort to discover the whereabouts of the eldest son.

In San Jose rain began to fall. When I stopped to raise the Morris's top, the grizzled canvas fell through the metal struts in three rotted pieces.

At speed on the freeway I remained dry, but off on Palo Alto's University Avenue Exit, at the red light nearby Whiskey Gulch the November rain drenched me with a vengeful will. On the floorboards water combined with dirt to make a grimy soup for my booted feet. My buckskin trousers stiffened like parchment as I drove the avenue of pole palms. A turn to the left, and I drifted alongside the incarnadine church in the shape of a fluted, triangular prism---the early work of Amos Jones, respected architect, Jones's sterling old man. The building's narrow, rectangular windows ran vertically from grass to towering apex, one every few feet the length of the church. Like his son, Amos Jones believed men were meant to act out their rituals in light, at any cost.

The family house sat on two acres of land in the older, shadowy section of Palo Alto. Oak trees bent and warped and hung over the structure's one-story sprawl. Muted colors everywhere: Naval gray. Next to the garage sat a covered garbage can painted the identical color of the house. Through the open garage doors I saw workbenches, tools, yard machinery, a rabbit hutch, sacks of concrete. All of it arranged with an expert's eye for balance and function. Nothing was out of place. Neatness counts.

Water dripped over my face. The car crackled with hot going cold.

I rubbed my stiff neck, fresh from five hundred miles of freeway, and reflected guiltily that I just might be in for some sort of mild Jones rebuke. I had been disappeared too long, had created too many squalid secrets, and some of my evasions, or lies, must be guessed at. I carried this inelegant mood past the spiffy garbage can, and came to what they called the back door, which led into the laundry room. Eight years before, Mrs. Jones had told me that the door was never locked. "It's open to you twenty-four hours a day," she said.

I opened the door and called out. The rain whispered behind me, but the innards of the house returned only a calm silence.

In the kitchen I took a bottle of milk from the refrigerator, as well as a jar of mayonnaise, a loaf of bread and a sealed can of calf's tongue. Clear preserving jell fell on my wet shirt, clung for a moment and then plopped to the floor. The Jones dog came silently from the deep of the house; an ancient, wheat-colored mutt, who limped into the kitchen and sniffed my damp boots. "Zero," I said, leaning down to finger his crown, "how's the boy? Where's everyone?" Without reply, he rolled onto his back and waved his stub legs in the air. After a while, having shared part of my tongue sandwich with him, I cleaned up, finished off the milk, carefully replaced all items where found, and flipped on the electricity under the glass coffee pot, still half-full of brackish liquid at four in the afternoon. I poured the heated coffee into a heavy brown mug, leaned against the stove and took quick sips while Zero craned up at me from below.

"Wolliam!" A single, hoarse syllable of my name: my diaphragm seized, my arms whipped apart, hot coffee splashed over my hands, my shirt, and the falling mug hit Zero's skull with a sad, hollow thump. The dog rolled on his side, as if in sleep; his shoulder trembled but he made no sound as I finished my backward dance and turned to the voice, still shaking the burning coffee off of my hands.

Amos Jones in the kitchen doorway.

In embarrassment I quickly stooped to retrieve the unbroken mug from beside Zero's still head, and as I rose my eyes made the trip from Amos Jones's tan desert boots to his skimpy brown hair in one suspended and pained second. Short, thick, quizzical, he was looking at Zero next to my sodden feet. "Get a sponge," he said, and walked the length of the kitchen to stand over the animal. Leaning from the waist, he prodded Zero's side with a hefty forefinger. Nothing happened. I grabbed a sponge from the sink. Now Amos squatted near the floor, raised one of Zero's eyelids, and together we saw an ellipse of white that was shot through with broken red lines. He allowed the lid to fall closed and looked over his shoulder, up at me. "He's dead."

I was suddenly conscious of the frown wrinkles on my forehead, the rectangle of sponge that rested in my hand like a block of cellular nothing. If I could only find the proper expression, I believed I would be all right. Amos Jones stood up; his face swayed a foot from my Adam's apple, his nostrils beat like wings---porous wings covered with a web of broken veins. I held the sponge between us until he took a deep breath and stepped aside so that I might clean up the amoeba pools of coffee. Useless phrases in my head, quickly destroyed as I stumbled to the stove, and before his oddly gentle eyes began to wipe the surface.

"Zero was an old dog," he husked.

"I know, I was here when you got him." I looked up. His eyes widened for a moment. Though all the puddles of coffee were now gone, I kept on wiping around the dog, and then took care of the front and top of the stove.

Zero's sphincter gave way; the stink blasted the spotless kitchen. I worried a piece of tongue from my teeth, and waited. Amos put a hand in his pants pocket, jangled change, gazed again and again at the dog. Finally, I replaced the sponge in the sink, squeezing it first beneath a stream of airy water.

"He should be moved," he said. "It was an accident." He seemed

208

to be telling himself.

"I guess I'm a little jumpy."

He turned his blue eyes on me. "Yes. Jumpy people *do* have accidents." His voice had passed beyond hoarseness to a whisper. The stink was overwhelming.

"I'll help you move him," I said.

"I've never understood you." His eyes remained steady.

"Sir?"

"It's not the dog. Perhaps you inadvertently put him out of his misery. He had rheumatism." A long pause, of the kind favored by his son. "Jeez." He shook his head slightly. "You've charmed my family for. . .what?. . .six or seven years."

"I—"

"Just wait a minute. I deserve a few minutes of your time."

"Of course," I nearly shouted, blushing through the depths of my head.

"Mrs. Jones, though, she's never been taken in by you. She referred to you as a psychological cripple."

I raised my hands into the air between us, palms up. And felt my jaw fall fool-slack. His entire body jerked impatiently, and then he kneeled to pick up the dog. Brushing by me with his burden, he tossed words—heaved them over his shoulder. "It's not Zero. You remember that. Sometimes my son can be a stone blind fool."

After he disappeared I leaned over and wiped up Zero's crap with my own damp handkerchief.

209

I stood by the Morris in the rain while Amos Jones worked in the garage. He took an opaque garbage bag from a toolbench drawer, flicked it open with one hand, and allowed Zero's carcass to slide from his arm into the plastic sack. He knotted the opening and carefully placed the entire business in the doorway, but out of the rain. Then he walked past my car looking not pleasant or unpleasant, just determined to pass by me and enter his house.

"Mr. Jones."

He stopped next to his immaculate garbage can and stared across the Morris and into my dripping face. "You don't know when to shut up, Wolliam," and the words came politely from his mouth as if he were telling me I ought to put my car top up.

"I'm sorry, sir."

He nodded and turned briskly to the door. "It's no good," he said, his hand on the doorknob. "You don't have the sense of. . .," but then his face crumpled up; he jerked open the door. "I'll tell my son you were here."

"Do you know where he is?"

Amos Jones stepped into his house. "Yes, I do," he said, and closed the door behind him.

North of Candlestick Park the rain stopped. Before me the Bayshore Freeway led its concrete way directly toward the sun. I clung to the steering wheel, a functioning parasite drawn dumbly to the light.

On Green Street, not two blocks from my apartment, I saw a tall blond man in dark pants and white singlet striding the sidewalk.

210

Jones, there you are! I hit the brakes, the car stalled, my mind unjammed and began to punish me like a dental drill gone berserk: *Look here, Jones, you've got to stop, talk to me, I've killed your dog in an incredible accident, and discovered a nemesis in your own father, who indirectly caused this death. Won't you stop! I never willed it, but I can explain everything, tell you all that I'm about lately, if you'll only cease this going away and listen to your friend, goddammit! You're still my friend, I returned the money--- a phone call will tell you. I wrote you a letter; the money had nothing to do with bloody dog shit on the floor, it was only a deal, you know, a little deal for making money from money. So money is shit, sure, but the rest of us need it! to get us out an away to that new life of grace and value, as you say, as you say, I'm so tired of listening to you. All right, I did go to Mexico, I didn't plan it that way. Something came up, a chance to make even more money, and I did it, you fucker! I sat in a hotel room for two weeks, sweating, murdering cockroaches. . . .Neurotic pursuit, you say---battery acid on the soul, Flute, but then you don't know my motives. You know them not, you know me not. You fucking myth. If you'd stop I'd tell you in a friendly fashion, in plain English, looking straight into your eyeballs, that I'm in love with Kate Ximines, and if she's not ready for me, she has surely turned from you. Can you understand me? The leap this simple fact forces me to make? It means I want to leave you alone with your impossible web of Christian virtues. . . .It means I want to strike out with Kate for a land less virtuous than the one you offer us. It means, my friend, you asshole, that I'm barely better than J.M. Bogue, or everyone else! What you refuse, I must deal with as I am part and parcel of it. Oh Jesus! You see my contra- dictions before I even speak them, or you could if you would only turn around and see me, hear my insanely blowing horn. I must have money, I used yours, but my one virtue is that I returned it. Ha! The morass of W.V. Flute, whose character---despite your old man---is shot through with selected ethics like a sponge full of spilt coffee. . .*

Slumped on the seat, suddenly conscious of the car at a crazy angle in the street---did the sidewalk stranger hear my howl?

idiot's rant?---I felt as if I had ejaculated into an open sewer. The Presidio Cannon shot off five o'clock with a hollow whang. I drove on. Through the trees above, the sky glared pink cellophane, orange lacquer.

In the foyer of my stony apartment building. Maybe I'm drafted again, and we can rerun all this with a different ending: The misshapen brass door of my mailbox swung by one hinge in the twilight. Not a thing in it. Upstairs, I unlocked the door, walked the hall to the bathroom, and vomited a terrible pottage of tongue, bread and coffee into the lavatory bowl.

I holed up on Green Street with my windows shut fast, like a man afraid of tear gas or his own world. The phone rang often. Sometimes I answered, sometimes not. From time to time I drove to Polk Street for a newspaper and dinner at the glum restaurant where Jones had discovered Kate Ximines. Among the peagreen booths and splotched mirrors. I did not.

The newspapers were simply, offhandedly violent.

My mail ramained uninteresting. From Orick, a village north of the city of Eureka, and no strenous distance from *Eureka* proper, came a postal card decorated with an artful photograph of an enfogged Golden Gate Bridge. Overside, the handsomely scripted message:

> *Crumpled orange girders lit by firestorm*
> *While Flute-Voyeur twiddles his moustaches*
> *And the Northern shores crumble gayly*
> *Into the bubbling sea -*
> *Are you there? We are here.*
> *A Merry Christmas to you all, and good night*

Bogue's signature was fitted between two leering cartoon faces--- quite likely inked by Molly Noel, witnessed by Phineas Clingsmythe.

And Julius Stein too sent an early Christmas greeting, a card which split open to reveal a multi-hued *Eureka* scene never, not ever to be seen: a translucent yellow dome in a purplish batik meadow, a trace of the sea in the distance, and above the glimmering dome stretched the superb head and shining neck of a giraffe, a bemused, elegant and graceful giraffe.

Stein's message:

> *Jinkies, America grows to be not a very funny place.*
> *Peace & joi, Julius*

And no joyful urban pleasure for me in my suspended moods: no movies, books, television, music. No conclusions. Just an aching for Kate that began to seem absurd, as if I were carrying someone else's dulling pain in the pit of my groin and between my eyes. I possessed my own kinds of regret---of the accidental killing of an animal; of aborted if self-justified financial manipulations; of Jones's discoveries---and I surely must have been distressed that a man I respected---Amos Jones---should be driven to stab me with words. But the truth is I *felt* nothing at all. An emotional cripple. . .at least. If there ever was a true *Bogueian Funk*, this was it.

Kate called me on December First: my arbitrary decision to answer that set of rings after three sets not answered probably has much to do with where I am now. Never mind that. When I comprehended the voice coming through to me my hands shook and dampened the phone instrument; her voice caused the dead weeks to fall away to nothing, and, despite every proper sense of disaster, I *knew* again what I wanted, that perhaps I could have her.

"Hi." The first syllable shot into my head. Outside my kitchen window fog-muted sunshine played in the trees and on the sidewalks. "Flute?"

"Yes, this is me. Good afternoon, how are you?"

214

"Fine. Yeah, I'm fine. I've been calling."

"I've been here for weeks."

"Sure," she said, dubious. "Tell me how you are."

I laughed, and heard the thinness of it echoing back at me---
goddamn telephones! I felt a wrenching desire to *see* this lady
approaching my rickety, unbaited snare. "Where are you?" I
asked.

"We should get together."

*Kate!* "Why?"

"Why! What the hell do you mean, why? I haven't seen you for
three months. You sure you're all right?"

"City paranoia," I said quickly. "Uhh. . .it's a good idea, us. I can
tell you. . .my adventures, like that."

"Like that." A bit of mockery? Yes.

"I still don't know where you are. There was a telegram from Jones
asking *me* that."

A massive electrical silence.

"I've been with Sandor Moody."

"Oh." My right hand rose and its fingers invaded my hair, clawed
for scalp, quickly made a fist of trapped hair and tugged for
anguish and the destruction in my brain of the perfectly focused
image of Moody's blackjack cock poised to enter her unknown-by-
me vagina. And after racking moments of this, I whispered, "That's
dangerous."

She laughed, gently. "He's safe, he's out of it."

"I hope that's true. Are you in the city?"

"No."

She didn't go on. Suddenly I was shouting. "Where the fucking hell are you then!"

"Flute, don't do that, Flute."

"I'm sorry. . .I'm preoccupied or something. . .edgy."

"No shit. I still think you need company," she said with some vigor.

"Maybe so, I'm a fraction nuts."

"You're alone?" Arch. "No *spiffy* courtesans there?"

"God no, but if it's Molly Noel you mean, I happen to know she's happily in the lowest circle of hell. . .I am alone."

"Okay."

"So please come, I'd like that."

"Okay, couple of hours." She hung up.


Later, in the living room, seated near the shadeless windows, my bold opportunism fell apart like a handful of old leaves. Fuck fate, I said aloud, and glumly regarded the outside, where the sun had fallen behind the Presidio, and Green Street lay in twilight---an empty hallway, it seemed, until a car door clunked shut once, twice. Ahh, I thought, sitting forward in my chair, at last it has arrived: a strange arrival just in time to prove Kate's call never took

216

place, that in fact *I* have never taken place. Rising slightly from the chair, I peered around a window sash and glimpsed my own carcass of a car. And in front of it the skimpy tail end of a red Mercedes. Who? Loman Pence of Paraguay, Jones's first worshiper, long ago a suicide, now come to enghost his belovéd's scurrillous vassal? Or perhaps Captain Lu Pei, bailed out and toting a sackful of the illicit dollars due me. Or Jones himself, bent on abstracting temporary theft and dog-murder into a philosophy of forgiveness? *There are more things in heaven and earth, Horatio, than are dreamt of in your philosophy. . . .*

I stepped back to the chair and sat down with my set of self-pitying delusions. Since I heard no foyer buzzer in my hallway, I seized upon the confidence that if there were any strange arrivals on this day, it would be Kate Ximines. But would she come? And did it matter? If she does, I mulled, perhaps I shall confess, present her with the details of my recent misadventures; and if she will hear me out I'll declare to her the only reason I possess for doing what I have done: Herself. Will she fall into my arms in a paroxysm of sweet irrationality? Kiss the nose of the crippled renegade fuck-up? Jump into bed with the hypocritical son-of-a-bitch? And would we then cuckold our only saint?

Not a chance, maggot brain.

The two men never pressed the downstairs buzzer. They simply lock-stepped up the stairs and tapped at my door, which I opened to a blurred sense of expensive suede jackets and identical sulphur yellow turtleneck sweaters. The leading edge of the twosome was a man with cropped hair the color of butter, and a face of harsh angles stretched over with sunlamp-burnt skin. A Stanford man. Who smiled tolerantly upon whatever sign of recognition I gave. "Hello, Flute," he said pleasantly as I took in the other, a shorter, thicker one whose rounded and heavily shadowed chin thrust at me like a small mace set dead center between the pointed tips of his immaculate mutton-chop sideburns. "Nice to see you again," said the sunlamp face.

217

"Uhh-huh." I opted for neutral sounds and searched for his name, a long way back.

"John Light," he offered benevolently from his height. "And this is David Leather."

"You're kidding," I said.

"Not at all." Light pursed his chapped lips. "May we come in?"

"Not unless you have an Emergency Warrant."

"We don't need one." Leather's first statement. His eyes were as close together as two boysenberries in a shot glass.

"I'm not playing," I said.

"We just want to talk," Light explained. "It's important."

"It?" I asked. "What the hell, I deserve you. Come in."

Light looked surprised. "Thank you very much," he said, and they followed me down the hall and into the darkening living room. I turned and found him examining the empty corners of the room with sparrow eyes, while Leather stood next to him like a post. "You have a nice place," Light said.

"Come off it, John, what're you up to. Are you still part of the Minor Trust Fund Aristocracy?"

"I beg your pardon." He was nonplussed.

"You went to Stanford," I said, "so you must have been part of that success syndrome, and successful now, for sure. Weren't you going to be a *writer*?"

"I was a year ahead of you and your crowd."

"Oh. That explains it. What d'you want?"

He lighted a cigarette and gestured that I sit down. I refused.

Leather, without stirring, said, "Please sit down, Mr. Flute." Light walked to the window and pulled my armchair to the center of the room.

"You guys are subtle," I ventured.

"Please," Light said, smiling, gesturing at the chair. I smiled in return and walked past him, intending to bring some illumination to the room, but Leather took one remarkably long step and put his hand over the switch, without looking at it, or me, but instead at the floor, where his black tennis shoes had again taken root.

"No light?" I asked.

"Not now."

"The chair, Flute."

"What happens if I knock one of you down and run like a bastard?" I was still foot-to-foot with Leather.

"A small violence," Light said gently behind me. I watched Leather rise on his canvas toes a time or two. His legs were very short.

I turned around with some care. "Kafka," I said. Leather snorted. His jacket creaked.

Light whispered dramatically, "You *would* say that."

"Would I? I was kidding. I really meant a kind of pale imitation of John Hawkes, who is an even paler shade of Graham Greene."

"Sure, Flute," Light said. "Will you have a seat."

I passed Light, sat down. He went to the empty bookcase, into the shadows that now occupied nearly every part of the room---except where my chair caught the feeble window light. A vacuum seemed to exist between my stomach and the lower regions of my throat. In one hour Kate Ximines would walk through the door and discover me asleep in this chair, a rime of fresh sweat above my eyebrows, a dream of *fuzz* balancing dangerously in my head.

"Your name is Wolliam Victor Flute?"

"Christ!"

"Keep it simple. Answer."

"Yes, it is my name."

"Are you gainfully employed?"

". . ."

Leather spoke, "Who pays for this place, your grungy car, your trips?"

"I work for a man named Jones. You know him, John."

"Yes. Talk about trust funds. What exactly is it you do?"

"Whatever," I answered.

"Factotum." Light spoke as if this were an accepted fact.

"We're friends," I said stiffly.

"No other sources of income?"

"Nope."

"No dope to high school kids? Acid for Russian Hill?"

"No."

"Do you use drugs yourself?"

"Not any more."

"Why not?"

". . ." Night fell. "Am I arrested?"

Both of them laughed. Light's cigarette illuminated his sunburnt chin. "We don't arrest," he said.

"That's encouraging."

"You're psychologically unfit for the service. Can you explain?"

"No."

"He's a cool son-of-a-bitch," Leather observed.

"I'm role-playing," I said, a little too breathlessly. "I mean, I'm responding as I'd respond to any machine."

Light made a huffing sound from his corner. "Have you ever been beaten?" he asked.

"Oh god. . . .am I going to be?"

"We're interested in several people you know. Would you explain what's going on up north?"

"No. Who the hell is this we?" Light cleared his throat, dropped the cigarette to the floor and ground it out with an invisible heel. I decided to tack: "Aren't you the prose stylist who wrote, 'at the door there was a loud, insistent knocking'?"

"What of it?" Slight catch in his placid voice. "We aren't interested

221

in your sophomoric memories."

"I guess not. You were a shitty writer though."

In the dark the energy of his flinch carried across the room and made me shiver. "Turn the kitchen light," he said to Leather.

Illuminated, his face was impassive, boiled. "That's a nice car you guys have," I said flippantly. "Maybe you do intelligence work for someone's private army. Or maybe you *are* a private army."

Light said nothing. Leather returned from the kitchen with a bottle of milk, which he placed on top of the bookcase. Light moved towards me. His face hung half-way between the floor and the ceiling, detached from the dark clothing. His teeth showed briefly— wide gaps between the shining pegs. "Where is Sandor Moody, Flute?" He took a cigarette box from his chest pocket.

"May I?"

"Of course." He handed me a Marlboro, even lighted it with a kind of graceful stoop. I sniffed suede, as well as some vague metallic odor. He stepped back from my chair, dropped his lighter into a pocket. "Where is he?. . . .and don't say 'who'."

"I've seen him on the news, in the papers."

"Come on," Leather said, swigging milk, grimacing.

"Are you going to transport me?"

"Jacob Maven Bogue," Light pronounced.

"Ahh, him I know. I was his patient."

"That's a euphemism, but thank you for a positive answer. However, the small-fry don't interest us. What about Kate Ximines?"

As calmly as I could, I blew smoke up at Light. "I haven't seen her for two or three months."

Light frowned. "All right. No more games."

Leather actually chuckled.

"You guys are incredible."

A stream of smoke slipped through Light's lips. "Look, we know your connections with Lucius Pei, we know your past history with Christopher Owl. We can have you under arrest within an hour if you don't come across for us."

"Come across with what, John?"

It was Leather who sang out, "Information as to the whereabouts of one Sandor Moody, as well as his co-conspirator Kate Ximines, and any other persons connected with Moody's interstate flight to avoid prosecution for treasonous crimes against the United States of America."

"No, no, no, I am not in this movie, rewrite the goddamn script and just fucking come back later. Jesus, Light, you went to *college*!"

And then that gentleman stepped aside with a gentle, reassuring smile, as if he were merely re-introudcing me to David Leather, who immediately inserted himself between my spread-apart knees. An open palm whistled past my nose and knocked the Marlboro stub into the window. A tiny thud. I attempted to rise but he snapped his own knees apart, and thus undid me. As I fell back to my seat he bent forward until his stoney kneecaps jammed into my thighs, pinning me like a sack. His coat creaked as he raised his short arms high, ten fingers locked together, and brought a flesh-mace arcing down on my skull with a crack that paralyzed my very Adam's apple. The double-fist plowed down my forehead, snicked my nose and fell into *his* lap, where it rested briefly, and I

223

was permitted to hear him snort once through his dark nose before the arc reversed and, rising, slammed into the underside of my chin. Fuzzy, dull pain arrived only after I had noted that my upper and lower teeth met halfway through the tip of my startled tongue.

Leather hopped off me. I experienced blood, swallowed and spat the salty hot; then a liquid splashed onto my head for all the world like a breaking egg. His tennis shoes squeaked. The end of my tongue swelled, subsided, in time with the slow awful pulse at the top of my skull. Leather was not in the room. "A difficult fellow," someone observed. Door slammed. I must have slept. Phone ringings did minor violence to my fractured ears. The zzzz of my buzzer. Doors opening and closing in my poor head, and my mouth dried up like an afternoon nap. Sourness and salt caked and sealed my lips. Wasn't I being pushed, prodded, shaken?. . . ."Fuck off!" The icebox door gently shut. And I was sitting on my hands, which had gone quite clearly to sleep. When I reached to unseal my glued lips, the hand employed missed and fell out of the chair. My boots dropped, socks hit the floor like virgin sponges, and cold crept the length of my legs for the sole purpose of invading my belly, which was yet a vacuum: an explosion resulted.

Molecule by molecule, the homogenized milk evaporated from my unconscious flesh.

And isn't that Kate on my kitchen phone? Must I declare myself? The dilemma of the pummeled evesdropper. ". . .Hi, is Jones there?" I must rise for this; why, she'll tell him I'm in a stoned fog. . .the satiated dog-killer. "Hello, I'm in San Francisco." I tried to call out through the plaster-of-paris that was my mouth. ". . .at Flute's. He's. . .I know but I got hung-up." Kate's telephone voice struck me as having great authority. "Has it been that long? Time, what a burgle. . . .No, I just got here."

Ahh, I figured, she doesn't know about *me*. "He's passed out in the living room, kind of bloody but breathing well and smelling right." At least there was that; she might have found me beshitted and unholy. I was perking up. I must shout a warning about my functioning ears. "Well, maybe he bit his tongue in a dream, or just passed out in the dark. . . .The door was wide open. . . . . Money? Does Flute have *money*?"

I tried to stand out of the chair, and failed miserably because the damned fissure had opened in my skull again; some molten and shameful substance poured into it. ". . .I don't care about you guys' business, and I don't understand you either. . . .No, I won't come down there, I like being alone. . . .What? . . .No, that's crazy; I came here to *see* Flute, don't be ridiculous."

Click, slam-click.

"Miss Ximines," I called out in what I thought was a stern and meaningful tone. And she did then step into the kitchen door's square of light, which became my total world at that moment. With her hair pulled back, downturned mouth, dark jacket buttoned to the throat, hands jammed into the pockets, she looked like a tough little navvy. Whatever she said escaped me, stuck in my chair as I was, sunk in my woozy desire as I was. Some beginning, I thought.

"Some welcome," perhaps she said.

In my doorway she fell out of focus. "Call off your goons," I commanded with some venom.

She advanced behind her pocketed hands. "You okay?" she called, quite chipper despite her serious face, her now shadowed eyes.

"Do I lie to you? That's my current problem."

"I don't know that you've had the opportunity. What I'd like to know is what happened to you, why you're all damp and bloody."

225

A narrow blur before me. "I've been violenced," I finally said.

"Mugged? In Pacific Heights?"

"It was more *personal*, I'd have to say."

"Oh. Should you go to a hospital?" she asked matter-of-factly, and without much sympathy, I thought. "It's no fun getting around tonight. I went through three police lines, another bombing or something." She sat down at my nerveless feet.

"In that case, I'll die here," I said, "I feel silly, like a hangover."

"Giddy?"

"That's it. It's so dark in here. . .no, no, leave it that way." I was afraid even the dimmest light might reveal the more-than-giddy gleam in my recovering eyes.

"So you're done in, and even more elliptical than ususal."

"Lips, laps, collapse."

"Let me clean you up at least."

"I would like that, please."

The cold washcloth first soothed, then stung where something had scraped a neat furrow down the bridge of my nose (she said).

"Open your mouth."

I watched her being gentle with my ravaged tongue. "I love you," I tried to say, but with the washcloth in there and her fingers gripping my jaw, it came out, "Ahh-ov-ou."

Her dark eyes remained fixed on her task. "What?" She leaned

226

back on her haunches, done with the patient.

"Nothing."

"You should change clothes, your shirt at least. What is this. . . milk! Come on, Flute, who did this?"

"I've lost my ability to plot. . . . .I mean, to figure out how to answer that. Do you know John Light?"

"Nope," she answered, scratching an ankle with a sound simple and intimate enough to make me even dizzier. But clearly as I could I told her what had happened, including the fact that Light had asked specifically about her in connection with Sandor Moody. This fairly objective report of the story acted upon me as a balm (an anti-aphrodisiac); enough to cure me of the mad impulse to blurt out all my involuted and private longings.

"So the feebies are sniffing around," she said casually. "Well, Moody's out of it, that's all that matters."

"But what about us?"

She brushed a swatch of hair out of her eye. "Us?"

The pain of this double-ness, this courtly dance we were doing without moving a muscle; but wasn't I dancing alone, and was I about to be discovered for a fool? "We Jones people," I clarified.

"If they really are feebies, when they find out Moody has split they'll leave us alone. We're not doing anything wrong, much."

"But maybe they're sort of *outside* the law."

She shrugged. "Then we better watch out, hadn't we?"

"They knew everything," I said with some anxiety.

Kate laughed and surprised my knee with a stiff tap. "Your other lives, Flute?"

And again I thanked circumstance for the hugging darkness that concealed my hot blush. "I think I can get up now. Shall we have some dinner?"

"Will your poor tongue permit it?"

"Yes," I lisped, and made to rise from the chair. The movement set off triphammers in the top of my skull, but she caught the coming swoon and used her hands to bring me wearily erect in the reeling living room.

I managed the bathroom by myself: a shower, shave, some bracing witch hazel and a refreshing change of clothes. When I entered the glare of my kitchen I found that she had prepared plates of spaghetti positively gleaming with butter, and in front of each plate a water tumbler containing the dregs of my only red wine.

"Sit down," she commanded. I did. "You're low on staples here, I'd say."

"I'm a recluse these days," I muttered.

"It's sad about Zero."

"What?" The steaming spaghetti suddenly looked like an evil nest.

"Jones told me on the phone."

"He did," I said stupidly. "I heard you talking."

"Oh," She approached and sat down across from me, brought her lovely face on my level for the first time; if only I could control the emotions playing tag in my putrid brain. "No big thing," she said mysteriously.

I stayed quiet. There are no lies in silence. Not true. She began to twist her spaghetti on her fork, the fork tines uptight against one of my large spoons. *Does she lay Moody, or doesn't she?*

The spoon of pasta entered her wide mouth, the fork retreated, she smiled at me in the midst of chewing, swallowed. "Don't stare at me like that. Are you all right? Can you eat?"

"No, yes, I don't know."

"I don't have much of a sense of you," she said. "You're kind of *smoky*. What do you think of yourself?"

"Jesus." And I probably groaned out loud.

"May I stay here?"

My invisible double-take; the fissure at the top of my skull seemed to widen and I nearly fell apart behind my rude kitchen table facade. "Sure. . .sure you can."

"Thanks. I'm at loose ends." She laughed. "I've got a sleeping bag."

"That's nice," I said weakly. "I'm an opportunist."

She took another bite, chewed it slowly---watching me with those clear eyes. Could I really see myself in them? See the tiny, foreshortened image of my scoundrel self?

Kate said, "Everyone wants something. It's screwing up that I can't accept."

"Ahh, don't they always do that?"

"Do they? Have you? You seem very flexible. I have an image of you peering around corners, never committing yourself to even the possibility of screwing up. You rise and fall, but never sink."

"You mean I'm a chameleon," I said numbly, remembering the words of Amos Jones.

"Probably not," she pronounced, "not if you can say it."

What a fine girl, an original. Why waste it on me?

"I like you," she said. "But I don't know exactly why. I think you've done some strange things."

Hung in the kitchen's brightness, her head appeared to recede, zoom in-and-out of my vision. The sentence leapt at me again and again: IT'S KATE. IT'S KATE I WANT. I rushed, sped into dark blue space. "Listen, Kate, I love you."

"Oh, no, be careful." Her eyes were gigantic. "Go carefully. . . please."

But her fear---or whatever it was---pushed me on. "I'm not rising and falling, or even sinking; I'm stuck. What did you mean about Sandor Moody on the phone? Tell me, I'm scared shitless."

She looked at me for a long time, and under her gaze I began to slide from desperation into ridiculousness. Finally she said, "Sandor's my friend. He needed me with him, he needed all the help he could get. But that's not what you want to know." This, to my relief, was gently said. "He's not my lover. He used to be, before I knew Jones or you or any of the people. . . .But it got complicated." She gave a kind of rueful smile. "We're friends, Flute. Is that enough for you? I don't think I have to say any more."

My body relaxed; the livid images disappeared into their hole. "Thank you," I said. But, without warning, I was rushed again. "What about Jones? What about him?"

"Yeah. What about Jones?" She took the time to bite a fingernail. "I guess Jones is beyond me. . .beyond all of us, if that's what you mean. . ." Heart-thumping pauses for me. "And if he's beyond me, and us, then perhaps he doesn't even exist. I haven't seen his physical shade since September. . .since I last saw you." Once again, her mouth bent itself into a strange smile. "You didn't miss my little signs, did you?" I shook my head, pretended more confidence than I actually felt. "Small, significant gestures," she went on. "Jones hasn't slept with me since we met Claude."

"Really?" My voice cracked. I was incredulous, I was gleeful, I was overjoyed. *Kate!*

"Flute, don't be small, Flute. You don't know so much! If I've drifted from Jones, and been watching you, it doesn't mean I want you. . .or even know who the hell *you* are, let alone that other lunk."

"I'm sorry. I'm a little mixed up about my motives here. I have to tell you---"

She sighed, as if worn out. "I'm washing the dishes first. You can't eat?"

"I don't think so."

"Will you help me?"

"Yes." And I did. In the context of this physical task, I managed to keep my mouth shut at her request. While we carried and scraped and rinsed and wiped, I sensed that for once I was doing the right thing in keeping silent.

"Do you have any booze?" she asked when the kitchen was as clean and neat as it had ever been.

"I have bourbon. Would you like some?"

"With lemon, please, and some ice."

In the living room she took the chair, and I stood with an elbow on top of the bookcase, now ill-at-ease in the silence. Where would we go now? "Do you keep candles?" she asked after what must have been several sips of her drink.

"Indeed," I answered, every bit as formal. I would *fit* to this strange, self-possessed woman no matter what it cost me. "I'll find one." I did, lit it, turned to her for approval, and discovered that she was crying.

Almost relieved, I went to the chair and kneeled beside her. The candlelight made reflecting prisms of the tears, and one of them came to rest---winking---in the soft down laid invisibly over her upper lip. Like a drop of enchanted sweat. "What's the matter?" I said, and knew exactly then that I had embarked upon an unavoidable habit---a verbal tic, directly responsive to her moods.

She shook her head. "Nothing." As she sipped the drink, her lips pursed away from the bitterness. "What do you have to tell me?"

"Excuse me?"

"You said," and she mimicked my confession voice, " 'I have to tell you some things.' " She swung her face to mine. Eyes pinned me.

"Well, don't cry," I said.

"Why do you hide so much?"

"I'm not."

"Then what are you, dammit?"

"A thief, a liar, a. . .psychological cripple."

She blinked. The tears had stopped. "Is that it?"

"And I'm in love with you."

232

She laughed icily. "What's to love? What does it mean, *I love you*? You don't know me. You think I'm some tough little *chick* come along to pummel the self-pity out of you."

"You sound tough."

She hit me square on the cheek with the flat of her wrist, and the drink smashed to the floor beside me just as I caught the wrist coming at me again. "Damn you, damn you," she hissed, and I intercepted the other hand before it struck my face.

"Kate, what's the matter with you?"

She stopped, her body simply stopped, and when I set free her hands she slumped back into the chair. "I am more than a man needs me to be," she mumbled, and suddenly seemed even more exhausted than she had. "Don't you know, don't you know? Or are you no different from Jones?"

". . ."

She closed her eyes. "I don't know, I'm tired. I don't want to talk."

"Kate, what can I do?" I asked. But I was thinking that she would walk out and the whole confusing business would be over and done; I could go back to my less strenuous fantasy-life, free of blows from the David Leathers, and women like this.

"You can get my sleeping bag from the hall and clean up the broken glass you're kneeling in." As I rose, she grabbed my hand, squeezed it for a moment before letting go. "I didn't know this would happen. Be a little patient. I told you. . .I'm at loose ends."

"Okay."

I carried the non-violent impression of her palm on mine with me into the kitchen, the hallway, and then back into the buttering yellow light of the living room where she was---absurdly---asleep.


In the morning. She stood beside my cot holding a glass of frothing yellow, and was smiling with a pleasure or mirth unknown to me. Behind her, behind my bedroom window, the sun broke its way through Green Street's morning fog. Coming into being, I was surprised to see that she wore not the pants and peajacket of the night before, but my own plaid and moth-eaten robe instead. Her hair gleamed wet from the shower. "Drink this," she said.

I sat up out of the chocolate puff. "Thank you."

"And thank you for putting me to bed."

"You're heavier than you look."

She sat on the edge of the cot, arranging the robe over her legs while I moved against the wall to keep us balanced. "Oop. At least you could have taken off my coat." I grunted, and drank the juice straight down. "No, timid Flute would let the lady perspire in her whiskey sleep."

"You weren't drunk."

She fingered the thin wool of the robe. "No, I wasn't. How's your tongue? Why don't you brush your teeth, carefully, and I'll fix you some breakfast."

"Right." I gathered the puff about me and stood out of the cot, cloaked.

As soon as I was up, she laid herself out where I had been, her head propped up with one hand. Wrinkling her up-turning nose, said in mock-fierceness, "This thing reeks of Molly Noel."

"Come on, she hasn't been here since. . .since I went off to be inducted."

She combed her fingers through her hair and flipped out the ends; a gesture of absolute dismissal. "Well, I won't stay in this *love nest*."

"Suit yourself."

She folded her body with some speed---a glimmer of sound thigh--- and was off the cot, past me, and rattling things in the kitchen before I could decide not even to guess at what the bloody hell this mood was. "Did you brush your teeth?" she called.

"Shit, Kate, they're my teeth," I said from the doorway.

"Maybe so, but I'd like to make love now."

"Oh dear."

And in that morning kitchen my blood's circulation abruptly stopped, became unable to tolerate the horrendous shifts of my present-tense life, simply decided it could in no way adapt, and so refused to move me in any direction. Frozen, I was nothing, not even protoplasm in secret motion. Still, from a great distance, I was able to view Kate Ximines in all *her* stillness, or whatever she was in the process of knowing about me as I confronted her statement, mummified in my inane chocolate puff. But, of course, protoplasm can only be still for so long before it manufactures, in whatever mysterious way, electricity, and that in turn a resurgence of thought of word, and the word was *Jones*. "Forget him, he's nothing." Did she say that? My hand was taken, and I floated from that kitchen, and into another room of sunlight, of silvery down sleeping bags, of books that I had once owned but now forgotten, and certainly all content was forgotten as I was led to lay myself down beside this robed woman who, in the moment after casting aside my cloak, used her impossibly soft lips to label me a peakéd mantis. . . .

235

Later.

"Are you going to stay here?" I asked.

"Why not tell me what you want?"

"I want to marry you."

"Why?"

"Why not?"

"That's no answer. Will we always do this on floors?"

"I pray not."

"Then go and buy us a bed. If it's satisfactory, I'll think about marrying you."

"That's easy."

"It won't be easy," she said, blowing a soft Merry Christmas in my ear.

And later.

"Will this bed do?"

She flopped, groaned, spread her fair limbs. "Yes, it will. Throw out the other, please."

"I've done that," I said.

"You think about me from time to time, I see."

"Most of the time."

"You know. . .a lot of romantic bullshit goes down during holiday seasons. What do you think about when you make love to me?"

"I wonder what you're thinking."

She laughed and left the new bed. "Where's pleasure then? You never say anything in the midst of it. . .of screwing. I think you *see* things."

"Don't you?"

"I do, I see signs, which I read to myself, and laugh---silently--- about. Don't look shocked. If I *thought* about orgasm I'd never come. So tell me what you see, Flute."

"What do your signs say?"

"Last night I saw one that said, 'Flute misses the point.' "

"Okay, okay. I see Fog, rocks. . .flames, sometimes. But it's all out of my control."

"Absolutely," she said. "But when you come, you're *here*. It can't be beat. That's all there is."

"You've got me. So marry me."

She looked out the window. "What would that be like? Would I ever see you? Which of your lives would you live with me?"

"Goddamn!"

"Men come and go. Some don't come at all." She held her forehead between thumb and index finger. "Do you want children?"

"I don't know. Do you?"

Her eyes rose up and caught me. "I'm considering it. It's a way of knowing you better, isn't it? Yes, I do."

"Okay then."

"Everything is *okay* with you. Will you tell Jones?"

"Tell him what?" I said too quickly.

Her short laugh was like a bark. "See, you're so tied to him you freeze at the mention of his name."

"I think you do, too. Yeah, I'll tell him. Why not?"

"I'll marry you sometime. For now, let's christen this bed of ours. We are finally off the floor, Mr. Flute."

"Okay," I said, engaged, and the father of Ann though I didn't know it.

Jones came to Green Street after midnight, five days before Christmas. For late night reasons, now forgotten, Kate and I were eating French toast. But the fact is that he simply appeared. As always, the looming nocturnal visitor, as if his four months absence had been but a day. The ramrod body stepped lightly into my kitchen, and all was in order: the blond hair combed back from his forehead in precise, wet lines; the pressed and faded jeans; a nylon windbreaker of some darkness over the standard white jersey—all of it puny drapery on his exaggerated body. Like my betrothed, he maintained his enormous hands in the pockets of his coat. "Hey, you guys," he said, and the eyeglasses he wore only at night shone in my kitchen's glare, lending to his face a most gentle perplexity. "You want to fly north for Christmas with Stein and me and Robert Quell?"

238

Dumb but not uncomfortable, Kate and I regarded him. Clean as a whistle, straight, taut, he *occupied* the silent room.

"You guys. . ." He smiled, or grinned, or chuckled.

Our syrupy trance. How long could it last?

One of us said that yes, we would indeed like to go in the airplane. And we each took a bite of French toast: our synchronized act of communion.

"Where've you been?" I asked.

"Oh, around here."

"Would you like a cigarette?" I asked, nodding toward my pack of Camels. He looked pleased. A hand came from the coat pocket and took one from the pack, used my lighter. Very still, he stood smoking in that tight-lipped way he had. The smoke shot over our heads in thin trails. He refused Kate's offer of food with yet another smile, but did then accept some bourbon whiskey, about three fingers of it.

"You know," he said. "I came here to listen to what you have to say." He looked at me. "Don't drift, Flute. Tell me what's what."

And in turn we gazed at him.

Kate gathered the dishes.

"You're something of a toad," he said to me. Gentle words floating in the kitchen air.

I have never seen a man stand so still.

We waited, for what I don't know. Each time he inhaled, his head bobbed slightly. The exhales were powerful and peaceful sighs. Until, finally, Kate and I each took a glass of bourbon. He lifted his own glass, held the amber mash to the light.

"Nepenthe," he said.

I stood up. "Kate and I are going to be married."

She was beside me.

Jones lowered his glass, held it toward us. His face was a field of honest pleasure. "Yes."

Our glasses tinged together. The three of us drank. He set his glass on the table, and turned to the doorway. "Halfmoon Bay Airport at noon on the 24th," he said as he left.

April First. Indubitably. The proof is a simple raising of my head; outside my window the sap is indeed rising, the grass once again begins to live. The snow has retreated to thin necklaces encircling the bases of a few distant trees, and the stone well now stands totally exposed, gleaming darkly against the poking grass. And inside I am racing for my imaginary ending. Inside I am telescoping the fierce past, and even now making bright projections into the mute future. No one beckons to me anymore. I am not visited, cajoled, prodded, chided or even challenged. Kate and Ann may well have given up on me. . .

. . .who writes with such facility of the lovely natural changes, but who cannot see his way to going outside to feel of the, or smell the smells with his wife and only child. . .

. . .who is racing against an arbitrary deadline in future time, April 14th, with his backbone bent from morning to midnight in an attempt to outrun a date that here in New Hampshire holds meaning only for me. Kate herself probably remembers---but chooses not to worry about---everything of that spring last year when pain exploded everywhere; and never would a *date* cross the on-flowing threshold of her guiltless mind. She is right. Her way is the better way. But I am stuck; stuck with more *knowledge* than she can have, stuck with this DATE, stuck with myself, and with all the others, wherever they may in fact be---all unwitting subjects of my scattergun conjectures, misconceptions, injustices and even labels.

April 14th, this unwelcome anniversary.

Open the windows!

Raise the roof!

I will be done!

I shall come out!

Re-born Jones. . .

Jones!

Jones---as I advance fearfully on this imminent first anniversary of your *untimely* death I try to think that you will hear me, hear my fiction, that just maybe you will note the sound of my ghostly words of homage and atonement.

Kate, will you smile in relief, or will you charge me with a complete lie as you stand in the spring sun of our yard, this April day? If you do so charge me, then you may burn these pages in a pyre of your own making, and the banana boxes as well. A conflagration of all the people who never existed.

Yet they did.

Claude D'Mambro. I can only guess where you might be. Will you wipe the sweat from your sunburnt face, thinking all of a sudden: 'If I'd remembered about that peacock Flute I'd of shot him myself.' And will you then look blankly to your left, to your right, and realize once more that Bobbi Love has not been within your sight for three hundred and sixty-three days? And with a grunt, return to your work, your salvation, whatever that may be.

Sandor Moody. Black Man of all my dreams. Will you be allowed to celebrate the aniversary of the day on which your vision of both the natural and the human was so disastrously verified? Is there room for such celebration in your detention camp? Are chained prisoners of the State allowed to exercise their vocal cords as well as their bodies? No. I don't believe that the American Government will allow Utah Camp No. 7 (is my racist information

242

correct?) the privilege of celebrating April 14th as any holiday. Just shuffle on a little slower that day, Sandor; I know that I am white.

Ahh Bogue. Jake. Old mentor. I don't need to ask about you. If Kate and I possessed a television I'm sure I'd find you on it that very morning, Phineas Clingsmythe's script tumbling from your lips like sweetened lye, your body within the studio no doubt guarded by a certain Leather, a certain Light. I fancy the early news, afternoon of April 14, 197_, your patrician face in extreme closeup: "In catastrophes such as those we have seen, the magnitude of which we can only begin to fathom there is a lesson for all freedom-loving people. . . .We must continue to guard this West, what is left of it, from those who would further weaken its shores, crumble it into the sea. . . .The results of anarchy tell us that the Rule of Law *must* prevail. . . .I remember. . ." At which point I would switch you off, destroy you, you son-of-a-bitch.

Stein, I know you're in Asia Minor. Where else? And perhaps Bobbi Love is with you in that place. She'd be watching you sketch, watching you cross-legged on a mountain top dotted with midget trees. Or you both could be in Kenya, you perched on a stump beside a single, stately giraffe, tethered to you with a length of string. Whichever, on the afternoon of the 14th, you will descend from your mountain, or dismount your stump, and in the village you'll find an old fart of a man to whom you can say: "Jinkies, America sure is a funny place." And eight thousand miles away, I won't laugh at you, man.

Robert Quell. Robert? You're lost again.

But Molly, I know you. Wake up the morning of the 14th; apply cream to your skin, remove curlers from your hair, look out at your quickly dying Saint Louis world, watch the goose flesh that rises from your navel to discover your nipples, nubble your neck, and finally violate your arms. So, you abandon your mirror, drop the silken dress over your head, walk into the kitchen and tell your newest master-psychologist that you'd like permission to lay the first intellectual punk who walks into the office this morning.

Only Kate will know where *I* am. And none will hear my laughter, the thud of my ass falling off, the ehh-ehh sound as I choke on my year old freedom, my new life.

Except you, Jones. Forgive me. For what was. For this so far. And for the end to come.

I, Claude, am living.

Even when the shit hits the fan a caretaker keeps his facts straight.
It is now a full day since the earthquake---if that's what caused me
to wreck the weapons carrier, and this morning to lose Bobbi
Love, not to mention all the rest of the Jones people. It's Tuesday,
goddammit, the morning of April 15th, and I am still alive, wandering like a barefoot ignoramus in the redwoods. Where are facts?
I am looking for Bobbi. Was she evacuated while I spoke with
Margaret Pickel? Did that mooning Quell snatch her from the barn
loft while I was gone? Did Bogue and his bunch shoot Jones? Margaret Pickel said they did. I don't know very damn much, but I
believe that after the wreck I carried Bobbi through the trees.
Hours. We came to the house, but the house was burned to the
ground, and not a soul anywhere. The pool was empty and cracked
across its cloudy blue bottom. Up in the loft of the barn ashes
hung in the air, and I put Bobbi on a bed of burlap sacking and
wrapped her in her moldy parachute. She was out of her head; the
blood in her hair flaked off just like pieces of cold, dried bacon.
I was the cook at that place, and this is a fact. I don't know how
the night passed, but the next morning, this morning, I told Bobbi
to wait there in the barn, that I would walk to Margaret Pickel's
house and call a doctor. "O blow the doctor," Bobbi said. So, I
have been to Mrs. Pickel's, and I have been back to the barn, and
Bobbi is not there. I hid from the helicopter, and now I go on
bloody feet through the trees, making for the beach, keeping the
facts straight, the way caretakers do---even in bad times.

On my way back to *Eureka* from Mrs. Pickel's, I met a man on the
eastern edge of the Redwood Park. He showed me a knapsack full
of whiskey fifths, and I could see he wore a wedding ring on eight
of his ten fingers. "Gold and whiskey is just the ticket when the
shit hits the fan," he told me in a whine like Piro's. Spittle bubbled
in the corners of his mouth. He asked me for food, information,
tips on where what was left might be; he meant empty houses
and gold and whiskey, I supposed. I told him I myself had had no

food since breakfast the day before, which was true. He scrambled a few trees away from me, crabbing backward so as I wouldn't send a rock through his skull in trade for his precious goods. "There's snipers all around here," he called out. "A fat lady up the river shot my buddy Tom in the nuts with a deer rifle of great power. Watch out for her, o boy you better watch out. . . .There's some others too, three of 'em in a big grey Caddy." I thanked him for his tips before he disappeared into the still woods. But that might not have happened anywhere near as peacefully as I now recall it. Still, I'm positive a talk of some kind took place; a fellow did come along and speak to me sometime before the National Guard Helicopter came hovering over the busted pool and smoking pile of house. The house was growing colder every minute as I watched the chopper from my hiding place near the second dome. Where Bobbi was not.

I walk on, still looking for her sweating face beneath some spongy tree. Me. Fumbly carpenter, high caliber caretaker through ten months of thick and thin; and a pretty fine cook all the while: Jones's good ol' boy, now surviving in a stove-in countryside where either Margaret Pickel could shoot me dead; or the National Guard bastards could lasso me from their chopper, or maybe stick me with no enemies in the world.

There are figures in the treetops. Others grab at my ankles from root hiding places, or leer from those damn mirages above and behind this ridge. It was only a few minutes ago that up, up in a giant redwood, Oyd Fikes hurled mummified noses at my head; and behind him MaryJane squeaked transparent words: ". . . .KILL YOU!" But I don't hear them any more. Sandor Moody's angry hands burst from a crowd of tree roots, got hold of my bare feet, and only let go when my old friend Piro swelled up over the ridge, bobbing in the air like a circus balloon shaped like a man—— with a bloody trench between his eyes. And half-way up the ridge, intending to prick Piro out of my seeing, I spotted Dr. Bogue hustling from a grove of trees, followed at heel by Clingsmythe and the prickteaser Molly Noel. They jogged along the ridge-line carrying a huge and glowing chainsaw, its silent, speeding teeth

246

spitting in all the soft light of the morning. They stuck it right into Piro's balloon gut, and all three men disappeared in a poof, which left Molly Noel hanging naked from nothing; and Robert Quell's Bobbi-loving laughter came from nowhere like a booming drum, while I saw pieces of Piro sucked by the wind toward the sun and the sea. Ha! Ha! Ha!

These are the facts.

At the top of the deserted ridge I stand under a madroña tree and feel of the bark. None of this ever happened, I say. And the tree is as smooth as the sole of Bobbi's foot. At Christmas, when all of them were here together, Jones said to me before he left for Nova Scotia, "Madroña trees bear edible berries that put me in mind of Chinese Checkers. Do you think you could get some for Kate and Flute's wedding feast?" Now I strip a handful of orange BB's from a low branch, let two rest on my tongue. Without spit, they taste of hardness, like chick peas left months in a jar. Well, I cooked for all those people. I was cook enough at a hundred dollars a week, four hundred dollars a month, plus dome, board, and a girl for a few days more than ten months---all this in exchange for my hands did not ever seem a bad deal; but who will pay me now? Cooking is as fair as anything I've ever done; if you do it well, the rewards come quick. "If you're not going to do it right, don't do it," Jones told me a hundred different times, and I reckon it's the truth to say that on the morning of April 14th, yesterday morning, I cooked, like always, a decent goddamn breakfast for all ten of us. I tally it up: Bogue, the prickteaser, and the lawyer had arrived, unwelcome, in the Cadillac the night before. A gathering of ten for the spring plowing, and it even includes a pregnant Kate and her dandy husband. Twenty medium eggs just barely fit into the glass jar of a Waring blender. And there was no fog, no sir. At about 5:30, the day had slid up from behind the Humboldt Redwoods, and not even a film of haze hung between the sun and the wedge of Jones's five hundred acres; such clear, unfiltered light hadn't struck Bobbi's and my dome, at least before noon, since the people's Christmas visit, when Quell joined Bobbi and me for the winter. Well, we ate. In the sunshine of the house the whole lot of

247

them swallowed my feathery eggs, snappy bacon, muffins and filtered coffee. Most of them sitting there knew that some of them were nuts, but spring was here, and they sat at the table in front of all the food they could want, and seemed as happy as pigs in shit. I have to spit away what is left of the madroña berries, and stumble on towards the noon sun.

"You stay here," I told Bobbi this morning. "I'll find somebody, I'll find Jones."

"O blow Jones," she said. "King mother fool. He's dead."

"Take it easy." On the parachute and burlap she was lit up with sweat.

"Make some popcorn," she was saying. Pieces of her bloody hair curved into the corners of her mouth like wires. "Take the goddamn sponge off my chest, Jones, soaks up all my air."

"No," I said, "I ain't Jones, Bobbi."

"Then fuck you, fucking Jones, go ahead and die!" Tears and sweat.

"You're making it up," I yelled, but she only laughed, funny out-of-breath laughter that blew the shining hairs away from her dried lips. "You stay here," I told her, hobbling off barefoot to meet the man with the American whiskey and marriage gold; stupidly running off to visit Margaret Pickel some four miles away. I knocked at her door, which was not thirty yards from the Mattole River---water the color of old blood rushing like the dickens for the Pacific.

"Where are your shoes, boy?"

"I don't know." In the doorway she cradled the thirty-ought-six, its polite, needle-point end aimed precisely at my feet. "I don't know," I said again.

"Well?" Filling up the doorway to the five foot mark, she wore elkskin hunting boots, thick khaki pants that flowered from the boot tops and kept bulging outwards until they finally caught her hips, got tied to her waist by a cartridge belt full of thirty-ought-six steel-jacket suckers. Her bosom, shoulders and gut were covered in the plaid I'd yet to see her without. "Hey!"

"Do you have any food, ma'am?"

The point of the rifle grazed one of my big toes, swung up along my shin line. She chuckled; I watched her rumble through her thickly-painted lips until her jowls rattled in the morning sun. "Who has? Do you know this state is almost wiped out?" Her eyes turned to mucous behind the glasses. "They were naked, you know. . .sexual activities."

"Excuse me?"

She allowed the rifle to fall, now smiling at me. "So, no, I don't have no food for you, sonny, or any like you. How long you think I've watched you?"

"I don't care. I need. . ."

"Maybe you think ever since your little shriek stole my car, but I've got a surprise for you. You should be ashamed." I just looked at her. "You were on the beach."

"What's the matter with you?"

"She spread her legs in the sand like a crab. . . .She engaged them all naked as a jay."

"Have you seen anybody?" I very near shouted at her. "Mr. Jones? Or Flute or somebody!"

"Huh!" She took a step back and raised the rifle with both of her sausage hands. "That grey-headed psy. . .psychologist cock shot your Jones dead, boy."

"That's not true, goddammit! Where is he? *You* did something to him."

"Got to flush out your house if you don't expect to be housin' flushes, right?"

"Listen, don't point that thing at me. Bobbi is back at the house and she's hurt."

"Where? You tell me exactly or I'll blow your nose off, like you did that poor Piro Webster."

I backed off. "She's in the barn. She's got a concussion."

"Fiddle-dee-dee. So she's got one of those diseases, does she? What do you want me to do about it? You people got every bit what you deserved, especially that big blond boy. . .whew!" She laughed high and long. "You know, I can't even use my own telephone now." She took a step back into the darkness of her house.

"Mrs. Pickel, please, I don't know what's wrong with her. I don't know. . ." I was shouting at the top of my lungs, ". . .what's WRONG!" The door slammed. I ran for the trees. Did a rifle shot ca-runk! and make smithereens between my ears?

"So she shoots my buddy Tom in the nuts with a high-powered deer rifle of some reliable vintage, you understand? When the shit blows, you just can't rely on nothin' but all the whiskey and gold you can carry on your back. As a matter fact, you got any tobacco? If you did I'd trade you one of these rings; see that one, look at that mother, I'd trade you for a bunch of tabac, right now."

I came on over the last hill just an hour ago and saw the three domes squatting like strange helmets in the morning sun. The light played over the dark plastic so that the struts and triangles stood out like a body's bones. I followed the stream to the barn. Halfway down the hill I began to run, the charred beams and blackened wreckage of the house bounced and blurred in my vision. The ruin became a haphazard blur, a tiny no-see-um bug in my left eye. I sensed a faint blue outline of the buckled and empty pool. But beyond the burnt timbers and torn pool, our dome hung bright and whole. "This is an organic structure," Jones would say, "very solid," and he would press his thick fingers into the polyethelene stretched over one triangular form. "Colder'n shit right now," Stein might add. "I'll bet D'Mambro and his sweetie don't stay in this thing all winter, what'dya say?"

And in the barn loft I found the burlap sacking and the parachute. I pawed through the yellow chute, empty, as empty of Bobbi as the rest of the stinking barn. I sat down in the ashy barn dark and beat my skull with my fists. Picture shows flitted through my head; sometimes real live events, but then only blobs of color like fires in a fog. Either way, beyond my control: falling parachutes, yellow flowers from the sky; Bobbi drops like a shot, is swallowed by a pool without water, gulped whole by a chasm like a giant's yawn; no Bobbi, but the green airplane is corkscrewing for the sun; it disappears into blinding aluminum foil. . .becomes a Christmas tree sprouted whole from the roof of a shiny dome set upon a peaceful field; and all of us are mirrored, silvery, in the glare of the crazy tree. . .then the plane flies once again over my skull's landscape, but fails to let fly at the tree the girl intended for me on this crisp fogless morning.

But no, that's not what happened at all. When I saw that she was not in the loft I began to search in the domes, and among the trees. Chunk-a, chunk, chunk. . .engine sounds: the weapons carrier carrying Bobbi and me up the dirt road to Honeydew twenty-four hours ago. Bobbi sang a song, "a trisket, a trasket, a green and yellow basket," as we chunked along. Margaret Pickel stepped out on the road's hump carrying a rifle hooked under one plaid armpit. I stopped. "Howdy," she said, pointing a crooked grin at Bobbi beside me. We said hello, waited. "I'm going to tell you kids something." Bobbi started up singing again. "Your friend Piro Webster, I've got him in my basement."

"Baloney," Bobbi sang. "Get a move on, Claude. Time's wasted with this fatty." Mrs. Pickel struck the vehicle with her rifle, made a sound like a whinny, but we were off, laughing, for Honeydew and groceries. Chunk through the road's jagged rain gulleys.

While I was in the second dome, the U.S. Army chopper came from no where to hover over the remains of the house and pool, two hundred yards away from me. I ran like a mother for the trees, hunched down against the spongy bark, and listened to a machine talk to the countryside.

About three miles from the house, on the way back from Honeydew, the steering wheel suddenly went mushy in my hands. We slewed left, I punched the accelerator, we fishtailed left to right, ditch to road, rocking to and fro, goddamn out of control. . . slithering across slick road mud, now sideways---the wheel was useless in my hands. Into a red tree wall, but so slowly, like watching it all on the TV. Bobbi rose out of her seat, so slowly I could have reached out and caught her up by the scruff of her neck, but I did not, and she rose silently into the windshield.

In the sky the helicopter blared electrical words. The windshield blossomed like spiderwebs encircling her head. And as I walk on now I hear electrical words, the same chunking helicopter sounds, and I begin to run for the ocean ahead of me -

. . .AREA RESIDENTS. . .MUST EVACUATE IMMEDI-
ATELY. . .EVACUATE IMMEDIATELY. . .A SEVERE
EARTHQUAKE. . .THIS IS A DISASTER AREA. . .YOU
MUST GO IMMEDIATELY TO THE CIVIL DEFENSE
CENTER IN RIO DELL. . .RIO DELL. . .TRANSPORT. . .
THE AIRCRAFT WILL LAND ONLY FOR THE IN-
JURED. . .SIGNAL. . .SIGNAL. . .AREA RESIDENTS
MUST. . .

I am running. I hear the chopper behind me. . .chunk chunk chunk. But I'm skimming the *Eureka* meadows for the sea. Stop on the cliffs. I know what I know. I know Bobbi's alive. It couldn't be any other way. I, Claude, am alive. The chopper flashes over my head, tilts, rushes on over the roaring ocean. I raise my fist, middle finger up. Standing out clear as a lone cliff tree, I raise my finger at the dopes in the sky. I am up.

"What do you want?" Bobbi asks Robert Quell. "You want some apples?"

A fine, clear morning. Robert stands by the weapons carrier, speaking with Claude and Bobbi, who are sitting inside and eager to be off to Gooch Brothers Store, where Robert doesn't particularly like to go anymore. His shirt is off, and the sun tickles his broad back with heat. "No," he says to Bobbi, resting his elbows on her window sill, "bring me a box of Triskets, please."

"Okay." And she hums 'green and yellow basket' while Claude cranks up the engine. Now the truck is vibrating Robert's elbows. With the running board shaking against his shins, he asks, "Are you coming right back?"

Claude sends over a sneer, a look that Robert knows is not what it seems. "Yeah," he says, "Mr. Jones has a lot for us to do. Fact, you ought'a help him now." The engine revs, whines, and the truck goes away from Robert.

"See you guys," he yells, and watches them bounce out of the yard and disappear up the dirt road for Honeydew. Robert looks after, waves at nothing, and then walks past Dr. Bogue's Cadillac, past Flute's drooping Morris, and across the grass until he comes to the edge of the swimming pool, where Jones is kneeling to fiddle with some contraption set into a square hole in the pool-side concrete.

Jones, too, has no shirt this spring day, and for a while Robert just watches his back pulse under the shining white skin. "Who's that? Robert?"

"It's me."

Jones's head is practically all the way in the hole, in among the thrumming machinery. "How are you? How was your winter?" the invisible head says. Robert is speechless for a minute---this man, as far as he can recall, has never asked him a question about himself. "Well, was it cold? quiet? Hand me the ratchet, would you." A hand comes out, and Robert places the tool in it.

"I liked it, I don't like it in the city, thanks for letting me stay." Robert hears that the words have rushed from him too fast, as if he were out of breath; and he fears that Jones might take his haste for some kind of deception. He hurries to fill up the silence. "That's the filter, huh?"

Jones's shoulder muscles bunch, smooth out, bunch again as he works the ratchet thing. "Yep," he grunts. Then he's done with it. He stands up, his quiet face on a level with Robert's, and sweat-slick and glowing in the sunlight, he says, "A leaky gasket."

"We didn't run it while you were gone."

"I hope not." Jones bends to put the scatter of tools in their box. "You and Claude got along then?"

"Sure. We play checkers."

Jones smiles, hands Robert the tool box. "Good. You know, I went to Nova Scotia for quiet. I like to be alone there, but three months is a long time, and I fell to worrying about folks---all kinds of things. . .but my fretting is usually a trifle off-kilter. Why don't you take that box into the house and give it to Kate. There's a deal to do around here."

"What shall I do then?"

"You can help me cut wood in the grove. Where's Stein?"

"He's building a giraffe at the dome," Robert announces with some pleasure.

"Oh."

"It's a huge giraffe. He's going to paint it."

The other man laughs, and Robert feels positively joyful, as if Jones is really *there* for the first time he's known; and Robert laughs too. "Okay, leave the tools here, and go tell Stein there are more practical things than giraffes. Both of you can come up and cut wood with me. It's not summer yet."

"Okay," Robert says, putting down the tool box and turning for the ocean.

"If you see Jake Bogue or any of his guys you can tell them the pool is fixed."

"Okay."

Robert lopes through the trees and across the meadows to the second dome, which he and Claude had erected a week before. There is no one in sight. Even though he hasn't seen the Bogue family since breakfast he knows they are inside, but has no desire for the doctor or the others to look at him, and so, hardly pausing in his lope for the sea, he shouts into the black plastic: "Hey! The pool is fixed!" And he moves on, breathing easily, going on strong with the wind blowing over his face, whistling in his ears. Until he comes upon their dome, and Stein among his great pots and rising giraffe. Naked in the midst of his mess, Stein's black hairs lap down the length of him, from head to toenail, Robert sees.

"Robert! Lookee here, apprehend this." Stein points to the stick legs and swelling belly of his skeleton giraffe, which as yet has no neck or head. "I need a ladder. Or may I stand on your shoulders to mold the graceful throat and shoo-fly head of this statchoo?"

"Sure. . .Say, what's it made of?"

"It's made of art, can't you see? No, it's paper maché and chicken-wire, a most reliable medium, unless it rains."

256

"And you'll paint it?"

"That is an accurate observation," he says, reaching under his belly to scratch. "I shall paint it in dayglow yellows and blackest black, like your beloved auto, and then. . ."

"Jones has some work," Robert interrupts.

"Ahh! He must first see this. The king must look at my effort so as I can beseech him to replace his papery petrified image with the REAL THING. If not, I'll jump from this mother-humping cliff before I do a lot of work for him." He laughs, farts, dips his hands into a pot of what looks to Robert like gray porridge.

"It's too cold up here for a real giraffe," Robert says.

Stein looks around, squints behind his glasses, shows his amber teeth. "Do not. . .speak. . .like. . .a. . .rabid. . . REAL-IST." And suddenly he leaps into the air, arms and legs stretched wide, private part flying akimbo before him. "FUCK REALISM!" he bellows out to sea; and when he lands the ground beneath them is vibrating like a jackhammer, like the weapons carrier just a half hour before, but Robert is not *sure*. . .until the both of them, he sees, are swaying in a wind that is not there, pitching up and down, side to side, like men on a giant teeter-board. "What! What!" Stein is hollering, going down on one knee, trying to brace, while Robert's teeth click together like steel pellets in his mouth. There comes a low, far-off roaring which speaks of the arrival of a great ocean wind; and Stein continues to yell out---on his hands and knees now, trying to grab a hold on the sandy dirt, trying to dig in and find a lever that will shut off the mad earth. Still upright, Robert hears Stein's voice stammering into the air, ". . .Bogue!. . .it's that pig Bogue. . .making this Jee. . .sus MOMA !" It's over. Stopped. Still seconds, until Robert can hear the boiling and bubbling sea, and he is off and running, abandoning Stein to his handholds on the earth, running to pursue the strange idea that he must be somewhere else, and Stein goes on yelling, "It's not over. . .it's not over!. . .these are SHOCKS !" But Robert is going for the house, looking back just in time to see Stein's half-a-giraffe tumble on top of him; lay Stein out flat.

For Robert, it's a crushing, panic run---going like sixty towards the second dome with a head full of Bobbi and Kate Flute, or Jones twisted on the ground, needing him. Then another shock, like a rug pulled from beneath his flying feet, and the upheaval sends him crashing to the earth, crunch on his nose, his bare chest, but he is up again, beating down the deck of a pitching ship. His feet won't come down right; the ground is not there, but he's staying up, diving forward through bright green space. . .until dome No. 2 finally comes in sight. The vibrations cease again. Robert stops, to figure out what is rolling there by the dome: three twisting, crackling bodies meshed together at knees, elbows, heads. . .shrieking in front of his eyes. The staring Bogue, Molly, and the lawyer Clingsmythe who is like a stork among them: all tangled and squirmy in the flattened grass next to their queerly askew dome. Robert runs past them, exclaiming, "DAMN YOU! DAMN YOU, GET AWAY FROM HERE!"

On. Over the steady ground until he passes the dome belonging to Claude and Bobbi, and comes up in front of the house, which flares in his eyes and stops him dead. From the windows of the house flicker rosy cellophane flames, flames he can barely see for the wiggling sunlight that saturates even the porch, murdering its shadows. The house is whole, but not-there; impossible fire sprouts through the window screening, melting it like wax, while above, on the roof, chalk lines of smoke rise from between overlapping shingles.

Figuring. Robert is figuring, but the earth again palsies beneath his feet. A sudden violence, and the entire yard in front of the house becomes a grass trampoline. On his knees, he scrambles forward to do *something* about the people in that house. Kate Flute runs out on the porch carrying a bundle---a dress that smokes in her hands, but she's caught in the tremoring, is flipped off the porch in a slow somersault that ends her up on the ground, rolling in the grass toward the pool and Robert: a twirling mess of smoke and frightened hair. Robert is out flat now; and ground socks his chin, dribbles his head, but still he sees Kate tumbling, and hears. . .a terrific underground CA-RACK, a great splitting, and he knows without seeing that the pool is cracked, bottomless, yawning from end to end.

Kate's staggering toward him, soot and tears all over her face, carrying this smoldering. . .*thing* in front of the child he knows to be in her belly. She drops it in front of him, as if he's supposed to know what to do with it. He tries to bunch his limbs, rise. The yard stops. "Get in the car, damn you, get up and get in the car!" she shouts again and again and again. . .falling at him in slow motion, flames distorting and staining the air scarlet behind her head. Flute. It must be Flute. . .two hands digging into his armpits, lifting and pushing him hard in the direction of the barn. Kate veers, runs with him for the cars, and Bobbi's face flashes through his head clear as ever, but Flute. . .what?. . . Flute is not with them, though his voics gaffs the air as it moves away from them: "Stay in the car, I'm going to get Jones! And don't go back in there, Kate, look at me! Get the car away from the barn. . . right away from it!" And finally, Robert can see him as he dashes into the trees, his yellow shirt winking away from them. Now Kate is in the Morris, cranking away. "Damn. . .damn. . .damn. . . it won't start! Help me, damn you, you fucking idiot!" Robert extends his hands above the car, helpless idiot hands. "Do what?" He kicks the car viciously, the starter motor whining in his head. Nothing.

Glass is cracking, falling, splintering behind them in the house. "What about Bobbi?" he cries.

"Try the other car, Bogue's car!"

"No keys!"

Kate's scream flies into the air. Kate! She pounds the steering wheel with burnt fists, doesn't stop for the sound of running feet in the grass, but Robert swivels like a dumb machine; three stick figures streak across the lawn straight for the flames. The doctor,

Molly, Clingsmythe: veering, they run like hell past the spitting flame house, skim the stream, and float up the bluff into the red-woods, just as Stein flies howling into the yard, waving a giraffe leg over his wild head like a bastard club that shines yellow with fire in the flowery sunlight.

Hear me. Pay attention to my final, honest precision. Even if there is a Pacific Ocean rupturing three-quarters of a mile away, there is no substitute for aerial and landed accuracy. *Earthquake* may mean that within the earth's viscera years of growing strain gradually overcome the elasticity of rocks squashed along a fault line, and to relieve that excrutiating stress the rocks do then cleave, snap and hurtle past one another, telegraphing shock waves and creating traumatic fissures in the earth's crust; but for my wife Kate and me it meant, in the first jactitating instants, that *Eureka's* Sears & Roebuck propane cook stove snapped its copper tubes and bloomed a dozen blue and melancholy igneous fingers at our innocent, kitchen-bound faces. The floor moiled beneath us, and thigh to thigh we gripped the drainboard, both of us half-turned in queer fascination to watch a pale shoot of flame leap boldly from the stove to the ironing board that was surely two feet away; and on the ironing board Kate's Mexican wedding dress ignited as if it were made of cellophane. Before that first tremor had stopped, Kate seized the box of baking soda from the shelf and began to fling a white snow over the dress and at the stove. "That won't work," I said, and the house became still.

"Then turn off the gas," she whispered calmly.

"I can't get back there." The flames gave off the vaguest hiss as they rose to scorch the wall behind the stove. A gentle mist of baking soda enveloped my tic-ing face.

"Then go outside, Flute."

"What for?"

261

The yellow baking soda box struck my ear, caromed onto the stove's surface and wilted into orange flames, a black consumption of Arm & Hammer lettering, I noticed stupidly. Kate's voice continued as levelly as if she were in a bank, or a lawyer's office. *I think you should quit dickin' around, Flute.* "Turn off the gas at the tank."

"Oh." I turned and pitched for the back door on rubbery tip-toes, grateful for one fractured and silly moment that Jones was not there to adjudge my prowess in such an emergency. As soon as I was outside on the stoop, the screen door trembling in my hand, a glance to my left at the twin silvery tanks made possible this efficient observation: since there are no taps atop those cylinders, there is no way short of a wrench to turn them off, and this task is therefore aborted.

"Flute, the wall's on fire."

"Get a wrench then!" I backed into the house in time to hear the sound of her hasty feet behind the distinct pop and spit of burning redwood. In front of the stove's zigzagging tendrils of flame the ironing board and dress barely smoked---we've done something right, I thought.

"The tool box is gone," Kate yelled, invisible.

"Shit." She came through the pleated air currents from the living room, but before she reached me the second tremor, more like a shock, slammed against the foundation of the house, and I lost sight of her as the stove slid across the kitchen floor, upended the ironing board, and co'lided with the sink and cabinet. I held to the bucking doorframe, watched the cabinets welcome the flames, noted that the severed propane tube where the stove had been now pointed at me a small, tremulous spike of blue fire; and only then did I make the attempt to cross the kitchen. I fell beside the stove, felt heat like a brief sephyr over my face, and then was up to slam into the oak dining table, but was there in time to snatch Kate from under Jones's brick and board bookshelves just as they tumbled their useless contents upon the floor. I hauled her to the front door, and the infernal stillness arrived once again.

"All right," she said.

"Here comes Quell." He was running like a bald Marine recruit in the sunshine, bearing news, or building momentum for a gross cannonball into the pool.

"What do we take out of here?" She held my elbow and gave me a shake.

"The checkbook," I said. "Jones will come. He must be on his way." Behind us the fire went quickly about its business. For me, it was an entirely calm moment in our early marriage, there in the doorway. "He'll come and bust Bogue in the chops; he'll rout the fucking nay-sayer."

"Don't be an ass, the house is burning down." I saw sweat across the in-curved bridge of her nose. "You get the damn checkbook; I'll get my dress."

It appeared tremendously sensible. "All right. No!" But she was gone into the fiery kitchen before I could act to stop her.

"I've got it, I'm coming!" she yelled, and because I believed her I turned tail and flew down the hallway, and stood barely an instant in the middle of our room before gathering, in a wool purse, my retainer's tools: Jones's checkbook; his notarized power-of-attorney; our own checkbook; a cigarette lighter and carton of Camels; and a leather thong a'jangle not only with keys but also with a silver Saint Christopher medal and the five-holed Mexican cross Jones had given us on the occasion of our December wedding. Eminent sense, powerful foresight, W.V. Flute!

Back in the hallway, now almost opaque with smoke, I realized the living room had joined the kitchen in conflagration. I saw a ghostly Kate stumble through the front screen door bearing her lovely, ruinated dress in front of Ann who was even then in her womb. And BOOM! the third shock hit home with triple the force of the others, surely sufficient to break the very backbone of the house; enough to send me reeling the remaining length of the hall, ricocheting wall to wall in a pin-ball of up and down, side to side *battering* that made aching shards of my brain, made absurd syllables to explode from my mouth, a non-sense Stein cry, "Boomkitchwatt, you motherfuckers!" a rippling, fanciful bellow in the privacy of that smoked hall, before I bursted from the front door on to the rollicking porch. Kate was tumbling across the lawn like a teargas cannister aimed at Robert Quell, who sprawled full-face and twitching on the green, unfocused grass. I jumped. The ground met my feet at the wrong time, as if I'd flared out my plane too soon, and the runway socked me a good one. Yet I remained upright, and despite the bright outdoors ague made my way for Kate and Quell.

The pool went; it ruptured. And as I high-stepped past it I accepted onto my neutral retina the almost static image of hoards of bubbles rising ferociously from the pool's brand new fissure, the unseemly end of its pathetic tidal wave.

"Get in the car, damn you, get up and get in the car!" Kate's first proximity to the berserk in this ridiculously swift catastrophe, and I observed---as I ran on---that she was standing over Quell, and apparently about to shroud him with the fuming dress.

"I'll get him," I said, and circled to surprise his agitated flank. When I bent to seize his back Kate let go of the dress, and my cool eye once again froze for me the slow motion flutter of steaming, unbleached cotton gliding for the ground, which of course went dead still the moment the garment touched down; and gave me a proper footing for the job of hefting Robert Quell to his feet. I shoved him after Kate who was now heading for the cars, and at that moment in time---with the house hissing and snapping behind me; with the earth slowly sucking off the pool's water; with all the others unaccounted for; and with my head yet clogged with smoke and foolish booming cries---I made the brilliant, inevitable decision to go forth and seek my cuckolded friend and boss in order to ask him what he would like me to do. *You're something of a toad, Flute.* "Stay in the car," I shouted, commencing to jog diagonally away from the barn and the automobiles, in the general direction of the grove Jones had set aside for cutting wood, and from which, during most of our morning in the kitchen, we had heard the tip and whine of his chain saw. "Just get in the car, I'll find Jones." At that point I was perking up, running well, making edicts, positive that the worst was done and that the time for ordering the chaos was upon us. "And don't go back in there. Kate, look at me!" She was spitting on her wrecked hands, I now know. "Get the car away from the barn. . .right away from it!" Sparks, and the potential for explosion on my efficient mind as I abandoned them to the Morris, to the Bogues, or even perhaps to the mummers Light and Leather, for all I knew, or didn't know at that particular elevated moment. Surely Stein would incorporate, and together with Kate quench the lunacy until I returned with Jones.

I ran northwest until I came to the road that led to the Pacific, and once on it I settled my pace enough to notice that the trees along the roadway were set into the ground at odd angles, as if they were people slouching against one another for comfort, succor, some weary kindness. But so *normal.* Why were there no great splits in the earth? trees uprooted instead of merely off kilter? boulders spat into the sky like useless pebbles? Jones would know. I drifted left, turned off the road to follow the vague tire ruts heading toward the woodcutter's clearing. And suddenly stopped: there was no reason for this. If Jones had been in the clearing before the shocks, and I felt sure he had, there was nothing to keep him there now. And it came to me that if he were in the grove, it would not be because he willed it so. My feet sought the earth. A frozen sweat burst from my skin, I tried to move, but horribly, utterly, my brain was *dead.* I felt only cold, and somewhere far outside me my own distant voice: *I must keep my appointment with Jones.* I raced into the trees. The ground bent upward, crashing me into thicker stands of fir and spruce. Dwarf trees caught my feet, scraped my arms and neck, smeared my skin with gory pitch. I reached the ridge overlooking the clearing and stopped. Below me, someone was kneeling in the dark of a redwood. Below and beyond him the clearing was empty---jumbled logs, broken sawhorse, the chain saw---of Jones. Unless it was he rested against the tree. But no. That person kneeling with arms strangely thrust in front of a head sunk into brilliant plaid, was Margaret Pickel.

Oh. Is that all? I thought. I came within a breath of shouting a challenge. But I hesitated, unable to fathom what she was doing in that place at this time. She huddled against the tree---a colorful, perverse tuber growing from the redwood's trunk. Then, in a reversed-telescope line of sight that arrowed over her shoulder and down into the clearing, I saw Jones. A looming animal who suddenly occupies what was perceived to be empty space; but this animal staggered, lacked grace, and frozen, I watched him seventy-five yards off through a trick-viewfinder of my own making. Heavy boots, green jeans, no shirt, his torso and head spattered with grime. No, not grime; his blood, seeped. . .oozed blackly from a gash or *tear* which ran ragged from the base of his neck to the top of his beltless trousers. The distance. . .the woods murk. . .I'm trying for honest precision: I thought that the chain saw had somehow bucked into his chest at the first shock of the quake; of this I am still convinced. He stumbled, shaking his head so that the hair flew up into the clearing's sunlight like gilded ropes; and I say that his palms pressed over his nipples as if he were keeping his chest from falling in two.

Again, my mouth opened to call out. But he looked so far away. No words in the cave of my skull. I saw him as if he were an animal suffering in its final privacy. . .until my eyes tilted down, click-click, to Margaret Pickel, and the telescopic sight of her rifle became an awful tubular extension of an eye I could suddenly imagine. Of course, she's kneeled to shoot. Why hadn't I seen it before? Jones caught in the cross-haired circle. He can die. My mouth was saltpeter. *I will this not to happen.* Jump! I launched through absurd space, flew down the sloping earth and hit feet first just behind her, cocked my knees and, in the last moment of joy, I rose to save Jones, and even as I felt my chin crash into her soft neck from some far-off place the shot invaded my ears, thudded into my own brain. *Flute, you miserable bastard.* Margaret Pickel reared from her knees and shook me off her back like some paltry twig, so that screaming and blind I might tumble the rest of the slope and fetch up against my foolish and wondrous friend Jones, now dead.

Nothing. *I am a closet in his stellar sphere.* I was in the Morris with my wife Kate, with Robert Quell, and Julius Stein. *Suspended like a hairy seed in some burning liquid.* All my friends looked to me from behind blackened faces. The house was a beautiful inferno in front of us. The car started with a single twist of the key. Nothing obtained.

"Let's go."

"Where is he?"

"I don't know."

"We heard a shot."

"I did too."

I drove the lie away.

And came one day to New Hampshire, where it is now April 15th, and I am outside. The air is clear, my house well-defined against the blue of the spring sky. The grass is damp. At present I am sitting at a white table in the yard outside the kitchen. Inside, Kate Ximines Flute is at work on my lunch. Near the old stone well, Ann Arden Flute laughs through the wooden bars of her playpen, at me. At anyone who might come along.

What to say?

"Jinkies, man, endings went out with war," Stein would chide, but I ought at least to record a brief slice of yesterday, a day which of course didn't fulfill all of my expectations. Anniversaries seldom do.

I rose and ate breakfast with my family. Then we went for a walk around our land.

"I guess that's it," Kate said.

The wariness started in me like a reflex. "You've read it. . .the whole thing?"

"Yes."

"What do you say?"

"I say that's it."

"Now you know," I said.

She stopped and turned to me, and her face was absolutely open for me to see---as clear as every other time of clearness. "I always knew you were there when she shot him. Don't pretend the book's for me, Flute." She put Ann down on the ground and touched my arm.

"I could have. . ."

"But you didn't. You'll never know."

"Well, I got it all down, my many lives." But it was just something to say; she *knew* me. . .knew I was out of my room on this day, and on this day, that was enough.

"You did it," she said, smiling. "Put down your true, flawed version. Shh! What happens later doesn't matter. We're here. I'm here. And I tell you I chose this."

"I see."

"And now you're here, right?"

I nodded. "I think so, yes."

"Okay, Flute. When Ann goes down for her nap we'll find our bedroom and make love. . .with no airplanes or chemicals or queer books in sight."

HENDRIE LIVES IN SOUTH HADLEY,
MASSACHUSETTS, WHERE HE TEACHES
AT MOUNT HOLYOKE COLLEGE. HE
IS MARRIED TO SUSAN BLUE, AND
THEY HAVE TWO SONS, NATHAN AND ARDEN.

*Boomkitchwatt* IS HIS FIRST NOVEL.

## ORDER FORM

John Muir Publications
Box 613
Santa Fe, N.M. 87501

I enclose my check for . . . . . . . . . . . . . . . . . . . . . .

Please send me . . . . . . . . . copies of BOOMKITCHWATT by

Don Hendrie, Jr.
at $2.95 a copy

NAME . . . . . . . . . . . . . . . . . . . . . . . . . . . . . . . . . . . . . . . . . . . . . . . . . . . . . . . . . . . . . . . . . . . .
   *(Please Print)*

Address . . . . . . . . . . . . . . . . . . . . . . . . . . . . . . . . . . . . . . . . . . . . . . . . . . . . . . . .

. . . . . . . . . . . . . . . . . . . . . . . . . . . . . . . . . . . . . . . Zip . . . . . . . . . . . . . . . . . .

*Book Sellers!*
*Please contact Book People, 2940 7th St., Berkeley, California 94710*